Finding Leigh

Amy J. Hawthorn

Copyrights Finding Leigh, PUBLISHED MARCH 2017 BY AMY J. HAWTHORN, ALL RIGHTS RESERVED FINDING LEIGH Copyright © 2017 Amy J. Hawthorn Edited by Virginia Nelson Cover art by Laideebug Digital With the exception of quotes used in reviews, this book may not be reproduced or used in whole or in part by any means existing without written permission from the author. The unauthorized reproduction or distribution of this copyrighted work is illegal. This book is a work of fiction and any resemblance to persons, living or dead, or places, events or locales is purely coincidental. The characters are productions of the author's imagination and used fictitiously. The author does acknowledge the trademark status and trademark ownership of all trademarks, service marks and word marks mentioned in this book. All rights reserved worldwide. No part of this work may be sold, manipulated, or reproduced in any format without express written permission from the author, except for brief quotations embodied in reviews. Thank you for respecting the hard work of this author. Amy J. Hawthorn/Words by Night Publishing ISBN: 978-0-9968801-4-5

Dedication

For the Addies of the world...

Chapter One

Addie's thirteen-year-old heart beat against her breastbone so hard she felt it all the way to her ears. Palms sweating, she followed the creepy guy through the woods. Although she'd been on her own for a long time, living in what little was left of her family's old house, she'd never dealt with anything this scary. She didn't know what the bad guy would do if he heard her, but she knew it wouldn't be good.

There has to be some way I can help her!

The pretty woman who always left food and stuff for Addie dangled limply over the bad guy's shoulder. The setting sun cut through a break in the trees, glinting in brown hair so long it almost touched the ground. It waved back and forth against the back of his strong looking legs as he climbed the narrow path.

She wished she had one of her grandfather's old guns, but no, her good-for-nothing father sold them at the pawn shop the day after her grandpa died. She had the phone from the rich guy who always came with the pretty woman in her pocket. She'd been playing with it, learning how to use the camera and flashlight things. She hoped it would be of use now because she didn't know what else to do. She just knew she had to do something.

Addie thought she knew where he was going, but she didn't want to make any noise by using the phone to call for help. Judging by all the gunfire she'd heard, there still might be trouble at her house.

Her home.

She knew it wasn't much more than a shithole, but it was all she'd ever known. Now she wouldn't be able to stay there ever again. It hadn't been a true home since well before the police had come and taken her dad and his drug making stuff. She hadn't even cared as she'd hid in the woods and watched them put him in the back of the police car. She thought maybe she should have felt bad for him or something, but all she could think about was a long time ago when the little house had been a happy place. From the day her grandpa had died from a heart attack, things had only grown more bleak. After her mom had gotten drunk and crashed her car into a tree, there hadn't been anymore good memories born.

There's nowhere for me to go. My people are all gone.

The guy slowly stepped out into the clearing where her mom's older cousin used to live. Her trailer had burned down not long after she died and no one had ever done anything with it. With his gun in one hand and the other arm around the lady's legs, he walked to a shiny black car. He opened the passenger door and put her inside then quietly shut the door. Afterward, he got in the driver's side and started the engine.

A picture. She could take a picture of the license plate. Her shaky fingers fumbled over the buttons until she found the right one. She waited until the car turned around to pull out, then she snapped a picture. And then another, just to be sure she didn't mess up.

She blinked and the car was gone.

~

As the leader of Dark Horse Inc. and former Army, Rick Evans wasn't used to feeling helpless. But right then, his gut twisted with hollow panic he could neither control nor combat. He needed out of this ridiculous bed, needed to find a way to help Leigh, but instead they had him trapped in the damn emergency room.

His instincts clamored, urging him to get up and move. Leigh's hourglass was almost out of sand and her abductor, Marcus Sutton, was not the kind of bastard to twiddle his thumbs. He wanted Leigh for a reason that was anything but good.

Rick's own rules, the very base that he'd built Dark Horse Inc. on, mocked him. From day one, he and Trent Dawson—his closest friend and right-hand man—agreed that they would never take a mission if it posed a risk to anyone on their team. Years ago, when they'd served in Afghanistan, they'd lost one of their team. The pain had blindsided them.

When Rick had called in a few of their friends to help protect Trent's woman, his friend had urged him to make Dark Horse Inc. official. Over time Rick had, but they'd always agreed that their team's safety came first. That meant no matter how badly they wanted otherwise they never acted without proper intel, surveillance, and planning.

Trent would lock Rick down and start on all those very things they'd sworn to live by.

Deep down to the very center of his soul, Rick knew that would be a mistake.

He glared at the tray on the wheeled cart beside his bed. Covered with a crumpled paper drape, it held a mountain of bloodied gauze, antiseptic, and suture needles. The syringe containing lidocaine was still over halfway full. He'd refused more, afraid the medicine might affect his ability to move fast or think coherently. The doctor's stubborn insistence and his own impatience was the only reason he'd consented to even a small dose.

As it was, his anger burned so blistering hot, it was a wonder the ER physician had stayed in the room long enough to tend his wound. Rick had to give the doctor a huge measure of respect. The man's hand had been steady as he'd sewn a ticking time bomb back together.

Leigh. Mother fucking Marcus Sutton has Leigh in his filthy hands.

He looked up to the bags of fluid hanging on the pole beside him. The bag of blood had finally emptied and his second bag of saline was almost finished. Close enough. He undid the tape holding the IV in place then leaned over, stretching to reach the bedside tray. He pulled it closer and grabbed one of the two remaining mostly clean pieces of gauze. It was his blood, and he didn't give one damn about anything beyond getting out and finding Leigh. Holding it over the IV catheter, he slid the IV out and applied pressure. He'd never been a big bleeder. He wouldn't need more than a few seconds.

While he waited for the bleeding to stop, he cautiously stood, testing his leg.

Trent was going to be pissed and pissed good. But Rick couldn't wait any longer, and he couldn't draw his friends deeper into this madness. Having Leigh at the center of it brought him enough terror for ten lifetimes. He wouldn't risk anyone else.

The numbing medication was wearing off, so his leg throbbed like a bitch. He'd had plenty of injuries over the years. He and pain were well acquainted, and this injury might not be his worst, but it wasn't a walk in the park.

But none of that mattered.

Confident his leg would hold his weight, he took one cautious step then another.

He ditched the gauze on his arm and walked to the door. A glance into the hallway showed the ER was quiet. Certain no one watched, he clutched the ridiculous gown and hoped his ass stayed covered. He slipped out into the hall and made it almost to the ambulance bay before he ran into anyone. Wide, glass doors slid open as a security guard and nurse walked in. They carried a faint whiff of smoke in and that gave him the story he needed.

He ran a hand through his hair. "I gotta have a cigarette. I'll be right back. Less than five minutes."

Long used to patients sneaking out for a smoke, the nurse pursed her lips in annoyance and the guard rolled his eyes. When they moved out of the way, he faked a smile. Since they'd been caught doing the same, they didn't argue with him.

Where did Trent park my ride? He looked around the front lot and found his SUV. Clutching the stupid gown, he hurried over. The rough sidewalk and then the asphalt were harsh on the soles of his feet, but he didn't give a shit. He made it to the truck and keyed in the code on the door handle. The moment his ass hit the seat he lifted a cup holder insert and retrieved the spare key.

In less than a minute, he drove onto the main road. Impatient, he stopped at a red light. Where was he going? What would he do? In a bad habit that Trent's sweet Kate would scold him for, he reached for his phone. It lay in its usual spot, in the cubby beneath the dash. He blindly fumbled for it as he watched a long line of cars cruise through the intersection.

He hit a button and glanced at the screen. His heart

stopped.

Hopeful, but scared he'd imagined it, he closed his eyes. When he opened them, that number was still there under his missed calls.

Mary. Or Addie. Addison Jolene Potter. Thirteen years old. Pete, the young man who handled his computer searches, had found her birth certificate in the online county records. Her mother hadn't given the girl her father's last name. They'd had a hell of a time finding any info on her. He couldn't imagine having a child and not making sure that they had everything they could hope for, including his name.

Tom Caudill was a bastard of the highest order.

She'd called him. After what felt like years of waiting, Addie had called. His hand shook. Not good. He checked traffic and, making sure the lane beside him was clear, he pulled off the street and into a gas station. He parked and took a deep breath.

It couldn't be a coincidence that she'd called him yesterday evening after everything went to shit.

He took another deep breath and pushed play.

A small voice spoke in a hushed, jittery jumble. "Uh. Hey. I hope this thing works. I saw him take her. That guy with the blond hair. He carried her over his shoulder like a sack. Um. I took a picture of his license plate." She paused a moment and then her small shaky voice provided him a miracle as she recited the info.

He listened to her message a second time, committing it to memory. He'd memorized the plate number on the first pass. The second time around, his focus was all about Addie. After expending so much energy and time searching for her, she was right there in his ear.

Yet, like a ghost, he couldn't grab hold and catch her.

Afraid to hope and expecting the worst, he dialed her number. He held his breath and hoped with everything he had left that she'd answer. After the fifth ring, it went to a generic voicemail box. He exhaled and tried one more time. As badly as he wished differently, he wasn't surprised to get the same result. His wandering little orphan was determined to stay lost.

The only thing that kept him from crushing his cell in his hand was the very minute possibility that she might call again.

He closed his eyes, did his best impersonation of a man whose world wasn't crumbling around him, and backed out of his parking spot.

He had to get back to his place, grab his computer, his gear, and lastly some fucking clothes. As badly as he wanted to rush in and find Leigh, he couldn't do it without intel, and he couldn't run in with his dick flapping in the breeze. He pulled back onto the road and hurried as fast as he could without getting pulled over.

He figured Trent and the rest of the crew would be looking for him by now. If they found him, he wouldn't be able to shake them loose. As much as he needed their valuable support, he couldn't put them at risk for something he was responsible for.

Demons always returned when you least expected them.

He had a few things at the new house he'd just bought. It wasn't much, but he'd make it work. He couldn't chance getting caught at Trent's, where he stored most of his gear. Even if he managed to get in and get out before the Dark Horse crew, Harlan wouldn't hesitate to sit on his ass and hold him until Trent came home.

Harlan Walker might be a couple of years past his prime, but the man was still a force to be reckoned with.

Fortunately, he hadn't told his team about his latest purchase yet. That might buy him a little more desperately needed time. Though, the reprieve would be a short one. He'd be in trouble once they set Pete on his tail. There wasn't a damn thing the kid couldn't find with a little time and a computer.

He'd locked a little cash away in a safe, along with an extra pistol and ammunition. In another futile attempt to bring him back into the fold, his father had sent him a sample pack of his legacy's finest wares. It was far from ideal, but it would do.

~

The world around Leigh shook violently. Her head felt as though it might snap from her neck. Pain screamed through her brain and vicious light sparked behind her eyelids.

"Hey there, gorgeous girl. Wake up." *That voice. Dear god, that voice.* She'd only heard it a few times, but each experience had been followed by either electric pain or the nauseatingly sweet smell of chloroform. Repeatedly, she'd wakened only to be sent back to unconsciousness.

Now he wanted her awake.

Cruel fingers dug into her upper arms with bruising pain. On another jarring shake, her teeth snapped together. Wanting absolutely nothing to do with her current nasty reality she tried to fight her way back to oblivion. Her head lolled on her shoulders. She fought the urge to stand on her own feet.

Her instincts screamed at her to flee, run. She needed to get as far away as fast as possible and stay there. But she couldn't. Her ankles were bound and her wrists tied behind her back with a merciless lack of play in the ropes.

With every ounce of will she had, she forced herself to stay limp with her eyes closed.

He crooned in her ear. "Come on, precious. This will be so much more fun with you awake." Bile rose in her throat, and she prayed she didn't choke on her own vomit. Swallowing her revulsion, she struggled to remember what happened. She'd been out at Addie's with Rick and someone else. There'd been trouble. Jumbled, random, blurry images came to life then faded into each other.

Blood. There had been so much blood on her hands. Sheriff Hawkins shot Rick and he'd lost consciousness. Then the world had gone black. The blood was all her fault. She'd insisted they make a trip out to little old house to drop off groceries for the little girl.

Joe. An image of her fierce older brother wavered in her mind. She reminded herself that Joe would leave no stone unturned. He was smart, determined, and stubborn enough for ten men. He and Cara were unharmed the last time she'd seen them and they would have taken care of Rick. No one was more competent than Joe.

She'd always hated that about her brother, but she couldn't be more thankful now.

Rick. She knew they would have gotten him to a hospital. She had to believe that he was okay.

Something wet and hot trailed up her neck. He bit her earlobe. Pain exploded, light bursting behind her eyelids.

Oh no oh no oh no oh no.

"I know you're pretending."

Her breaths came in short shallow pants. Her heartbeat

thundered in her ears.

A man yelled in the distance. Something loud thundered against a door, startling her. She lost her focus and whimpered.

"Ah. There you are. I knew you were awake. Let me see your eyes." He spoke against the hollow of her throat making her cringe away from him. Only she had nowhere to retreat.

"Yo, boss! We got a problem!" Someone yelled through the door.

"Not now!" She flinched and turned her head away when he shouted. "Handle it without me or consider yourself a dead man."

"Boss, it's Wen. He got himself into trouble. He doesn't look good."

Her captor growled low and menacingly. "We'll finish this later, princess. It'll only be sweeter for the delay. I promise to make it worth your while." He bit her ear again and dropped her, leaving her to crash onto the hard floor.

Tears pricked her eyes as the door slammed shut. Gritty and cold concrete bit into her cheek. Her body throbbed in one screaming, twisting, knot of pain.

Muffled voices trailed off as the men hurried away. "I think he got into the supply. I know you don't want any attention here, but he really looks bad, boss. If it were anyone else we'd just toss him in the river but, well, it's Wen.

Chapter Two

A flip of the coin. Two locations. One choice obvious, considering the time, 4:25am. The other option, a long shot. If he chose wrong, Rick could tip his hand and run the risk of alerting Sutton. He figured the bastard might think he'd bought himself some time.

Marcus likely thought Rick was down, maybe even dead or dying. Dark Horse would grieve, lick their wounds and regroup. Or so the bastard would assume.

He would take Marcus's underestimation and use it to his full advantage. The elements of time and surprise were Rick's biggest assets.

He sat on the marble floor of his new, virtually empty home and typed the two addresses into a map. With his good leg bent cross-legged and his injured leg straight, he balanced his notebook computer awkwardly on his lap. The screen's bright glow cast shadows and gloom over the cavernous living room. Pete might be Dark Horse's technology expert, but Rick wasn't without his own skills. He'd traced the plate number Addie had given him to L and S Consulting. Among other things, the company touted a reputation for donating half of all profits to providing medical supplies and services to third world countries.

Rick's longshot for finding Leigh? A smaller branch of the so-called consulting firm, called Beating Heart Industries. It used a large warehouse on the outskirts of town near the river to receive, store, and ship secondhand medical supplies and equipment for the nonprofit arm of the business.

Then there was the obvious choice. He'd found residential property recently leased by L and S. The home sat in one of the most expensive neighborhoods, just outside the city limits. Any normal person should be at home in bed, oblivious to the monsters lurking in the dark, waiting to attack.

Tonight, Rick was that monster, and heaven help the sorry bastard who got in his way.

He memorized both routes and closed the computer's screen. Using his good leg he awkwardly stood, ignoring the pain in his wound. The lidocaine used for his stitches had worn off, leaving him with an itching, screaming ache.

He'd leashed his impatience while focusing on his search, but now it raked at his insides, fighting for control.

Leigh was alive. Marcus, the sick fuck, would want to play with her first. Rick's only hope was that he got to her before Marcus had any significant time with her. Hopefully, with one portion of his heroin distribution operation in shambles, he was busy tying up loose ends. Rick's gut said that he'd likely hidden Leigh somewhere until he had time to savor her.

Nausea and blistering anger roiled up inside Rick until he had to swallow the urge to vomit. He fought to slow the air rushing in and out of his lungs, focusing on a mirror hanging on the wall until his vision cleared.

He tossed the laptop in his duffle then slung the bag over his shoulder. Exiting his home, Rick locked the door behind him and paused. His jeans stuck to his thigh. He ran a palm over the spot and cursed. The wet denim felt warm against his palm.

How long do I have before I fall flat on my face?

Anger, adrenaline and raw, burning determination

would only get him so far. *I'm not invincible.* Even now, exhaustion grabbed and pulled at him with greedy fingers. Pain pounded at him with every single heartbeat, each pulse stronger than the one prior.

But, damn it all. This was his mess. It was his fault that Marcus had taken Leigh.

He opened the door to his SUV and threw his duffle across to the passenger side. The circular driveway led to an even longer path through his silent and empty property.

What would happen if he didn't survive the night? He had confidence in his skills, his equipment. He knew enough about himself to know that he'd rescue Leigh or die trying.

But, he wasn't a superhero, not even a mortal one. If he didn't survive, he knew Joe and Trent would pick up his trail and take up where he left off. His crew would miss him, but they'd be okay. His father, his only family, would be fine without him. In fact, he had been for over twenty years.

Guilt and worry swallowed him into a yawning, hollow pit. He could make all the justifications he wanted, but if something happened and he didn't make it out of this, he'd be leaving a huge—possibly the most important responsibility he'd ever claimed—hanging out to dry.

He fished out his phone and dialed number at the top of his call log. Just like every other time he called it, the generic voicemail greeted him.

With a croak in his voice, he answered the robotic request for him to leave a message. "Hey, Addie. It's Rick. I just wanted to let you know that I'm going to get Leigh back. I promise you that." He carefully swung his leg into the SUV and his wound protested with a burning, ripping pain. Stars spun in the periphery of his vision. "If something happens to me, I want you to know that you can call Kate and Trent. Trent's number is stored in your contacts. He and Kate are the people taking care of your foal." He closed his door and started his truck.

"They're good people. The best people I've ever met. If I…if I don't come out of this, if you don't hear from me by lunchtime today, I want you to call Trent's number and tell him everything. If you need even the smallest thing, you call them. I…goodbye, Addie." He swallowed the basketball in his throat and disconnected the call.

Contemplating his choices, he pulled out of his driveway and onto the main road. The dark, moonless, early morning sky settled heavily over the landscape. Acres of shadowed pasture lined with white fencing appeared to run beside him as he flew by his sprawling property. Trent would laugh his ass off when he discovered Rick had bought the old Underwood horse farm.

To this day, I still don't know the first thing about horses.

Yet, he'd chosen to stay close to his friend. It hadn't hurt that the sprawling property with a myriad of stables and barns could conceal any number of things. Vehicles, equipment, training rooms. Hell, he could even construct and hide a helipad or two, if he wanted. Like Walker Farms—it would be secure and no one would question the tight security because of the assumed value of the horses housed on the property. Kentucky, particularly this part of the state, was home to some of the most expensive horses in the world. Of course, he didn't actually have any horses, but the neighbors didn't need to know that.

With his blue blood pedigree, he'd fit right in. But he

knew on the most basic level, he didn't deserve to be here. He knew nothing about horses or animals of any kind. He likely couldn't cut grass or hay without making a total fool of himself. Equipment? A wide assortment of tractors and trailers had been included with the sale of the farm when the former owner retired due to a health scare that changed his priorities. When they negotiated the sale, he'd assured Rick that everything was in good working order. Rick couldn't even put a name on the odd vehicles, let alone operate them. Maybe he could have Cara show him without telling the guys? The woman could drive anything.

The road's end came into view, signaling that the time to make his decision had come. A dark, empty intersection beneath a highway overpass never seemed so surreal.

Left or right?

The highway heading right led to the city's eastern outskirts and Marcus's neighborhood. The path to his left would take him to an onramp for the westbound freeway that would take him to the warehouse.

Most people would be at home in bed. The approaching dawn waited—warm, muggy, and impatient around him.

His time was limited. Trent and Dark Horse were breathing down his neck. They'd track him soon and, when they found him, it would not be pretty. Yes, absolutely, Leigh's safety would come first. But after they had her safe?

Trent would kick his ass, injuries be damned.

He turned the steering wheel right and drove onto the highway headed east.

~

Marcus stormed down the dim hall toward his office. Anger ripped through him, hungry and fierce. A living fire searched for a target, ready incinerate anyone in his path.

No one in his employ dared come between him and what he wanted.

And he'd wanted her badly. Still wanted her, with a hunger so savage that it made him pause for a moment. He never denied himself anything.

He wanted. He took, and there was no help from heaven or hell for those who hoped to deny him.

He took a deep breath. This was Wen. He needed to chill. He took another deep breath.

Nope. Still pissed. Ready to tear the head off any living thing that was stupid enough to get in his way

Fucking Wen. His brother. Both the only person he loved and the biggest weight around his neck.

One more reason he was happy to be a cold-blooded bastard. Not having a heart meant he felt no guilt, no responsibility toward anyone but himself.

Except, twenty years ago, he'd been a child and dumb as a box of rocks when he'd fallen in love with his baby brother. Truly, he'd had no choice. He'd been forced to raise Wen, even though he'd only been a child himself. So, in a fucked-up sense of love, he continued to care for the weakling.

Marcus threw open the door to his office. He allowed only one person entry to his space when he wasn't present— his brother.

Denny knelt on the floor, his hand on Wen's neck,

checking for a pulse.

He snarled, "Get the fuck out."

"It's bad, boss. You want me to call an ambulance? He needs help, like, yesterday. I know we don't want to risk the heat, but..."

"I said *get the fuck out*." No need to raise his voice. From day one, he ruled with an iron fist. He paid well to ensure their loyalty, but they were also aware right from the start, no one defied him. His brand of pink slip came attached to a bullet and ended with a trip into the river.

Denny had been with him for almost three years, longer than almost anyone in his employ. And he wasn't stupid. He blinked and then he disappeared, shutting the office door behind himself.

The moment the door closed, Marcus hurried to a potted plant on an antique table in the room's corner. He lifted it and twisted off the false bottom. Setting the pot's top half aside, he watched his brother's thin, t-shirt covered, chest. Hoping he saw a faint rise and fall, he pulled a box from the bottom half of the vase. He dropped the base on the floor where it landed with a dull thud. He tore open the box of Naloxone nasal spray.

Unfortunately, it wasn't the first time he'd had to use the opioid overdose med. *What a shitty thing to have to be a pro at.*

He popped the caps off both pieces and assembled the kit. He dropped everything on his desk except the spray, then knelt at his brother's side.

This was his fault for leading them both down this path. The money. The drugs. The power. He wanted it all for them both. Demanded it. And in the process, he'd brought his not-too-bright brother along for the ride.

Wen didn't deserve this. But if he was too stupid to at least listen to Marcus, there was only so much he could do for the idiot.

This was the last fucking time he'd do this.

He felt for a pulse and found a weak one. Tilting Wen's head back, he sprayed a half a dose into each nostril. Rolling his brother on his side, he cursed. "Man, you better fucking wake up. You have no idea what you just interrupted." He smacked his brother on the back of the head. "Wendell!"

"Wendell Alexander Lewis!" *Fuck me, what a stupid name.* Their mother had said that he needed a name that would sound proper when they attended parties and expensive schools. She hadn't been any brighter than Wendell. He smacked his brother harder. "Wake the fuck up." It summed up their life. Born dirt poor, grasping, fighting for more.

"Ow." His brother groaned weakly. "Don't." He tried to roll to his back.

"No way. You stay right there. I'm not getting puked on again." Angry and maybe even a tiny bit scared, Marcus smacked Wen again, this time far less hard. "You did it again, motherfucker. Almost killed yourself."

Eyes closed, with a weak hand, Wen swiped a hand over his brow, clearing the mess of greasy dark blond hair. The moment he dropped his hand, it fell back into place. "I know. Think I saw mom. She would make a pretty angel." Squinting, he blinked his bloodshot, dark brown eyes several times.

"Bullshit. Whores don't go to heaven." Holding Wen's shoulder, he fought to keep the memories of a grasping housekeeper with the skills to get what she wanted but not enough brains to keep it. Each time he looked at his brother, he saw their mother in Wen's fine-boned features. He'd be a good looking male, if he ever got his act together. Marcus didn't see that happening any time soon.

"Come on, do you think I'd go to heaven?" His brother laughed, weak and rasping. "I said she *would make* a pretty angel, not *is one*. Don't think I was standing in front of pearly gates, Marc. I'd like to see her again."

He released his brother and stood. "She was worthless white trash. Get that shit out of your head." He toed Wen in the back with his shoe. "Get the fuck up."

"Chill! I almost died. Give me a break." As dramatic as it sounded, his brother was right. He swiped his messy hair out of his eyes and splayed his arms out to his side. This time, his too-long, shaggy hair stayed.

They wouldn't be in this boat if it weren't for their mother and Wen's father. She'd had the bastard in the palm of her hand, quite literally, at one point. When the time had come to use her brains instead of her body and display a little patience, she'd gotten greedy too fast. She'd lost sight of the big picture and settled for a minute fraction of what they'd been entitled to.

Then she'd blown every last cent.

Marcus sat in his desk chair and glared. "You look like shit. Would a shower and haircut kill you?"

"Hey. Chicks dig the bad boy vibe."

"Trashy chicks might, but if you want sweet, clean pussy then you need to show them you have class. You'd have them eating out of your hand. I can pick and choose from a catalogue of women eager to please me." Yet, the one he wanted waited, bound and gagged, in a storeroom.

He toed Wen in the side of his head to get his attention.

"Do I need to drop you off at the ER? How much did you take? This one was bad. You can't do this shit again." They'd been lucky this time. If he hadn't been nearby or had the Naloxone handy, things could have had a far worse ending.

He'd be dumping his brother's body in the river.

Resignation darkened Wen's tone. He knew what was coming. "Not much, I swear. You're going to make me suffer for this aren't you. Last time was bad."

"Yup. We'll go back to my place. You can suffer through the withdrawal there. I'll lock your ass in the bathroom again."

Wen visibly shuddered. "Fuck. Me."

"Man. I love you, but I don't have it in me to keep this shit up. I'll throw your ass in the river before I let you ruin everything I've built."

His brother responded as if he understood it was only a matter of time. "I know you will."

Chapter Three

Joe MacDonald stood on his friend's front porch, completely oblivious to the sliver of dawn kissing the horizon of Trent's horse farm. He listened to the phone pressed against his ear, praying that Detective Bowie with Kentucky State Police had something. Even the smallest crumb of news about his sister's abduction might give them somewhere to start their search.

"We've got two men on Boyd, and they'll let me know the moment he blinks. Right now, it's not looking good. He's on a ventilator, so even if he wakes, he won't be talking. The doc is worried about possible brain damage due to severe blood loss and lack of oxygen. Even if his condition improves, there's no guarantee he'll have anything useful for us. I don't know much about Sutton, but I have a feeling these two aren't the best of friends. Sorry, Joe. We've exhausted every possible lead. I swear, I'll update you the moment we have anything at all." The call disconnected without another word, but Joe clutched the phone, unwilling to release his hold on hope.

A gentle presence pressed into his side as Cara wrapped an arm around his waist. He shifted to bring her closer, and she laid her head against his shoulder. God, how he loved this about her. No meaningless words or false promises. All she offered was her love and support. He squeezed her tightly and kissed the top of her head.

He'd be lost without her.

"How are your parents and Kylie?" Her soft-spoken

question punched him in the gut.

He'd checked on them first. They were saying up at the big house with Harlan and Sandy Walker. They'd only balked for the briefest moment before conceding that, with so much going on, he would have one less thing to worry about if he knew they were secured at the horse farm. "Upset. Confused. And terrified. But my parents are two of the strongest people I've ever known. They'll keep it together, just to keep things as normal as possible for Kylie. They haven't told her yet, and I agreed. Maybe once we know more... but we don't see any point in scaring a six-year-old. They've told her that her daddy is working extra. She's used to that. God, their trust in me is staggering. My father told me not to worry about Kylie, that she'll be fine with them while I concentrate on finding Leigh. He was so confident that I *would* be able to find her. I mean, there wasn't the slightest shred of doubt in his voice. Their faith in me brings me to my knees."

Cara squeezed him tighter. "They know you won't stop until she's home. That's all they need, a little hope and their trust in you. They're not the only ones who believe in you, and you're not alone in your search."

"I know." And he did. Until he'd fallen hard and fast for his sweet little soldier, Cara, he'd never understood the power of having someone walk by his side. Not just in the sunlight, but who was also willing to fight beside him in the darkest hours of his life. "Let's go see if the guys have had any luck."

Hand in hand, they went inside, where an exhausted and frustrated Trent was answering his cell. He turned on the speaker function and laid it on his dining room table. "Pete, tell me you've found something, man." The small black device held everyone's attention.

Pete's voice came over the phone as Trent braced his arms on the tabletop, wide shoulders tense and palms flat against the surface, as if willing the phone to give him the info he needed. "Okay, I've run multiple searches, and you're not going to believe this. I found a property, not more than eight miles from your place. Underwood Stables. It was sold recently and—"

Trent shook his head, making his sandy, near-to-shoulder length hair, shake. "What?"

"Underwood Stables. It's a large horse farm. The map says it's about—"

Trent straightened, planting his hands on his hips and looked up at the ceiling. "I know the farm, Pete. I can spit on it from here. Who purchased it from Bill?"

Pete's voice quieted from its usual exuberance to an uncharacteristic muted drawl. "Richard Frederick Evans purchased it, almost a month ago."

Holloway stood, his chair legs scooting across the floor. "Son of a bitch."

Noah asked, "Do you think that's where he went?"

Joe spoke up for the first time since they'd gathered at Trent's home, their usual, if unconventional mission planning headquarters. "He's planned his own rescue op without us. He's going after my sister alone. I haven't known Rick as long as you all have. I've only known him long enough to learn two things. One, he shoulders enough responsibility for ten men. And two, he's ridiculously stubborn. It's an honorable, but potentially deadly, combination. I don't like this." And he really didn't. Dread sat low and heavy in his gut.

Pete's voice came through the phone connection. "Are

you sure you don't want me to come home? My wife and girls will understand. Crystal would do anything for Rick. If I leave now, I can be home in about six hours. Quicker if I can find a flight."

Trent answered. "It's best if you stay put and connected at all times. Just keep your phone on you and dig up anything and everything you can on L and S Consulting and Marcus Sutton. I need every grain of intel, Pete. That'll keep you occupied for a while." Trent ran a hand over his exhaustion stamped face.

"Got it, boss. I'll call the moment I find anything. Stay cool, man."

Trent shook his head and disconnected.

Everyone stood, looking to Trent and waiting for his next command, even though every person in the room knew where they were going.

~

Leigh took a slow breath and exhaled, testing her ribs for pain. She'd been drugged and tossed around like a bag of trash and had the aches and pains to show for it. They hurt, but considering the shape the rest of her body was in, she considered herself lucky.

Closing her eyes, she listened intently. With nothing to keep her company except the thunder of her heartbeat in her ears, time crept by. Everything was quiet, except for a few muffled voices.

A door slammed open and her captor barked one last

order, dashing any hopes she had of escape. "Boys, you're working over tonight. No one leaves until I return. Keep your eyes and ears open for trouble."

Why, she didn't know, but she counted the replies as the men spoke.

"Sure thing, boss." *One.*

"No sweat. We're nearly finished loading this shipment, but we'll find something else to do." *Two.*

"No problem." *Three.*

"We expecting trouble?" *Four.*

"I don't know, stay alert just in case. I've got something important stashed in the old office. I'll be back for it as soon as I take care of something. Don't leave."

"Got it, boss man." *Five.* There were at least five men out there. Even if, by some miracle, she managed to untie her wrists and legs, she'd never be able to sneak past five men unnoticed, especially not ones who'd been instructed to watch for trouble.

A door slammed in the distance, and the voices continued dimly.

"Can you believe what happened out at the Riley Creek operation? What a mess."

"I heard, but didn't want to believe it. I asked the boss if he wanted us to make a second trip out the quarry to retrieve the rest of the supplies, but he said no."

She stared at the dull, yellow light shining through a small widow near the ceiling behind the desk.

"Yeah, the place is probably crawling with cops by now. Can you imagine how much product he lost out there? It's unreal."

"He didn't even blink over the loss. The man has more

money than God. He doesn't take shit from anyone, but he's fuckin' smart as hell. He's always saying to never keep all your eggs in one basket. Always thinkin' two steps ahead of everyone else."

"Yeah, forget plan B, he's already got plans C, D, E, and F mapped out."

"I only wish he'd let us in on the scoop. He's as secretive as he is smart."

Leigh closed her eyes in despair. This was her fault. Her kidnapping. *Rick.*

God, I hope he's okay.

Cara would have seen to his injuries as soon as Joe took care of Sheriff Hawkins.

And Addie? So far, the girl had been beyond difficult to find. For once, Leigh hoped that she stayed that way for a little longer. Safe and hidden from harm. If only she hadn't pushed Rick into doing something he'd known was a bad idea.

"No, shit. All I know is that I never want to end up on that man's bad side."

Music that had been playing dimly in the background rose in volume until she could no longer hear their conversation. She couldn't say that she minded, other than the voices had offered her a distraction, something to focus on besides her miserable situation.

Tears ran down her cheeks. What could she do? Wait patiently for him to come back for her? *No. Absolutely not.* She opened her eyes and looked around the dim room. God, she hated being helpless.

As a social worker, she watched people in difficult situations try to climb their way out of despair and into something brighter nearly every day. She offered every bit of help that she was able and encouraged them to keep trying. *Never give up.*

She'd be a hypocrite if she didn't do the same.

She tamped down her helplessness and focused on the dark room. The only light shone through a small window in the wall behind the desk. She assumed the artificial source to be a streetlight or lamppost from the lot outside the warehouse. She arched her back and craned her head to get a better looked at the old desk. It didn't look like much, but maybe she could find something to cut the ties around her ankles. She refused to lay in the floor, like a damsel tied to the train tracks.

Carefully, on her side, she inched her toward the desk and hoped for a miracle.

~

Rick stared out the window at the monstrous stone home surrounded by a six-foot fence that, at a first glance, defined subtlety and grace. Rick wasn't fooled. Before he even shifted into park at the curb across the street, he'd counted six security cameras. All in all, Marcus Sutton's home didn't look any different from the other homes on this side of town. Sure, the color and style was a hair different than the one beside it, but it appeared no more sinister than other homes in the neighborhood full of McMansions.

Rick would bet his last dollar that the place had more security than most banks, not that it would matter. One way or another, he was getting Leigh back, but over-the-top security aside, something was off.

The scene was just *too* normal. To think the house hid a wealth of crime, including kidnapping, just didn't feel right. Aware that evil often lurked in the most unlikely places, he fought to clear his unease. He placed his hand on the key to turn off the ignition and stopped cold.

It wasn't the seemingly normal house that nagged at him. His gut, the very instinct that had kept him and his friends alive time and time again, beat at him. The only other time it failed him had been the day Justin died. The reason they'd been attacked? Rick hadn't listened to the instinct telling him to turn their convoy around. He'd squashed it and listened to their orders and common sense.

A good man died because of Rick's mistake.

He sure as hell wouldn't take a chance at repeating history with Leigh's life at stake.

He shifted into drive and pulled away from the curb. Shifting in his seat, he carefully adjusted his leg as he raced through the silent dawn. He'd wasted strength and precious time.

Breaking speed limits, he flew through the quiet early hours, oblivious to the empty world around him. When the looming brown brick warehouse came into view, he weighed his options. How could he approach without detection? Where did he make his entrance?

On his first pass, he drove down the main street running through the industrial park and by the warehouse. Observing the lot, he counted five vehicles, all parked near a door on the building's east side. Two large, truck-sized doors marked the shipping and receiving bay at the building's north end. Following the road around, he noted that the building's west and south walls were similar to the others, except that the lot was a little more polished on the west side. Landscaping sprinkled with small trees and flowerbeds bordered the entrance. The door was glass and marked with a Beating Hearts Industries logo. He assumed that the business offices and reception area waited through this door. At this early hour, the parking spaces sat empty and the lights inside were off.

He'd found his entrance.

He parked behind a building a block away. He locked his truck and half jogged, half limped through the eerily quiet industrial park.

He made his way through the shadows and, assuming the people who worked there parked closest to where they worked inside the building, around to the west entrance. He pulled on the handle and wasn't surprised to find it locked. He pulled his B&E kit from a pocket on his cargo pants and made short work of the surprisingly challenging lock.

But then again, if he was a heroin smuggling criminal, posing as a legitimate business owner, he wouldn't skimp on security. Not only did you have to keep out authorities, but also competing criminals.

He held his breath and pulled the door open. Thankful for diligent maintenance workers and silent hinges, he eased inside the reception area and shut the door. He scanned the dim surroundings. He gripped his weapon in one hand and quickly made his way through the generic reception area and down the hallway. The passage came to a head at an oak framed painting of a little girl in a wheelchair reaching up to hold a doctor's hand. On the left wall was a door with the word *Meeting Room* etched on a glass panel in the door's upper half. A quick look inside revealed a large conference room and a framed map on the far wall. On the room's opposite side was a framed poster of the Beating Hearts logo with its slogan, *Charity makes the world turn.*

No windows. No exits.

He closed the door and turned to the door labeled *Office* on the right. Inside sat a large, elegant desk that spoke of leadership. The room was so generic it could have been used for an office furniture catalogue. The only thing out of place was a potted plant that someone had set haphazardly on the desk.

One closed door was on the left wall and another on the wall to his right. Silence hung heavy in the darkness. He walked lightly on his feet, senses alert.

The injury to his thigh throbbed with each step, but he refused to give it any of his time or attention. Each painful jar brought him one step closer to finding Leigh. When this was finished, and he had her safe, he could curl up and die. Until that, his needs meant nothing. Opening door number one, he was rewarded with the view of a bathroom. Behind door number two?

He pulled out a penlight and looked into a short, pitch black hallway that ended in a metal door, complete with locks that would make the most experienced locksmith quake in his boots. Rick put his ear to the door and heard the faintest hint of music.

Perfect.

He tried the door and, surprisingly, found it unlocked. The knob turned and when he pulled, the door opened silently. Light barged into the hallway making him squint against the artificial glow.

He quickly looked around the door's edge. The cavernous warehouse sat silent and mostly empty. He let the door shut softly behind him and scanned shipping and receiving area. A few scattered pallets holding plastic wrapped equipment waited to be serviced or shipped.

Ages ago, Rick had suspected that the business was a front for opium smuggling out of Afghanistan, but they had never found any evidence. Even though they'd had assignments with their unit, they'd tried keeping a watch when they'd been able. No question, Marcus was a sly bastard and covered his tracks, but he often popped up in locales not far from Rick. It happened far too often for it to be a coincidence.

Making his way through the equipment, he worked his way back to a heavy door. It opened easily, revealing a wealthy supply of cleaning chemicals. Judging by the names on some of the containers, he had to wonder if they might be used for something far more sinister.

Like cutting or manufacturing heroin.

He closed the door and moved onto the next. Marked *Utility,* this one was locked. He quickly unlocked it and found what he was looking for. He went straight for the electrical panel and building's main power switch. When the large lever took both hands for him to flip, he knew he was in trouble.

His strength was flagging.

The moment the breaker tripped with a loud thunk, the room went dark.

Without missing a beat, he pulled his night vision goggles out and continued on his path. He exited the utility room, quickly locked the door behind him and made his way toward the sounds of confusion. With the music silenced, male voices were distinguishable.

"What the hell, man?"

"Did someone forget to pay the bill?"

"I can't even see my own hand. You think we should call the boss?"

Go ahead and call him. Please.

Rick smiled into the darkness as he moved closer.

~

After what felt like hours of inching her way across the floor, Leigh made her way to the backside of the desk. She rolled over onto her belly, bent her legs beneath herself and used her forehead to push against the floor. She rose awkwardly to her knees. The old desk had four drawers, three down the side and one centered beneath the desktop. Cursing her captor for tying her wrists behind her back, she inched her way around until her backside was facing the center drawer. Leaning forward to lower her shoulders and raise her hands, she fumbled around until a couple of fingertips grazed the handle.

She lost her balance and fell. She turned her head and just missed smashing her face on the concrete as her shoulder broke her fall. The rough floor, cold and stinging against her temple reinforced her determination to find a way out of hell.

She braced herself with a couple of deep breaths. She fought the urge to gag on the stale and dusty air. Spreading her legs the bare few inches her bindings allowed, she rose to her knees. Slowly, testing her balance, she tried again. She found the drawer, and bypassing the small knob, she extended her hands, tucked her fingertips under the bottom edge and snapped her hands closed, pulling the drawer with them.

A shockingly loud screech stopped her in her tracks.

Holding her breath and listening, she hoped for all she was worth that somehow, against the odds, no one heard the noise. She counted to twenty and when she heard no change in the distant sounds coming from outside, she released her breath. Reminding herself that in the tomb quiet room, every sound seemed magnified, she took another breath and reset her hands for another pull of the drawer.

Her heart thundered. Air rasped in and out of her lungs. Her knees shushed over the ground. To her ears, each sounded as though she'd been hooked up to the largest microphone in the world.

She worked her yoga-magic and was rewarded with another scoot of the drawer, thankfully, with a quieter squeak. She wriggled her hips and knees, moving a couple of inches forward, this time pulling the drawer with her fingers hooked under the drawer's bottom as she moved.

Her shoulders throbbed and burned, begging to be free of their uncomfortable position.

But her only hope lay within the mysteries of the desk.

She couldn't allow herself to contemplate the challenges she'd face if she somehow miraculously found something sharp inside the desk.

One step at a time. I have to focus on the here and now. Nothing else matters.

No matter how much faith she had in Joe's abilities and determination, she'd be naïve to think that if she waited, help would magically find her. It was possible, maybe even likely, that he didn't know who'd taken her. Even if he did know, that didn't mean a blinking neon beacon would appear over her location. After finding her, he'd have to get a search warrant, wouldn't he? With all that had happened in the Riley

Creek Sheriff's Department, everything would likely be a mess for some time.

I am well and truly screwed. If only I could get my hands and feet free.

The faint sounds of music abruptly died, as if the radio's cord had been yanked from the wall. The men complained about the darkness with assorted curses.

She turned and looked into the shadowed drawer.

Nothing. The only things inside were two paperclips and an old gum wrapper. She sank to the floor. In the yawning silence, everything, even slightest movement, seemed magnified until each breath sounded like a windstorm.

"Shit. Where's my phone? I can't even see it." She heard scrambling sounds as the men looked for some way to provide light.

"Hang on. I got a lighter somewhere. Yeah. Here."

"Got it, thanks."

"Use the flashlight app. Light this place up, man."

Filled with a sudden sense that time was wasting, but not knowing what else to do, she decided to try and open the desk's side drawers. If nothing else, it might give her something to concentrate on.

She stopped when the general confusion in the outer room abruptly changed to alarm. "What the fuck! Did you see that?"

"No. You're just freaked."

"Yeah, Jim. You're just seeing shadows."

"Screw that. I saw something."

"Man, put your gun away. Pussy."

"I know I saw something moving over there."

"Put the gun away, Jim. If you blow your toe off, boss

man won't be happy. If anyone hears gunfire and calls the cops, he'll be supremely pissed."

"Whatever, man. How much longer do you think we gotta wait around here?"

"Don't know. Don't care. As long as I'm getting paid to babysit whatever special cargo is in the old storeroom, I don't care. Ain't got nowhere to go except bed, and I like my paychecks."

"I hear you, man. Best part of this job."

"Don't you wonder what he has stashed in there? I mean we're sittin' on a ridiculous amount of product here. What do you think? About 15,000 dollars' worth of H?"

Derision dripped from another voice. "You never could add two and two. I'd say it's closer to seventy grand."

"Shit. But that's my point. What could he have hidden in there that's worth more than what we've got here and packed into those old exam tables? I mean, I've seen him ticked off before, but he was pissed. Like, ready to murder someone mad."

"Don't know. Don't care. And don't even think about peeking. Gil, let's try the breaker. This building is ancient. Maybe a fuse is blown or something. Tim, don't fuckin' touch anything and don't shoot any shadows."

This is just wonderful. The goon squad is armed and stupid.

Chapter Four

Bingo.

The idiots had just given him Leigh's location. Hopefully he could keep it together just a few minutes longer. He cursed his injury and weakness. He wasn't able to move with half of his usual stealth. Fortunately, luck was on his side and the only one who'd seen his movement was the kid. No one ever believed the new guy.

The maintenance room's locked door might buy him a little time. Then again, if someone had the keys, the few seconds wouldn't be enough. Regardless, his time was running out. He'd pushed past his limit.

He stayed as low as his leg allowed and made his way along a wall, toward the door in the back corner.

"Why are you so jumpy, man?"

"I'm not. I'm cool."

The kid was anything but cool. He was one jitter away from a panicked eruption.

It gave him an idea.

He pulled out his lock pick kit and took out a couple of tools. Reining in his impatience, he waited. The moment the men relaxed, he threw his smallest pick to the opposite side of the room. The sound of metal hitting the floor was quiet, but clearly audible in the large, mostly concrete room.

As Rick had hoped, the kid's anxiety only increased. "Did you hear that? Dave, is that you?"

"Chill. It was probably just a mouse."

"No way. I heard the office girl say that everything in

here has to be extra sanitary, because of the medical stuff. There aren't supposed to be any rodents or bugs. I thought it was funny at the time, because of what we do back here. There's nothing clean about what goes on here at night." The kids voice rose in volume as his words tumbled out faster and faster. "Maybe we should leave. We'll go in the storeroom, get whatever the boss is keeping in there, and take it with us. We'll keep it safe and call him to come get it."

"No. No way. It's just a little darkness. Man up, for fuck's sake. Just because it's supposed to be clean, doesn't mean it is. It was just a fucking mouse."

Rick threw the largest pick in the same area. Then moved a few feet closer to the door. He was making progress, but this method wasted time he didn't have. If they got into the utility room and turned the power on, he was screwed.

He threw two more picks, one right after the last. He needed something larger. Then he pulled the pocket mirror he used for seeing around corners. Useless in the dark, he wouldn't miss it. He threw it just a few feet from the tools. In the silent, cavernous room the clattering sound clamored and echoed.

Finally, the kid lost his slippery grip on his remaining composure. "Shit!" Someone fired three shots fired in rapid succession. Light flashed in Rick's periphery. He raced to the door and hoped for all he was worth that it was unlocked.

The world behind him erupted into chaos as someone else yelled. "Shut the idiot down before he kills us all, or worse, brings the cops!"

Rick shut out the cacophony and narrowed his focus onto one small pinpoint. The handle. He blocked out the pain, awkwardly running the remaining distance.

"What the fuck is going on here?" The guy who'd gone to look for the electrical panel had returned.

Out of options, Rick aimed at the ceiling and fired his own shot. He hoped the echoes would confuse them further.

"That wasn't me! That wasn't me! There's somebody in here, I swear!"

He grabbed the handle and twisted. Thank the heavens, it turned. Yanking the door open, he lunged into the room and pulled it closed behind himself. The dim world spun around him as he leaned against the door and gasped for air.

He ditched his night vision goggles and peered into the spinning room. Looking for any sign of life, he listened to the chaos outside.

"Shit, I saw it, too."

"I told you!"

The senior guy snapped at the kid. "Give me that fucking gun."

Rick stood in a ghost town. His stomach dropped like a stone to his feet. He limped further into the room. To his left, he saw nothing but old file cabinets and a stack of cardboard boxes. To his right, a wall of shelves filled with industrial cleaning supplies and an array of chemicals. He might not be able to read all the warning labels in the dim room, but he suspected it was the kind of stuff you wouldn't put in just any janitor's hands. The entire wall was lined with gallon sized jugs. When he'd heard the men talking about special cargo, he'd been so certain they meant Leigh. Had they only meant the shit they used to cut the heroin?

Now what do I do?

He'd barely made it in there alive with the hopes of finding Leigh. Saving her was the only reason he'd had to keep himself together. Without her? He had nothing. No reserves left. And Leigh? God. Where was she? Could he have screwed this up any worse?

He smacked the back of his head against the door. "Fuck. Me."

~

When gunshots barked right outside the door, she dropped like a stone to the ground. She had no idea what caused the commotion, but she wanted nothing to do with it or any stray bullets. When the door opened and closed just a moment later, she held her breath. Fear sent her heart racing, fighting to get out of her chest.

Then she heard two magical words. Six perfect letters.

"Fuck. Me."

It wasn't the words so much as the weak, rasping voice that spoke them. Before her brain could tell her mouth to stop and be cautious, quiet, the stupid orifice opened.

"Rick?" For all she knew, she might be imagining things. She struggled to rise, but in her haste, she fell.

Footsteps rushed over and then big hands were on her, turning her until she sat on her backside. Then in the murky darkness, she heard the voice that she'd worried might be gone forever. Rick's. "Thank Christ. Are you okay?" She wanted to sob with relief, wanted desperately to wrap her arms around him and crush him to her.

Yet, she couldn't. She was as helpless as a turtle on its back.

"I'm fine. Please tell me you have a knife?" Her head

buzzed with a hundred questions, but their situation went above and beyond dire.

Low, a little bit gravely and a lot tired, he spoke into her ear. "Yeah. I do. Don't move." She ached to lean closer and absorb his presence, his everything. He cupped her lower legs in his big palms and examined the ties around her ankles.

His hands shook as he pulled out his knife.

"Rick. I—I'm so sorry. This is all my fault. Your leg? I—"

"Not now. And it's not your fault. Never. Let's concentrate on getting out of here alive. Okay?" He sounded so tired, utterly drained of his usual strength. He should be in a hospital bed, not running a Dark Horse operation.

Speaking of which... Something didn't add up.

"Rick. Where are the rest of the crew?" It might be Rick's newly formed team, but considering the shape he was in, she didn't think Trent would let him participate in a rescue mission. She might have only known him for a few months, but she knew enough about Trent Dawson to understand he would lock Rick down if he wasn't up to a job.

His hands trembled on her legs. Alarmed, she looked at him closer. Was it the yellow tinted light casting the sickly hue to his skin? When sweat beaded on his forehead she feared it wasn't. His breaths were short and shallow. He didn't look up to walking out of the room on his own steam, let alone running an op.

Not to mention her overprotective brother Joe who, at the minimum, would be right in the thick of things, if not barging in and taking over. Something stank to high heaven.

"Sweetheart, don't move." Despite the noticeable tremble in his hands, he positioned the blade with precision beneath the tie.

"Yeah. You already said that. What's going on?" When he wouldn't meet her eyes, her stomach sank.

His only response was to cut her bonds loose. A million pins and needles stabbed her legs. An excruciating rush of feeling returned to her lower limbs. It was all she could do not to cry out. The trembling in her muscles made Rick's hands look like immovable granite. He sat the knife down and, starting at her ankles, tried to massage some feeling back into her legs.

Outside the room, one voice rose above the others. The one who'd taken charge and seemed the most capable had returned. "What the hell is going on here? Give me that fucking gun."

All the other voices started talking at once, spilling a tangled story.

"Something's up. The door to the utility room is locked. It was unlocked when I got here. I found the key. Don't let anyone out, nobody fucking move until I get the lights back on. Not a fucking millimeter."

"We gotta go, babe. We're sitting ducks."

"Okay." The only thing she knew was that she had to trust Rick's abilities.

He considered the window then he looked back to her. "It'll be a tight fit, but I think we can make it."

He hooked his thumbs into the waistband of her jeans and helped her to her feet. He didn't have to tell her to hold still. She willed her shaking legs to remain steady so he could free her arms. A moment later, her arms dropped to her sides. If she thought the pain in her legs had been bad? The agony in her arms was about ten times worse.

She kept her misery in check by reminding herself that Rick had a gunshot wound, and he'd come to rescue her. His torment had to be a hundred times greater. And his willpower? Apparently, the man had more than a wounded superhero on a mission to save the planet.

"Help me move the desk, babe. We're running out of time."

He hurried to one end, and she went to the opposite. In unison, they lifted the heavy monstrosity and shuffled it over to sit beneath the window. His shoulders heaved with deep breaths as he straightened.

He braced himself with a long, steadying breath and used his arms to climb up onto the desk with an awkward hop. He pulled an odd hammer shaped tool from a pocket on the side of his fatigues and broke the window's glass. He ripped off his tee, wrapped it around one hand and used it to clear the remaining shards from the frame.

"All right. Let's go. You first."

"But—"

With one look, he quelled her objection. He made a step with his clasped palms. She stepped up with one leg and swung the other into the opening. When it was through to her knee, he supported her so she could put the second leg through.

He grabbed her hand and slapped a set of keys into her palm. "Turn left and run one block. My car is parked on the far side of a red brick, two story building. Wait one minute. If I don't show, go without me. Count to sixty, then get out of here. Find somewhere to call for help. No arguments."

The soft light of dawn highlighted his hard features. A new, darker light entered his eyes. In the few months she'd known him, she'd learned he lived life far too serious. She could count the number of times she'd seen him smile on one hand. Kylie, her six-year-old niece, had been responsible for most of them.

But this darkness? It scared her on a bone deep, visceral level. She didn't know this man. A stone cold, merciless warrior's eyes stared into hers, demanding her obedience. She was a stranger walking in an unfamiliar world. He lived, even thrived here.

She'd be an utter fool to disobey this new, somehow impossibly darker, Rick.

"Leigh. Promise me."

"Okay. I promise. One minute. Please don't make me leave without you. Please."

"I'll be right—"

Voices outside the door broke into their conversation. Unsurprisingly, they heard the kid above everyone else. "Light! Finally. I can see. Hey, the door's locked."

"Move out of the way, idiot."

Rick crushed his mouth to hers in a hard, brutal kiss.

Then his mouth was gone, and the dark eyes returned. "Go."

Her feet touched the ground. As if they heard his order, they ignored the screams in her heart and ran across the parking lot. When the first gunshot rang out behind her, she didn't stop to look. She put her faith in Rick and kept running.

And praying.

Several more gunshots followed the first. Tears ran unheeded down her cheeks as an iron fist squeezed her heart. Following his directions, she ran to the truck as the soft morning world blurred through a wet shimmer. The moment his vehicle came into view, she fumbled with the keys until she found the one with the unlock button. The car chirped at her and she threw open the door and jumped into the driver seat. She put the key into the ignition. Thunder rocked the earth, shaking the seat beneath her.

Reflexively, she ducked her head and covered her ears. *Oh my god. Oh my god. Rick.*

Her head popped up. Smoke billowed from the warehouse.

Forget waiting.

Forget waiting and driving away from that blast, from Rick.

She threw the car into drive and stomped on the gas. Tires squealed, but she didn't stay to smell the burning rubber. She cut the corner and drove over the curb, driving back the way she'd just come.

She would not leave without the idiot.

Where the hell are Joe and Trent?

Racing around the corner, she half expected to run into him. But he wasn't there. Other than the smoke pouring out of the warehouse, the early morning scene sat silent and still before her.

She braked, halting the car in its tracks. Wiping the tears from her eyes, she scanned the area. Then she saw him. Up ahead, lying on the far side of the parking lot was a body. Black pants, no shirt, dark hair.

Rick. Her Rick. Lying face down in the parking lot. She put her foot on the gas, speeding across the pavement. She pulled up directly beside him then braked to a hard, jolting stop. Hopping out, she raced to his side. She dropped to her knees and checked for a pulse at his neck.

Relief washed over her when she felt the rapid flutter

against her fingers.

"Rick, come on. We have to get out of here. Where is your cell?"

"In the truck. Battery's dead." Each word spoken seemed a struggle.

"Then we have to find a phone and call an ambulance."

He raised his pale face to meet her gaze. He was sweaty and filthy. Abrasions marked one cheek. She'd never seen a more precious sight than the light of his dark eyes staring back at her. "No. Get in the passenger side. The blast knocked me down, but I'm fine. We have to get you somewhere safe."

"Rick, you need a doctor."

The muscles in his upper arms bulged as he braced his arms against the pavement to push himself up. "Now, Leigh. Get in." He stiffly rose and gripped her upper arm. "Marcus will arrive any moment. Who knows what his men are doing? We have to get you out of here."

"Are you crazy? You're hurt! I'll drive." A gunshot rang out.

"Leigh, damn it. Get in!" He barked the order and ushered her inside the vehicle. Once she was in, he slammed the door and limped at a run to the driver side.

A moment later, they were on the way.

He shifted in his seat, as if to find a comfortable position for his leg. His hand shook as he put it back on the steering wheel.

"Are you sure you're okay? I think we're far enough away for me to drive." She prayed he'd let her take over. He looked ready to pass out. God, he'd been shot what? Twelve hours ago? This was crazy.

She couldn't believe so much had happened in such a short time. All she'd wanted to do was drop off food for Addie. He'd warned her against it, feeling it might not be safe. She hadn't listened and nearly gotten them killed. Rick had been hurt. Her brother, Cara, they'd all been shot at. She could have accidentally drawn the orphaned girl into a shootout!

Another terrible thought punched her in the belly.

She'd assumed everyone had made it through that mess, simply because the alternative was unthinkable. But any number of horrible things could have happened to them. What if Rick was the only one capable of coming after her?

Nausea roiled in her belly, pushing bile higher and higher in her throat. The edges of her vision wavered and grew dim. She had to know, but couldn't make herself ask the question that might trigger an answer capable of breaking her in two.

"Leigh? Stay with me. You're safe now. Just a few more minutes and we'll be in safe territory. Morning traffic is rolling in and they won't chance a scene in front of witnesses. Marcus has too much to lose. C'mon, baby. Breathe. Slow deep breaths in and out."

How pathetic was she? She was physically fine, safe, and here she was, on the verge of a panic attack. He'd been shot, was likely bleeding everywhere, and he was taking care of her.

Time to get my shit together.

"I'm okay." She closed her eyes and forced the words out of her mouth. "Joe? Cara? Kate and Trent? How is everyone?"

"They're fine. Truly. I was the only one injured. Well, not true. Cara's ankle is probably twelve shades of purple, but it's not broken. She refused crutches. Joe didn't have the strength to fight her over it. Your parents are staying with Kylie up at the big house on Walker Farms."

All the worry and fear whooshed out of her in one long exhale. Beyond a bomb shelter, she couldn't think of a safer place for her family than the Walker's horse farm. The place had always had an extensive security system in place. After her cousin Kate's kidnapping, Trent had only increased its safety measures.

There weren't words in the universe capable of describing the amount of relief those few words had given her. Yet it didn't answer all her questions.

"Are you sure you're okay?" Her words softened with worry. "You look like hell, Rick. Really. I don't know how you're still upright."

He was quiet, subdued. "I'll be fine. Promise." She wondered if he were trying to convince himself as much as he was her.

"What happened back there? I mean what caused the explosion?"

"Me. One of them shot out the lock in the door. They barged into the room, armed and ready to kill. They fired at me as I climbed out the window. I suspect all the chemicals in there didn't mix well with bullets. There's no telling what kind of flammables Marcus hid in there."

"What do we do now?"

"We get somewhere safe until I can figure out what to do about this shitstorm."

What could she say to that? She had nothing.

Despite the warm morning, shivers racked her body. She wrapped her arms around herself and waited. Wondered.

The morning world raced by as he drove them to God only knew where. They exited the highway and, just when she thought they were headed to Trent's, the familiar scenery changed. The sprawling horse farms looked similar to Walker Farms in size and grandeur, but they didn't have the same comfortable charm she loved.

Rick slowed the SUV at a set of enormous of gates. Black, elegant scrollwork surrounded the letter *U*. He pushed a button on the truck's sun-visor and the gates opened. He drove them onto a long, winding drive flanked by towering oak trees. The setting would have any movie producer weeping with envy.

While she looked around slack-jawed, he drove them practically to the front door and parked. He grabbed the keys then his phone from the cubby under the radio. "I need to charge my phone. I have something for you."

What planet was he on? Had blood loss made him loopy? "Are you crazy? I couldn't care less about presents. You need a doctor—better yet, a trip to the emergency room. I need to call Joe. My family will be half mad with worry." Stubbornly, he limped inside the ridiculously huge mansion with a single-minded focus that scared her. He looked well past ready to collapse. If she didn't have nightmares from the guy who kidnapped her, the sickly pallor of Rick's skin would surely bring them on. White as a sheet, trembling, she feared he'd pass out any moment.

He hobbled through the empty halls until he came to an office furnished with a desk and single chair. Like the rest of the home so far, it seemed cold and lonely. He stalked to the desk, attached a charger cable to his phone, and laid it on the desktop. His focus was scarily narrow. Nothing but getting that phone up and functioning seemed to matter, not even his life. She couldn't imagine how whatever it was could be so important. *Has he grown delirious?*

As much as she hated interrupting, she had her own desperate needs. Her family. She had to let them know she was okay. "Do you have a house phone I can use? I really need to call Joe." *And an ambulance for you, big guy.*

"The line works, but I haven't gotten around to purchasing the actual handsets yet. My cell will be ready in just a moment or two. I need it for one or two minutes and then you can have it. Promise. Five minutes, tops."

"Okay." Hopefully, he'd cooperate with her after he took care of whatever madness held him in its tight grip. She rearranged her priorities and vowed to call 911 before she called her family. Her heart caught in her throat, blocking her argument.

He swayed a little on his feet as he stared down at the dead phone, waiting. She felt unsteady, shaken as her hands trembled. She couldn't even imagine how terrible Rick must feel. He'd nearly driven himself to the grave in order to rescue her and he continued to forge ahead when it appeared a stiff breeze could knock him over.

He pushed a button and the phone lit up. He touched the screen a few more times, but she was more concerned with making sure he didn't pass out than with whatever he was doing with the godforsaken phone.

Then she heard it and understood.

A small, timid voice filled the air. "Uh. Hey. I hope this thing works. I saw him take her. That guy with the blond hair. He carried her over his shoulder like a sack. Um. I took a picture of his license plate." The world around her tilted, and she placed her palms flat on the desk for stability. *Addie.* In the midst of all the chaos, Addie had called him.

Bright morning sun poured in through the large window, casting Rick in shadow. He touched the screen and the sound of a ringing phone filled the tomb silent room. She held her breath, waiting through two of the longest rings Leigh had ever heard. Then the line connected.

Addie spoke, getting right to business. "Did you get her back?"

Rick nodded his head once to the phone, indicating that she should answer.

Leigh swallowed the grapefruit in her throat. "Hey, sweetheart. He did. I'm safe. What about you? How are you?" What Leigh really wanted to know was where the girl was. Was she hiding near her home? A million worries raced through her head.

"I'm okay." Addie paused, as if uncertain. "Um. You're really okay? He didn't hurt you or…" There was another pause. When something dark and sinister filled the air, Leigh didn't know whether to vomit or punch a hole in the wall. "He didn't do anything to you did he?" The stark fear in the girl's quiet voice put a stranglehold on Leigh's words.

As far as Leigh knew, there was no reason for Addie to be so scared of someone she'd never met. Unless she'd run across him at some point.

Rick cursed. A string of vile, hate-filled profanity filled the air, shocking Leigh out of her stupor. "No. I'm fine, sweetheart, really. Whe—?"

Anxious terror laced Addie's words. "Is he in jail? Did they catch him?" Her small voice rose in pitch and volume. It was a fear not born of suspicion, but of experience.

Leigh's blood drained to her feet as she answered the girl. "No, Addie. Not yet, but we will. We'll get him."

An oppressive cloud of panic filled the atmosphere as the girl's words tumbled out. "He's still out there? Oh no. I gotta go. I gotta get out of here." The panicked chant continued for a few seconds longer then abruptly cut off as the line disconnected.

When an invisible, yet palpable snap of rage lashed through her, Leigh looked up to the source. Rick. He stepped away from behind the desk, a juggernaut, hellbent on murder. That's when she saw it. One leg of his black pants was darker down the front, soaked through. With each step, he left smears of crimson in his wake. She rushed to stop him, putting herself in his path. "Rick, you can't. You need a hospital." *Like, yesterday.*

"Move." The gentle hold on her shoulders contrasted with the barely leashed violence straining his voice.

"No, Rick. You can't." She braced her hands against the hard muscles of his chest.

"Leigh. Move, baby." His hands left her shoulders and went to her waist. She was tall, and had never shied away from meeting a man head-on. Rick's six-foot-plus frame easily dwarfed hers.

Drawing on every bit of her patience and determination, she cupped his face in her palms. "You have to get your leg tended to. You won't be able to save anyone when you pass out." She implored as she tried in vain to catch his focus. She met his gaze with hers, but he wasn't seeing her.

Sweat broke out on his forehead. "I have to find her." He swayed on his feet as he moved her aside.

"Damn you. You can't go. You don't even know

where she is. You don't know where he is. You'll be lucky to make it out the front door." Again, she raced to stand in front of him. Chest to chest, they danced a dance of fear and anger. Leigh feared for his life and his anger burned hot enough to blister the skin from her bones. Yet, she knew she was safe from his rage. Though his fury might be enough to drive him to his very grave, he'd never lay a single finger on her. Placing her hands on his shoulders, she tried with all her might to stop him.

The door behind her burst open and hit the wall with a bang. When she whipped her head around, Joe and Trent stood there.

"Joe! Help me stop him!"

Rick swayed again as he tried to move her out of the way. She followed, trying to block him. He gripped her hips and tried to lift her. She wriggled from his hold, braced her shoulder low against his chest and planted her feet on the floor, linebacker style.

Then she held her breath and prayed to the heavens.

Then he toppled backward, taking her with him until they both fell to the floor with a bone shaking crash.

Thudding feet raced to them. Large hands gently grasped her upper arms. Male voices spoke hurriedly. Dimly, she heard one of them calling for an ambulance.

For the second time in less than twenty-four hours, she placed trembling fingers on Rick's neck. Holding her breath and concentrating with everything she had, she thought she felt a faint flutter. Hopefully.

Chapter Five

Leigh paced over a small stretch of linoleum inside a room in the intensive care unit. The monitor's steady beeping reassured her that Rick's heart still beat. Anxious, she sat in the chair beside his bed and took one of his hands in both of hers. She looked at the differences.

Her normally neat nails were chipped with ragged edges, but her fingers were narrow, feminine and, well, nothing special. In them? She held the definition of everything a male should be. His fingers were long, sturdy and, even in deep sleep, they represented limitless strength and confidence.

They'd been thrown together in the oddest set of circumstances and, through every single step, he'd walked beside her. He'd taken care of everything. He'd often been two steps ahead of her, addressing things she hadn't thought of.

God, what would she do without him?

They'd met months ago, when trouble had found Kate. From the first minute Leigh laid eyes on him, she'd been suspicious.

Rick and Trent, two complete strangers to her, had wanted to take her cousin away, swearing to keep her safe. She'd thought they'd been full of shit, but they hadn't been. The two men had known exactly what they were talking about. They also had the skills to back it up.

She hadn't known whether to be thankful for their knowledge or annoyed that they'd been right. Since Kate's life had been on the line, she'd happily settled for appreciation.

On that same night, as the fire department extinguished the fire that had brought them all together, a little raggedy waif appeared in the dark. She'd been determined to check on Bonnie, Kate's foal.

They hadn't known it at the time, but the orphaned horse and young girl had a great deal in common.

Leigh caught a small, pale face and wide, pale blue eyes peeking around Kate's barn. Like an apparition, she'd vanished. Wondering if she'd been responsible for the fire, Leigh chased after her. Rick had chased after them both. He caught Addie. They'd questioned the young girl, and she'd answered them with lie after lie. To say they had been suspicious would be the understatement of the year. They'd tried to return the girl to her home, but she'd given Leigh the slip in a convenience store.

In their rural community, it hadn't been hard for Leigh to figure out where Addie had come from and the situation was anything but good. The girl's father was in jail and would likely be incarcerated for a long time, leaving her alone. They'd gone to her home, with the hopes of getting her into the foster system, but the thirteen-year-old was a wily thing, determined not to be caught. She lived alone in a pitiful little house not fit for animals, let alone a child. She had no one to care for her, no one to provide food, clothing. The child hadn't even had access to running water or electricity.

Leigh had never been so heartsick. And as a social worker, she had seen enough heartache to last a lifetime. She'd dropped off food and water for the girl, but Rick had gone two steps further and paid to have the electric and water turned on. While Leigh had been forbidden to go there alone by both her brother and Rick, Rick had gone alone taking her all manner of things. Art supplies. A desk. A mattress and pillow.

He'd deny it to his dying breath, but his heart was as soft as his will was iron.

Crazy man.

She'd be lost without him and so would the entire Dark Horse crew. She laid her forehead on their joined hands and stayed long moments, listening to the steady rhythm of the monitor. She looked up at the sound of quiet footsteps.

Cara Gregory walked in, carrying a large tote bag. The petite strawberry blond looked like a preschool teacher when, in reality, she was a force to be reckoned with. Nurse. Soldier. The woman her brother loved.

If she had a catalog filled with a million candidates, she couldn't have chosen a better mate for her stubborn brother.

Not knowing what to do, Leigh stood in greeting. "I'm guessing they're not going to let me escape any time soon."

"No. But, if you're okay with it, I can escort you. Joe will likely hover nearby, but Kate brought you a change of clothing and toiletries. You can even shower if you like. There's an empty patient room down the hall you can use."

A shower? Oh, dear lord. She'd never heard a more tempting proposition.

"A shower and clean clothes sounds wonderful."

"Great. Joe's going to order pizza for an early dinner, if that's okay?"

Food? When had she eaten last? She looked at the clock on the wall and realized she hadn't eaten anything in over twenty-four hours. Her brother had given her a sports drink from the vending machine when they'd arrived at the emergency room and that had been hours ago. If she didn't get something in her and get some rest, she wouldn't be of any use if Rick woke up.

When, not if. She refused to give her fear any power. It might be silly, but she worried that if she gave that fear any credence, terrible possibility would feed the smallest kernel and grow into reality.

She stood and bit back a groan as every muscle in her body protested. Her arms, her legs, her lower back. "That's fine."

"Good. While you get cleaned up, Trent is having them bring in something for you to stretch out on. He wants you to stay here until he has a plan in place."

Fatigue muddled Leigh's senses as she asked, "A plan?"

"A security plan. The entire team is wiped. Most of us have been awake going on thirty-six hours. It'll be easier to guard one location, this room, than it would be two. You just shower, take something for pain, and get some rest. We'll take care of everything else."

Leigh looked from Rick's unconscious form to the sweet face of a hard-as-nails soldier. She'd totally underestimated the situation. "The guy who took me, he's not going to let this go, is he?"

"No. He's not." Complete and utter certainty born of experience stared back from Cara's eyes.

~

Rick fought to open eyelids sadistically pinned down by sandbags. He'd lifted sofas that weighed less. He turned his head from left to right, struggling to shake off the thick fog of lethargy. Finally, he opened one eye and was rewarded with the most beautiful sight he'd ever seen.

Leigh, sleeping curled on her side, faced him. Her cheek rested on one hand, while the other held onto the rail of his bed. Relief washed over him.

Quiet, exhausted, and one hundred percent lethal, a familiar voice spoke from his other side. "It's about time you woke up. Lazy." Trent Dawson. He listened to his closest friend and apparently, now his guard dog.

Rick kept his voice hushed. "What time is it?"

Trent's dark blond eyebrows rose. "What time? Seven a.m. I think you should be more concerned with the date."

"Shit. How long have I been out?" He scrubbed a hand over his face, unsuccessfully trying to clear the haze of lethargy.

"Three days. Three long, cramped days in ICU," Trent groused.

"Which hospital are we in?" Details, ideas and plans slogged through his mind in a sluggish jumble.

Trent answered as if he knew where the conversation headed but was powerless to stop it. "Bourbon County Trauma."

"They have a couple of suites. Hell, I think Dad bought them an entire wing a couple of years ago. Why didn't you insist on a bigger room? Her arms and legs were bound for nearly twelve hours. She needs to be somewhere where she can get comfortable."

"She refused. Your girl insisted that we stay here. She's been determined that you stay in Intensive Care until you woke. Wouldn't hear of moving you, not even an inch. She's barely left your side. You scared her. You scared us all."

Rick didn't know how to respond, so he turned to look at Leigh. "She's not mine."

"Bullshit. Everyone has watched you two dance around each other all summer. You can't be that oblivious. Besides, I think she might have something to say about that. She's a MacDonald woman. You're screwed." Trent's words were laced with tired amusement. He made it sound as if being claimed by a *MacDonald woman* was anything but a punishment. He would know, considering he had claimed Kate MacDonald as his. Wild horses couldn't separate the pair. Rick couldn't remember the last time he'd seen Trent so content.

"Where is your pretty little Kate?"

"She's at the farm, spending some time with Kylie. Everyone is trying to make her stay up at the big house like a vacation, but the little squirt is too smart. She knows there's something going on. Joe and Cara may bring her by after they know you're awake."

"I'd like to see her." The words felt odd in his mouth, but he didn't see any reason to hold them back. Joe's daughter was everything a six-year-old should be. Bright. Happy. Energetic. And showered by love. Her father and family made sure she had what all children deserved.

Addie. She should have all those same things.

A tidal wave of emotions, all of them ugly, crashed over Rick. Anger. Sadness. Fear and worry. He'd been a witness to a hundred ways the world could be unfair, but no matter how many times he'd seen the uglier side of life, it still pissed him off when it touched those incapable of escaping a world threatening to choke the life from them.

He listened to his friend, hearing him shifting in a chair

that was likely too small for his muscled frame and long legs. Trent was a man made to be outdoors, not cooped up in a tiny room playing babysitter.

Though Rick was completely aware of his surroundings, his focus was fixed on one point. The pale face surrounded by a wealth of chestnut hair before him.

Damn, but she was a beautiful woman. Tall, lean, graceful. Long lashes rested on creamy cheeks. She'd been gifted with flawless bone structure and a mouth designed for kissing. If she'd wanted, Leigh could have given Kate a run for her money on the pageant circuit.

Her beauty went far deeper than the movie star smile and swimsuit issue body. Soul deep, because she had one of the kindest spirits he'd ever met. She also had enough bullheaded stubbornness for two men.

He'd never known both traits to be so strong in the same person.

Like when he told her to flee, to get to safety. She'd ignored his orders, going back to save him. He'd lied to her. He'd been in far worse shape than he'd let on. He might not have gotten up if she hadn't come back for him.

She frowned in her sleep, scrunched up her nose and released the bed rail to wipe away a stray lock of hair. As soon as her face was free, her hand immediately returned to its former spot.

She needed a gentle, loving man who'd cater to her every need. Her every whim.

He wasn't that man, and he never could be. He was hard, inflexible, and he lived in a dangerous world. He'd see her through this nightmare and then do whatever it took to insure danger never darkened her doorstep again.

Even if that meant cutting both her and Addie out of his life forever. Because surely the girl deserved to be with Leigh. He could think of no better guardian than a woman whose heart was as big as an elephant's and as soft as a marshmallow.

The only thing he could provide either of them with was a life of worry, stress, and danger. Both of them had already suffered too much. As soon as he could pry his ass out of this bed, he'd find Marcus Sutton and do whatever it took to ensure their safety. He'd find Addie, make sure she was permanently in Leigh's care, and then he would walk away, leaving them to the lives they deserved. Without him. Forever.

He ignored the painful clutch in his chest and closed his eyes. He might as well rest and gather his strength. He'd gotten by Trent once. It wouldn't happen again. When his friend left his side, even to use the restroom, someone else would take his place. He was well and truly stuck until he was better.

He just prayed that Addie stayed hidden and safe until he was free from his prison.

He listened to the sound of his friend shifting in his too small chair and focused on the woman asleep beside him. As long as the people he cared for—no, loved—were safe, he'd make it through this cold world alone.

This one time, as he made peace with his loss, he'd be honest with himself. Rick Evans loved deeply. If cutting ties with those closest to his heart insured their safety, then he'd make that sacrifice. He might not ever be happy, but he'd be satisfied with the knowledge he'd done the right thing for those he cared for.

~

"Excuse me. Is this a bad time?" Startled by the unfamiliar male voice, Leigh looked up from her book and across Rick's bed to see two men standing at the open door. Rick's condition had improved over the past couple of days, but Trent and James had opted to keep him in the intensive care unit for security purposes. Noah Ramsey stood next to a tall, lean male with salt and pepper hair. The unknown man's resemblance to Rick was unmistakable. The only difference other than age? Their eyes. Where Rick's were a deep, dark chocolate brown and always filled with an intense focus, this man's eyes were a lighter, softer brown. And they appeared tired, maybe even exhausted.

Leigh glanced at Cara and Noah before answering. "No. Not at all." Cara stood and stretched from her post on the opposite side of the room, closest to the door. Curiosity flashed across her features, but she seemed at ease. Combined with Noah's mostly relaxed posture, she assumed the man to be no threat to Rick. "He's resting, but you're welcome to come in."

Cara tilted her head toward the door. "Come on, hon. Let's go wait for Joe. He'll be by with lunch in a few minutes. We'll eat in the nurse's lounge." The older man stepped back to allow them ample room to exit. She followed Cara down the hall to the breakroom.

When they were inside, sitting at the table, she asked. "Was that Rick's father or some other relative?"

"Father. There's no denying they came from the same genepool, is there?" Cara pulled her cell from her pocket and typed a quick message, likely to Joe.

"He seemed tense...restrained, maybe? I'm not sure what to call it." Leigh didn't bother to hide her curiosity.

Cara set her phone on the table. "Their relationship has been strained for as long as I've known Rick. Trent probably knows more details, but as far as I understand, Frederick is Rick's only living relative. I think he's made a few attempts at reconnecting with Rick over the years, but Rick hasn't shown an interest. He can be pretty stubborn."

"I've noticed." She'd thought she was hardheaded. Heaven knows how many times her family had lovingly and sometimes not so lovingly cursed her for it. Rick? He had her beat by miles.

Concern and curiosity prodded her to ask for more. "Do you know what happened to his mother? He doesn't have any siblings or anyone else at all?" She couldn't imagine. All her life she'd been surrounded by family. Unlimited love and support waited, no matter which direction she turned.

"His mother died when he was a child. From my understanding, then he was sent to boarding schools. At some point, while we were stationed in Afghanistan, his father had a change of heart. I don't know for sure, but maybe the fact that his son was in a warzone served as a wakeup call?" Cara shrugged. "Frederick tried to reconnect, but Rick refuses to see that his father might be interested in more than keeping the business in family hands." Cara grinned. "I don't know if you noticed or not, but our Rick keeps his emotions bottled up tight and gives an entirely new meaning to the word stubborn."

Leigh picked at chip in the table's laminate top. "Yeah. I kind of noticed." She'd gone toe to toe with him more than once. Guilt still haunted her, and she doubted it would ever leave. He'd known that going out to Addie's house had been a bad idea. She hadn't been able to see past her own desire to help the girl. Rick hadn't been any less eager to help, he'd only wanted to keep them all safe. She had pushed and pushed until he'd given in and allowed her what was supposed to be a quick stop to drop off food and drinks for Addie. She'd gotten them all shot at, Rick injured, and herself kidnapped. Then he'd nearly killed himself rescuing her.

"What kind of business does his family have?" She'd never put much thought into anything beyond his time with Dark Horse and him being Trent's friend.

She thought about Dark Horse. Their equipment. The manpower and long hours Rick insisted on paying them for. Kate had said that everyone had offered to help. They all jumped in without blinking to lend a hand because a friend was in need, even though not one of them had known Kate when trouble found her. Not one of the members had given a second's thought to whether they would get a paycheck.

According to Kate, when things with former Senator Bailey escalated, Rick had insisted on putting the team on Dark Horse's payroll even though there really hadn't even been an official business yet. He'd wanted to insure his men were taken care of while they'd been taking care of Kate.

All that money had to come from somewhere.

Cara tilted her head and gave her an odd look. "You really don't know?"

"No. I never really thought about it. He's just Rick, a friend of the guy who's dating my cousin Kate." An odd feeling squirmed in her stomach. "What am I missing?"

"His father is Frederick Evans. Head of Evans Rifle Company."

Good Lord! When she'd been in sixth grade history,

they'd briefly touched on the Evans family's contributions during the second World War. Prior to the United States entering the war, Evans Manufacturing had been a leading name in sewing machines. They'd switched to weapon productions to assist with the war effort. Praised for their quality and reliability, they never looked back after the war ended.

The already prominent name had only grown more so.

Cara spoke again and Leigh realized she likely resembled a fish with her openmouthed gape. "Yeah. Rick never mentions his family history, money or connections. I doubt he ever gives it a second thought. It's a common enough last name that most people never think twice about it. It just goes to show, money can't buy everything." Sadness for her friend colored her words.

Leigh gathered her wits. Cara was right. Her upbringing had been relatively modest, but she'd never once lacked attention, a shoulder to cry on, or love. She thought of the hours she'd spent with her mother and grandmother stringing beans on the front porch or listening to music and gossiping with Kate. She wouldn't trade those memories for the world. "No, it doesn't."

Family was everything. The thought of Rick not having one was unacceptable. She was grateful he had Trent, Cara, and the Dark Horse crew, but they wouldn't keep his home filled with activity, laughter, and love. They wouldn't keep him warm in the cold, dark of night.

Something squeezed tight around her heart.

The door opened and her brother walked in carrying a couple of white paper bags. "Ladies. The finest carryout from the diner. You'll find a selection of their gourmet sandwiches, fries, and assorted condiments." He set the bags in the center of the table and leaned down to greet Cara with a lingering kiss. "Sorry it's not warm food today. I have to get back out on the road. Miss you."

Cara laughed, quiet and husky. "You just saw me this morning. That's been what five, six hours, tops? I think you'll survive until this evening."

"Too long." Joe stood and came to Leigh. "Brat." He gave her a tight side hug and kissed the top of her head. "I'll be back later this evening to pick you up."

Leigh looked from the bags of food and back to her brother. "You're not staying for lunch?"

"Not today. The Cline's and the other teens' families are meeting with a lawyer and asked me to come by. I assured Brayden I'd be there." He nodded to the food on the table. "It's not fancy, but there should be enough food in there for Noah, too. Holler if you need anything." He gave them a half-wave as he headed out the door.

Leigh watched the door shut and sighed. "He works too hard."

"Yep. You think we can break him of the habit?" Cara's smile was soft as she opened the bag closest to her.

"Not a chance in hell."

~

"Can I have a moment alone with my son?" Rick heard the familiar voice against the backdrop of chirping monitors.

"I'm sorry, Mr. Evans. I can't leave Rick alone, not even if the president himself comes through those doors. You can just pretend I'm not here. Everything will be confidential, if need be."

"Oh, it's fine, Noah. I trust you. It's just awkward." The source of his father's voice remained close to the door instead of coming to sit at either side of his bed, like Leigh or his team members usually did.

"I understand, and I wish the circumstances were better, but we'll just have to make the best of what we have, yeah?" The fake leather in the chair to his right creaked as Noah sat his big frame in it.

"Yes. You're right. I need to be thankful my son is alive at all. He's always been too hard-headed and self-reliant for his own good. Never could break him of that habit."

"We're all thankful he's alive. But can I offer a small piece of advice, sir?"

"Of course, Noah."

"Rick is alive because of that stubbornness. It's just another one of his many strengths. If he didn't have that, he wouldn't be the man that I know. I'd trust him with my life. Maybe it's past time you quit trying to change him."

His father was silent a long moment, so long that Rick wondered if he'd silently left the room. Then he spoke quietly. "Eileen, was the same way. Once she got an idea in her head, there was no shaking it loose. They are so alike. Everyone always said he's the spitting image of me, but he has his mother's strength."

"Probably a good thing, then, since he's always getting into trouble." Noah was always in tune with people's moods and often played the peacemaker. Rick had always admired him for his intuition.

His father's next words were quiet. "Yes. Probably a

good thing. I should be going. Thank you for watching over him, Noah. If he needs anything, please don't hesitate to call on me."

"Sure thing, Mr. Evans. I'll update you if his condition changes. He's going to be just fine."

"I imagine so." Without another word his father left with soft footsteps.

Noah waited about twenty seconds before speaking. "So. How much longer are you going to play opossum? He's worried about you. Leigh is, too."

Rick opened his eyes, glared at Noah and slipped back into oblivion.

Chapter Six

Rick carefully stepped down from Trent's beast of a truck and shielded his eyes from the midday sun. He smiled as a little hand waved high in the air from atop a red bike. "Hi, Wick!" Though excited, Kylie's volume was only half as loud as usual. She kept one hand firmly on the handlebar as she waved the other. She'd grown a bit since he'd first met her at the beginning of summer. He hated to see it and imagined how Joe must feel facing the dueling emotions of pride and loss every day.

Damn, his weakness had gone far beyond the physical and into the emotional. Totally unacceptable.

I sound like a Hallmark card.

Finally free of the hospital's confines, he needed to get his act together.

"Hurry up, old man! We've been waiting ages for you to get your lazy ass out of bed." Rick turned from a smiling Kylie to find Pete Taylor standing on Trent's front porch, smiling. Damn, but the kid was a brat.

He didn't know what he'd do without him.

"Even fresh out of the hospital, I can still kick your ass, Pete. Worse yet? I issue your paycheck, boy. You might want to remember that."

Pete's smile might be bright, but Rick would have to be blind to miss the worry simmering in the eyes of Dark Horse's youngest member. Guilt beat at him. He'd scared them all.

"Get in here. Kate's cooked enough food for an army

and it's getting cold. You know she won't let anyone eat until we're all present."

"Damn, Pete. Are you ever not hungry?" James Holloway opened the front door and stood there with his arms crossed over his chest. "You start dropping hunger hints before your foot crosses the threshold. I'm going to tell Trent you have designs on his woman." He wore his dark hair a little longer than he had when they'd been in the National Guard, but he still stood in the same arrogant stance.

"I have my own woman, thank you very much." Pete poked a finger into Holloway's chest. When the larger man glared, Pete took a big step back before continuing his goading. "Unlike you. Why is it women never stick around for more than a date or two with your ugly mug, James? Are you lacking in a certain department?"

Holloway took a step closer to Pete, dipping his head and glaring down until they were almost nose to nose. "The only thing I'm lacking is patience with smart-mouths." Then he ruffled the younger man's hair. He turned to watch Rick walk up the porch steps and the worry in his gaze contrasted sharply with his next words. "Get in here, Rick. We're tired of waiting on your sorry ass to heal."

"I didn't expect to find you all waiting on me." He'd be lying if he said he hadn't expected to be on the receiving end of their anger. He'd done the one thing he'd always forbid them. He'd gone in alone and unprepared.

They had every reason to be pissed at him. Despite his words, he saw nothing but concern in his friend's eyes. Holloway clapped him on the back and held the door open wide. "No one can resist one of Kate's meals." No truer words had ever been spoken. Trent's angel was the total package.

Gorgeous, softhearted, an excellent cook, and the woman had brains, too.

There was something far heavier, darker, in the air than a bunch of growling stomachs.

His crew was up to something. He'd bet his last dollar on it.

"Boss man! Have a seat." Noah's deep, yet quiet voice greeted him as he stepped into the cool, heavenly scented house. The big, russet haired male snatched a piece of ham from a platter Kate was loading in the open kitchen. She smacked Noah's hand, and he bent to kiss her cheek. Noah crossed the large airy dining room to look Rick over, scanning him from head to toe as if searching for any remaining bullet holes. "About time you got back on your feet. I can babysit this crew of knuckleheads for only so long. That's your job."

Noah took his usual seat on the couch. Holloway and Pete followed Rick inside then, without a word, they took their usual seats at the table. A table not set with china for Kate's meal, but a mission planning meeting. Trent's TV had been relocated to its workplace on the table. Pete's laptop sat waiting at the kid's spot beside the head of the table, cables attached to the TV.

"Smells amazing, sweetheart. You're spoiling the guys. They'll never leave." Rick turned at the sound of Trent's voice coming from the kitchen. He'd followed them in the front door and headed straight for Kate, his world.

For the briefest moment, as he watched Trent gently tug Kate's shiny brown ponytail, he thought he should be surprised at how hard and fast his friend had fallen for the former beauty queen. Their love shone bright, true and deep.

Then he remembered the faces that had left their

imprint on his heart.

All it had taken was one fateful meeting with a long-legged, stubborn MacDonald woman and a raggedy little waif, and he'd been a goner. But emotion and sentiment had no room in his life, especially now.

"Boys, why don't you fix your plates and eat while you work. Everything is ready. It's not fancy, but it'll fill you up." At Kate's call, the men all stood and headed for the kitchen. They grabbed plates and filled the air with appreciative moans and groans. As she watched the men load up with food, Kate's warm smile held enough light to power his home for a month. Yet, her happiness at watching the men didn't erase the concern softening her gaze when it circled back to him. "Rick? If you're tired, I can fix a plate and bring it to you."

"Thanks, sweetheart, but no. I'll fix something after the hyenas finish. If I wade into the mess, one of them might mistake my hand for food. Smells wonderful."

She pulled away from Trent and came to him. Placing a soft hand on his cheek, she paused as if hedging her words. But her eyes never wavered. "You scared ten years off my life. Don't you ever, ever do that again. We're all in this together. We might be an odd family, but that's what we are and always will be. Not co-workers. Not friends. Family." On the word family a fierce light blazed to life deep in her eyes. Her soft voice strengthened. "And if you ever scare me like that again, so help me god, you will regret it. You understand me?" She watched, waiting for his answer. Though he might weigh nearly double what she did, he wouldn't dare defy her.

His voice was a soft croak. "Yes, ma'am. Never again."

"Good." Just like that, the hardness left her. She leaned

in, kissed his cheek, and hugged him tight. After a long, heavy moment she pulled back. Her head tilted just a tiny bit as if reading him. Coming to some sort of decision, she gave an almost imperceptible nod and turned her head. "Looks like the kitchen's clear. Go fix a plate and take a seat. You don't have me fooled. That leg has got to be killing you."

Damn, but she slays me.

"Hurry up, old man. We've got work to do." Pete called from the table.

Still shaken by Kate's affectionate words, he did as he was told. He fixed a plate, grabbed a drink, and made his way back to the only remaining spot, his usual place. The head of the table sat vacant and waiting.

The only thing out of place? On the table in front of Trent sat a yellow legal pad and folders, all stacked neatly and waiting. The moment Rick sat, Trent tapped the pad and started the meeting. "Okay. You've rested long enough. We knew the moment you got your feet under you, you'd want every piece of intel. So, while you've been in the hospital, that's been our second priority. First was your and Leigh's safety. Frankly, that took a lot of manpower. But every spare minute we've had, we spent digging."

Just like that, Rick's brain fired up. Questions sparked to life, demanding answers. "What do you have?"

"Not me. We." There was a hard edge to Trent's tone, reminding Rick that they were all part of the same team and that included him. "We have updates on everyone involved in the mess at Addie's and info on what happened at the warehouse."

"You don't know where Marcus is."

"We don't have shit on Marcus."

Pete chimed in, full of guilt. "I kept at it until Crystal took my energy drinks away. After a thirty-eight-hour session at the keys, I didn't know whether to cry or to curse her when she dumped the last two down the drain. I slept six hours and got right back at it. We really tried."

Kate entered the room and leaned against Trent. He wrapped an arm around her waist and took her weight as if it were second nature. "Don't you dare curse Crystal. You needed the sleep. Good info is worthless if you don't have the focus to do it justice."

"Nah. I know better. And I made up for my grouchiness when I woke up. We—"

"No details, Pete! We're all glad Crystal's happy, but please. No. Fucking. Details." Holloway interrupted.

"Literally." Trent coughed.

Noah rolled his eyes and spoke up from the couch. "I contacted a Fed I know and called in a favor. She did some discreet digging. As far as she can tell, they don't have any leads on Marcus's location either. Until a certain, recent explosion at the warehouse, they didn't even have enough evidence to justify looking at him with any degree of scrutiny."

Holloway spoke, his voice full of dry sarcasm. "So finding a mountain of H inside a burning charity facility finally gave them enough to get a warrant?"

Noah swallowed a bite of the monstrous ham sandwich he'd constructed of Kate's offerings. "Apparently so. Now that they've finally amassed some evidence, they can't find the snake."

Rick slipped into his role as if it were a second skin. During his hospital stay he'd refused to ask for any updates and they hadn't shared. He would have been blind not to notice the guards outside another room at the opposite end of the hallway, but though it went against everything that made him who he was, he'd never asked. And they'd never volunteered. "Okay. What do we know? Let's start with Boyd." A member of their old unit in the Army National Guard, he'd been nothing but a thorn in their side since he'd resurfaced in the midst of Kate's trouble. When Cara Gregory, another member of their team, had returned to town, Boyd decided she'd make an easy target.

He'd been wrong.

Trent set his drink on the table and answered. "He's still in Intensive Care under guard. His condition's improved a little, but he's not out of the woods yet. No one can get any info from him and even if he wakes, no one's sure if they'll be able to. Either way, he's out of commission for a long damn time. I've talked with Bowie. He's agreed to keep us in the loop as much as he can."

"Rick, I haven't decided which team Bowie's on. He's seems like a helpful guy, but I haven't known him long enough to completely throw in with him yet." Holloway's opinion mirrored Rick's. "He seems awfully helpful. Which is great, but I'm not so sure he doesn't have an ulterior motive. It's not necessarily bad, but I think there's more to his good ole boy routine than he lets on."

"Agreed. I'm willing to cautiously consider him an ally, but I stress the word caution. Not a single piece of intel is to be shared, and not one person beyond this room is to be trusted with this unless we all agree." Far too much relied on their discretion, namely Leigh and Addie's lives. He would allow nothing short of a worldwide apocalypse to risk that.

Rick moved on to the next headache. "Dale Hawkins?"

"He spent four days in the hospital before they

released him. He's lawyered up and isn't talking. We can't get within a mile of him. The state understandably won't budge if it thinks anything has the slightest chance at jeopardizing its case against Dale."

"Jimmy?" Without question, the Potter County Sheriff's cousin was the weakest link.

"He had surgery to remove a bullet fragment from his shoulder and they released him to state police custody the next day. He thinks he can cut a deal and he's singing like a bird, but unfortunately he's a complete idiot. It's hard to sift the truth from the bullshit. Both Dale and Marcus had to be aware that he's not the sharpest tack in the box. Add that to his habit of sampling any and every illegal substance to cross his path over the years, it's doubtful that they gave him any useful info."

Holloway shook his head. "Junkies don't make the best co-conspirators. If he gives them everything now, he won't have anything to bargain with. Moron."

Trent finished with his final update. "So the DEA is dismantling Sutton's so-called charity. It's looking like they used the shipments of used medical equipment for opium and heroin smuggling. They refurbished second and third-hand equipment then sent it over to impoverished areas in Afghanistan, which as we witnessed firsthand eight years ago, there are no shortage of. Sutton is a smooth talker. In no time, they developed a relationship with area clinics. There's still a lot of speculation, but those clinics may have in turn been used to contact the opium growers in lowest income areas in Afghanistan."

Pete spoke up, his eyes unusually grim. "Only a shit-stain like Sutton can find so many ways to take advantage of those already in a sad situation. I can't wait until we nail his ass." For all of his exuberance, Pete's heart was just as soft as Kate's. He'd married young, started a family a few short years later and never looked back. His wife and two daughters were his entire world. He might seem immature at times, but he was a family man above all else.

"Basically, we have nothing on the men." Then he asked the questions that he both needed and dreaded the answer to. "What about Addie?"

Pete spoke up softly. "We can't find her. I've left messages. I've tried tracking the GPS in her phone. I've run every imaginable computer search. She's a ghost, boss."

James spoke. "If she doesn't have power to charge the phone, the messages won't do any good. Neither will computer searches, if she's lived virtually her entire life off the grid."

"We've got an even bigger problem. From some of the things she said when Leigh spoke to her, I think she's had contact with Sutton."

Sharp, angry curses filled the room.

"If he has the slightest inkling that we're looking for her, we won't be the only ones on the hunt. If he discovers she's important to us, he'll do anything to find her before we do."

"Fuck. Me." Holloway cursed. "She's just a kid. No one deserves to be in the center of this mess, but a little girl? Hell, no."

Noah asked the obvious question. "So how do we find her?"

~

Rick watched the last of the cars pull out of the

driveway and leaned against the porch rail.

The door behind him opened, and he knew without looking that Trent had followed him out. "I'm insisting that you and Leigh both stay here on the farm. You can stay here or up and the big house. I don't care which, but at least until you're in better shape, you're staying here." His friend's words were quiet, but unyielding.

Rick wouldn't fight him on this, at least not yet. He owed his closest friend peace of mind, if nothing else. For a time, at least, he'd give him that.

Plus, Trent was right. For now, Leigh was safer here. He just didn't know how long he could keep her prisoner.

"You're right. We'll stay here, at least for now."

"Are you two staying here or up with Sandy and Harlan?"

"She can choose where she wants to stay. Don't make it sound like we're a matched set. We're not."

"Are you sure about that? Even a dumb country boy can see the sparks flying when you two cross paths."

"You're anything but a dumb country boy. I hope you don't think you're fooling anyone with that act. And I'm certain. There's nothing more than friendship and worry for Addie between us. Once Sutton is out of the picture and Addie is safe, we'll go our separate ways."

~

"Please tell me you have a mutt that needs to be bathed or something? Poop to be scooped? Litter boxes that need cleaned?" As Leigh walked beside her cousin in the dusk, she knew she sounded a little bit looney. They'd walked down to the foaling barn to visit with Kate's horse, Bonnie. Having given the men ample time to do their thing, they headed back to Trent's.

Okay, so maybe I sound totally crazy. "I'm going to die of boredom. I understand all the reasons for the safety precautions, but I can only read so many books, especially when I have visions of the files on my desk at work multiplying like bunnies. Seriously, they're haunting my sleep at night."

"Leigh! Shush. I've never seen you like this before. Take a deep breath and calm down. We'll figure something out."

Leigh thought about her cousin's words and did as Kate said. Purple light lay over the grassy horizon as they strolled across the property. Most of the time, everyone drove across the property instead of walking, simply for time's sake. They'd opted to walk and enjoy the fresh air.

She couldn't imagine a more beautiful prison.

Leigh had wanted to be there when Rick come home from the hospital but thought it best to give him some space. As his condition improved, his mood had deteriorated. She'd thought that getting out of bed would have helped his disposition. For some reason she hadn't yet figured out, it hadn't.

Feeling like she was only making things worse, she'd spoken with Trent about leaving. He'd agreed to a point. The only way he'd allow—yes, *allow*—her to leave the hospital was if she promised to stay on Walker Farms. As much as it irritated her to do so, she'd agreed. She'd caused enough trouble. The last thing she wanted to do was add to Dark Horse's burden.

It had been a little over a week since she'd been able to come and go as she pleased, longer if she counted the short time she'd stayed there leading up to her kidnapping. Hers or any of their situations could be so much worse. She needed to remember that. She was safe. Rick had seen to it. He could have easily died from his injury. Boyd had held a gun to Cara's head and, although she hadn't known the former member of their unit like they obviously did, Leigh suspected he hadn't been playing around.

She needed to count her blessings and be patient. So even though she'd love nothing more than to find Rick and ask him a dozen questions, she forced herself to behave. And that had never been her strongest trait.

They came up behind Trent's home and around the side when they heard male voices. "There's nothing more than friendship and worry for Addie between us. Once Sutton is out of the picture and Addie is found safe, we'll go our separate ways." Rick's words punched a hole in her belly. Surely he didn't mean them? But there had been something heavy and final in his words that put a hollow ache beneath her ribs.

Breathless, she stopped in her tracks just before they rounded the corner and put her arm out to stop Kate.

She heard Trent's voice next. "You never did make a good liar. Damn good thing you don't do it often. Everyone has watched you two dance around each other all summer."

Rick's next words were flat, lifeless. "We don't have a relationship."

"Then you're an idiot *and* a liar. If Leigh is half the woman Kate is, and I suspect those two have more in common than either of us can even begin to imagine, any man would thank his lucky stars to have a MacDonald woman give him the time of day. And you know it. I'm not going to stand by and watch my closest friend make the biggest mistake of his life. What gives?"

Rick paused a long time before answering. "I don't have anything to offer her. Hooking up with me would cause her more harm than good, ten times over." Kate made a move as if she considered stepping forward and speaking up. Leigh gave her cousin a death glare that could be seen even in the growing darkness. Kate's face fell and she stopped, resigned to their fate as Rick continued. "I'm a loner, an asshole, and am starting a business which will require me to walk into danger frequently. She may be the most beautiful woman I have ever seen, but I would be a complete and utter bastard to tie her to me, to drag her into that kind of life. Every time she speaks, it's like an angel squeezes my heart. I won't ruin her life."

Leigh stared at Kate, holding her breath. Utterly clueless, he'd shredded her heart. She closed her eyes, unable to bear the sight of the one person she trusted with her most precious secrets.

Rick continued, swiping a few more slashes into her soul. "I don't know that I have ever met anyone that selfless and focused on helping others. With that gigantic heart of hers, she would willingly walk beside me into danger on a daily basis. I won't have it. I'll do whatever it takes to make sure she and Addie are safe and permanently together, but I won't be a part of that picture, even if it kills me."

A moment later the front door opened and closed. It didn't take a rocket scientist to figure out which of the men left his friend and the conversation alone in the night.

Shock. Anger. Amazement. A mass of emotions slammed home, fueling her with fierce resolve. She turned, finding Kate's worried gaze.

Her sweet cousin needn't have wasted her energy on worry. Up until the day she left for college, everyone in Riley Creek had said she was hell on wheels. Mouth of the South. One of her high school teachers had outright despaired over her "blatant sass. Young ladies should be gentle, well behaved and mannered." Mrs. Collier had warned Leigh that she'd never get anywhere in life.

She'd taken it as a challenge, determined to prove everyone wrong, going to college, getting her degree and working two jobs to keep her debt as low as possible because she'd hadn't had the grades for a scholarship. She'd just barely met the university's acceptance criteria but she hadn't let that stop her. She'd fought for what she wanted. Her success was all the more precious for that struggle.

Did I lose myself somewhere along the way?

Something inside her warned that she was in for the fight of her life. It was past time to unleash the real Leigh Ann MacDonald. Feeling waves of unconditional support, she faced her cousin and grinned.

In return, Kate beamed a cream-eating kitten smile, the likes of which Leigh hadn't seen since high school. They'd schemed, locking Sally Jo Carter and her crush, Sam Williams in an empty classroom after school. Not only had they succeeded in matching the pretty, quiet bookworm with the high school quarterback, the unlikely couple was still happily married to this day.

MacDonald women didn't know the meaning of the word quit. Rick Evans didn't have a clue what kind of trouble he'd just brought down on his own head.

"What are you going to do?" Kate whispered.

"What is it they do when they plan a mission? Observe, gather intel, and then plan their assault? I think I can handle that."

Kate raised her arm and did a fist pump. The excitement in her eyes contrasted with her whispers. "Oh, man. Rick is so screwed. I can't wait."

Chapter Seven

Rick read the email for a third time and, for once, didn't have an answer. How did he respond to a request for help when his team sat at a standstill until Sutton was out of the picture? He'd never shied away from a challenge. Turning away a request for help went against his every instinct.

He had to put his girls and his team first. Not *his* girls, *the* girls. Leigh and Addie. They weren't his, and they never would be. His only priorities were finding Addie and Marcus. He didn't have time to tackle another project.

Yet, the beginnings of a plan sparked to life. Maybe a challenge would keep him from going stir crazy. He looked down to his laptop and clicked the reply button.

A bloodcurdling scream erupted outside. His lungs froze even as his body moved. One moment Rick reclined on Trent's couch, poring over the endless backlog of email that had accumulated while he'd been in the hospital. The next, he was throwing open the front door.

Another scream met his ears, but then it was followed by a little girl's laughter.

Leigh stood with her hands on her hips, wet hair dripping in her face and a soaked shirt plastered to her torso. A pale pink, now see-through t-shirt. Denim shorts clung to her hips. Images of her long, tanned legs wrapped around his waist burst to life. He fought to swallow the hard lump in his throat. She called out to her niece, breaking the spell. "That's it, you little stinker! I'll get you. What's my rule?"

A smiling Kylie held a garden hose with the water

running full force and splashing on her and her aunt's shoes. Shockingly, Kylie's white sandals matched. Rick was stunned to find that he kind of missed her mismatched boots. Then again, cowboy boots didn't make for good water play. "Which wule?" Joe's daughter tilted her head in thought, not looking the least bit worried by Leigh's tone. "Gwownups have so many wules. Is it one of yours or one of daddy's?"

A mischievous, maybe even dangerous tone entered Leigh's voice. "The water rule, pickle. What happens when you get me wet?"

Kylie scrunched up her little forehead in thought. Then she looked up as realization hit. "You always say that I can spwash you, but if I do, you'll spwash me back double."

"Splash, with an L. And yes, that's right. Double." A wicked smile full of retribution spread across Leigh's face.

Kylie dropped the hose, turned and ran, all the while squealing. "Don't get me! Don't get me!"

Leigh grinned, waiting as if to give her niece a head start. After she shouted her war cry, "No mercy!" she grabbed the hose and ran after the madly giggling Kylie.

Kate stood nearby with a muddy dog on a leash. "I thought you two were going to help me give Pudgy a bath. Traitors." She smiled brightly, and the shaggy dog swept the grass with his tail.

"I will! I will! I wanna hewp!" Kylie ran in circles, ponytail trailing behind as she craned her neck to see how much lead she had on her aunt. Just then a line of water doused her back and she let out a squeal that matched Leigh's in both volume and shock. "It's cold!"

"It is." Leigh waved another rope of water over Kylie's back.

"Help me, Katie! Help me!" In the huge front yard, on an enormous horse farm with endless acres to flee, Kylie ran close circles around her aunt, clearly in no hurry to get far.

"I don't think so, squirt. You brought this on yourself."

Kylie dropped to the ground and rolled as Leigh continued to soak her. She giggled until Rick worried she wouldn't be able to breathe.

Leigh gave the hose to Kate and walked over to her niece. She held both hands out to Kylie, who readily grabbed hold so she could be picked up. "That was fun! Wet's do it again!"

Kate called out, "Leigh, when your delinquent asks for more punishment, I think you're doing it wrong."

Kylie looked from her cousin to her aunt. "What's a dewink…"

Leigh helped her out. "Delinquent. That's what you are, squirt." She picked her up for a hug and smacked a quick kiss her Kylie's cheek. The little girl wrapped an arm around her aunt's neck and then shocked him by waving his direction with the other.

"Hey, Wick! You wanna be a dewinkit with me? It's fun!"

He realized that, despite his intent to stay inside, as he'd watched the girls, he'd unconsciously migrated out to the porch's edge. "No, but thanks, little bit. It sounds like you're having a lot of fun, but not today."

"Does your weg hurt? How much wonger until you feel better?" Concern darkened her little features, and he hated watching the joy flee her face.

"It's getting better all the time. They took out my stitches yesterday." He leaned on the porch rail.

"Yay! We could some inside and pway a quiet game with you, if you want?" She rocked her body in the universal kid movement that signaled she wanted down from her aunt's arms.

He fought the urge to pick her up for a hug of his own. "Thank you. You girls have fun. I'm going to rest and do some computer work."

"Okay." She waved and then moved on to the next game. She looked up to Kate. "Can I use the hose on Pudgy?"

He turned, heading back inside. In his periphery, Kate froze. When her eyes got round as saucers as she probably considered the ramifications of allowing Kylie to wet down the dog, he smiled. When Leigh winked and gave Kylie a high-five, he didn't think twice. He shut the door as she questioned her aunt. "How'd we do?"

~

"Pwease, can we go swimming? It's hot outside, and Harwan said they would have to cwose the pool soon. Fall's coming. Pwease? I'm so bored!" Kylie's pleas reached a fever pitch, and she couldn't say that she blamed the girl. Leigh was an adult and her patience had worn thin. They were all going a little stir-crazy, so she could only imagine what a six-year-old must feel like.

"All right. Give me a few minutes to finish my work, okay?" She was trying to stay on top of her caseload as much as possible, but there was only so much she could do while stuck at a standstill on Walker Farms.

"Yay! I'm gonna tell Katie! She's still here."

"Sure, sweetie." Leigh saved her progress and shut the lid of her laptop. Standing, she stretched.

Yeah. I definitely need to do something other than stare at the walls.

She opened the drawer of her beautiful, but temporary dresser and pulled out one of the two swimsuits she'd packed specifically for swimming with Kylie. Some days, she thought her niece was part fish.

Just as she put her hand out to shut her bedroom door, Kylie came barreling in, bouncing with excitement. "Katie said she'd swim with us, too. She said to tell you to wear your 'kini for a suntan."

"Bikini, with a—b" But Kylie was gone as fast as she'd appeared. How long had it been since she'd done something as simple as laid out in the sun with her cousin? They used to slather themselves in baby oil, turn on her old radio and bake themselves crispy. These days she used sunscreen instead of oil.

Not sure why it mattered, she traded her black one piece for her simple turquoise bikini. She pulled her hair up into a high ponytail and grabbed towels. She wrapped one around herself and carried two extra. It never failed to amaze her how someone as small as Kylie could spread so much water.

Kylie, dressed in her cheetah print suit and cowboy boots, waited impatiently just inside the patio doors. Her niece hopped from one foot to the other. The moment she caught sight of Leigh, she put her hand on the doorknob and looked up hopefully. "Can I open it? Katie helped me put on sunbwock while she talked on the phone."

"Yep. We're ready."

Kylie jumped, then used both hands to turn the knob. She was out the door in a flash. No stranger to chasing after her, Leigh followed.

Kylie hadn't been wrong. The last days of summer were not going down without a fight. With temps in the mid-nineties mixing with high humidity, it was a day meant for swimming. Kylie kicked off her boots and jumped into the water so fast, Leigh wouldn't have been surprised to see her heels smoking.

Leigh didn't waste any time. The heat beat down in punishing rays, determined to scorch anything in its path. She dropped her things on a patio table and jumped in, splashing Kylie. The cool water sliding over her heated skin felt delicious.

The backdoor opened and Katie walked out, wearing jeans, boots and a sly smile. She held a tall glass of ice water up to her forehead.

Leigh shaded her eyes against the sun's glare. "The munchkin said you were swimming, too. Did she fib?"

"No, she was right. Trent's on his way up to discuss something with Harlan. He's bringing my suit. I've been out with the foals and need to cool off." Even now, flushed and sweaty, wearing old barn clothes, her cousin looked like a beauty queen.

She swam to the middle of the huge pool, letting her feet touch the bottom. Kylie swam by and Leigh couldn't resist. She grabbed her niece's foot and pulled her in close. She held her by the waist. Knowing what was to come, Kylie squealed. "Throw me. Throw me!" So Leigh did. Kylie flailed like she was attempting to swim mid-air, then water splashed everywhere when she hit the water. Like a buoy, she popped up, ready for another go.

"I don't think so, squirt. If you have your way, I'll be doing that all afternoon and night. Use the diving board." The door opened again and Trent walked out. Leigh had no trouble admitting that Kate had done well when she chose him. Tall, broad with sandy blond hair, the man belonged in a cowboy movie. Yet, he was as down to earth as they came.

And utterly smitten by Kate.

Kate greeted him with a smile that lit her entire face. Trent casually took her glass for a long swallow. There was something odd in her tone when she spoke. "Didn't you bring my suit?"

But there was nothing but pure trouble in Trent's when he answered with a grin, "Nope. It'll be here in a minute. I forgot the bag I put it in on the table."

Oh crap. There's no telling what they're planning.

He took Kate's hand, drawing her with him. He pulled two chairs into the shade of the wide, gorgeous patio. "Sit with me for a minute."

"Spwash bomb!" Kylie screeched just before water erupted just a few feet away, spraying Leigh's face. She waited for her niece to surface then grabbed her for a quick toss. Knowing how this game worked, she needed to escape before Kylie suckered her into more throws. She stooped, ducking beneath the cool water, then she slowly stood, with her head tilted back. She let the water pull the loose tendrils of hair from her face as she rose. Standing tall, she wiped the water from her eyes. Opening them, she met Rick's dark, hungry gaze.

He'd stopped mid-stride on his way to deliver the forgotten bag to Kate.

Already on her way out of the pool, she didn't see any

reason to change course. She walked to the steps at the shallow end, water running down, sliding over her skin.

But the sensation of water against her flesh had nothing on the raw heat of Rick's eyes.

Molten, liquid, desire brewed so heady, it stole her breath. His dark eyes devoured her as they made a slow sweep down her body and then back up until his focus caught at her breasts. When he swallowed, something deep inside her quivered under the attention. Her nipples beaded into hard points, and her top left little to the imagination on a normal day. Faced with the heat of that stare, the bikini didn't stand a chance.

When his hot knowing stare returned to hers, arousal pooled deep in her belly.

Hanging onto her composure by a thread, pride intact and spine straight, she pretended to be unaffected. Walking up the steps, she casually pulled her focus from the magnetic draw of eyes so deep and dark, she feared she might fall into a never-ending black hole.

In reality, he shook her to her core.

This kind of blistering chemistry wasn't supposed to exist. Sure, she'd read about, dreamed about fictional desires hot enough to scorch the earth, but never expected to experience it.

Damn him all to hell, he denied it, preventing both of them from getting what they needed. So be it. All bets were off. He wanted to stare at her as if he might throw her over his shoulder and carry her off to the nearest cave? Two could play at this game.

She'd never worn a crown like Kate, but she'd been by her cousin's side for countless lessons and practices. She could hold her own on a runway. She met that dark, hungry gaze with one of her own as she stepped onto the deck and let him see the pent-up desire she'd kept to herself for far too long.

With one long leg in front of the other, she strode past him and across the patio. She grabbed a towel and her sunglasses from the table.

She chose a lounge chair in the sun, bent over and covered it with her towel. She sat, spun her legs around, and as she lay back on the chair she found him. Her gaze clashed with his. She smiled, all challenge and feminine hunger.

He knew what he'd given up. Mission accomplished, she slid her glasses up to cover her eyes. Leigh shifted her focus to her niece, shutting him out. Raising her voice to be heard over the splashing water, she called out. "Let me see your best dive, Kylie." She might not have the man she wanted, needed, but, by god, she had her family and she'd never take that for granted.

"Okay! Watch this spwash bomb!"

Chapter Eight

Leigh heard the rumble of a vehicle coming up the long driveway and forced herself to remain seated on the porch swing where she and Kate had spent the last hour stringing green beans. The crew had left hours ago, and neither of them had been able to concentrate on anything that required the slightest bit of brain power. They'd grabbed a couple of buckets and picked Sandy's garden clean. Afterward, they'd turned on some music and set to work on the front porch.

It had taken every ounce of self-control she possessed to stand back and not demand that they take her with them. She'd learned her lesson the hardest of ways. Her phone lay silent beside her the entire time they'd been gone, but she'd reached for it countless times, wanting to call and ask for an update. She hadn't.

Leigh had sworn to herself that she'd step back, stay out of the way, and let him do what he did best.

It was killing her.

She prayed they'd found something, anything that might lead them to Addie.

Taking a deep breath, she reached for another bean. She positioned her knife at the tip ready to slice it off and pull the string down and gave up. She dropped the knife and unfinished bean in the bucket and stood.

Trent's truck and Rick's SUV park side by side. Early that morning, everyone had gone out to the search area, Addie's sad excuse for a home.

She stepped up to the rail and watched when she wanted to run to Rick and demand answers. She needed to know like she needed her next breath.

Somehow, through it all, she'd worried over Rick just as much.

Trent had assured her that they wouldn't be doing anything too physically taxing. She trusted him.

She had to.

Fighting her need to fuss over Rick, she walked straight to Holloway. As she and Rick passed each other in the yard, he drew her attention. As desperately as she wanted to ignore him, he caught and held her focus. An olive-green tee stretched across his shoulders. Black sunglasses shielded his eyes, masking any emotion. Sweat dampened his hair, making a sinfully sexy mess. They all looked like they'd spent a week in the forest, not a mere day. She had no doubt that he'd been with them every step of the way.

Maybe she needed to set her worry aside? The man radiated strength, endurance, and enough confidence for ten men. He looked nothing like a man who needed looked after.

But he'd been hurt, had nearly died, because of her.

Forcing her feet to continue, she moved until coming to a stop in front of Holloway, who reached for a pack of gear from the truck bed. When he nearly bumped into her, he placed a hand on her shoulder.

"Hey, sweets." He dropped the bag, freeing his other hand so he could further steady them both.

She didn't bother with pretense. Everyone knew where her head was at. The same place as theirs, focused on finding Addie.

"Anything? Did you find anything at all?"

He put his sunglasses on his head, so he could meet her eye to eye.

"It's not that simple, hon." Concern softened the hard angles of his handsome face.

She'd known that, but she'd hoped...

Angling her body toward James so Rick couldn't read her lips, she lowered her voice. "How did he do? He didn't push himself too hard?" *Stupid question. That's like asking a tiger to remove his stripes.*

"We didn't let him. Rick's good. I promise. He may be a little sore tonight, but it'll be the good kind. Don't worry so much, little momma." She'd known they would look out for him, but she hadn't been able to keep the words bottled up any longer.

"Thank you."

He lightly grasped her shoulders. "Nothing to thank us for. He belongs to us, too. I just wish we had better news. We'll get it eventually." He pecked her forehead, then grabbed his dropped bag and followed everyone else to the house.

Following the team with her gaze, she found Rick holding the front door open and staring at her. Circus clowns could have marched past him and he wouldn't have noticed for all the attention honed on her.

Despite his glasses, she felt the pull of his focus to the center of her being.

Unreadable, unforgiving and maybe even a little bit angry, the vibes emanating from him scorched her.

He's mad at me? Why?

"The boss doesn't like to share. He thinks you were making googly eyes at James. If you wanted to make him jealous, you scored a direct hit." Noah stepped in front of her, much in the same way she had James.

"I'm not trying to make him jealous. I promise. I just wanted to make sure he didn't overdo it out there. As desperately as I want to find her, I don't want him to hurt himself in the process. And you know he will, if he thinks there's even the slightest chance it might make a bit of progress."

"I know, love. I like that you're a straight-shooter. We all do. Life is complicated enough. Never did understand why most people need to make it worse by adding half-truths and lies to the mix." Looking down at her, he paused before speaking again. "Between you and me? Throwing in a little jealousy and shaking him up a bit might be just what he needs."

"That's your suggestion? From the man who just said that the world has too much drama? You want me to poke the wounded bear with a stick?"

"Yup." He grinned and then headed toward the porch where Rick waited with, if possible, an even darker scowl.

Oh damn.

~

He wasn't ashamed to admit that he might be a little pissed as he watched fucking Holloway kiss Leigh. Sure, he'd only briefly touched his mouth to her forehead, much in the same way he'd seen her brother do. Yet, he'd sworn he'd seen a hint of…something just before he'd done so. Amusement? Challenge? That quick glance had been to see if he was still on the porch and watching. He'd bet money on it.

Had he wanted Rick to see the kiss or had James pulled

back and not kissed her on the mouth because he was watching? Then after the flash of whatever and the kiss, he'd sauntered up to the door, whistling and smiling like a loon.

What. The. Hell.

Then Noah had taken a moment to speak with Leigh. Their conversation had been short, but when Leigh turned, her expression was no less perplexed. What were they talking about?

She'd probably just been impatient for news. He'd promised to contact her immediately if they found Addie, so she had to know they didn't have her yet, but that didn't mean the wait had been easy on her.

She'd likely been tied in knots the entire time they'd been gone. But why hadn't she come to him? She always had in the past.

Unless they'd been talking about him?

Damn, he was tired of being fussed over. Granted, in the hospital he'd had the most beautiful caretaker in the world before his grouchiness sent her away.

And it hadn't gotten by him that his men were neither idiots nor blind.

He had made it clear that he and Leigh were not involved and never would be. Technically, that meant she was available. A man couldn't ask for a better example of all things beautiful. Steady. Loving.

Were they already moving in?

They had a right to, and no matter how difficult it would be for him to watch, he couldn't say he blamed them. In fact, they'd be stupid not to.

He held the door open as she trailed behind everyone. When the crowd was inside, leaving the two of them on the porch, she stopped. "Anything at all?"

He closed the door, leaving them alone outside. "Nothing. The food, everything we dropped off that last time, down to every single bottle of water, was still there. She hasn't been home."

The pain in her eyes wrecked him. The graceful lines of her throat tightened as she swallowed. "I don't know if that's a bad sign or a good one."

"Honestly? I don't know, either. Until I learn differently, I'm just thankful that she's staying away from there. With Marcus on the loose, that's the last place she needs to be. She's smart. She's avoided us and him. It's as reassuring as it is frustrating." He stepped closer. "Are you joining us?"

She blinked hard and turned her head as if looking out over the farm. When she spoke, her voice sounded thick and strained. "No. I'll just be in the way. I'll let you guys do your thing. Thank you." She turned to leave.

Something inside him broke at the torment in her words, and he forgot everything except his need to comfort her. He grabbed her hand, stopping her. "Hey. You don't have to thank me."

The muscles worked in her throat before she spoke. "I do. Not many men would expend this much time, money, and put so much at risk for someone they don't know. She got to me, and it kills me that she's out there alone. I mean, I know that there are thousands of kids out there on the streets, but she's...."

"Yours. She's yours. Leigh. Look at me." He slid his hand to her nape and forced her to meet him face to face. The stark grief written in the lines of her lovely face gutted him. "It's okay. She got to me, too. We'll find her. I'm not giving up. Not ever."

"I know." She pulled away and jogged down the steps. Her soft words, even quieter as she stepped down to the lawn, incinerated what was left of his will. "I don't want this madness to devour you, too. You don't deserve that." Her quiet words shredded him on the deepest level. He couldn't stand it any longer. Stepping down off the porch, he quickly caught up with her. Gently grabbing her shoulder, he turned her into him.

Quiet, shuddering sobs rocked her soft body against his. Holding her tight, he absorbed her sweet, intoxicating scent. No woman had ever gotten to him the way she had. Her tears had the power to eviscerate him. Clueless, without any idea of how to erase her pain, he held on, waiting.

Stroking her back, he savored the gift of having her in his arms, even as he reminded himself that he couldn't have this beauty in his life.

"I can't work at all, can I?"

"No, I'm sorry. I won't let you off the farm until we find Sutton. I know that's taking so much from you, but it can't be any other way."

"Deep down, I know that. Even if I flexed my feminist muscles and argued that, Joe would take the same stance as you. In my head, I understand it all, but my heart is barely holding on."

"I wish I could make this easier on you, on everyone." He attempted to put a little distance between them, but he failed. "I can't."

"I'm trying so hard to stay out of the way and to be patient." The grief in her voice increased his own. His black heart bled, but he could only imagine how worse it must feel to her infinitely softer one. He'd do anything to spare her this pain. "I know you're doing everything in your power. I won't ever be able to repay you, and I don't want you to think that I'm impatient with you, but…"

"But what? Come on. Be straight with me, beautiful. No teasing. You know the rule." He tipped her chin so she had no choice but to meet his gaze.

Her words tumbled out, a rapid-fire confession she had to expel before she lost her courage. "I don't know if I can stand another wait like that. I mean, I know you can't just rush in. Patience and planning and all that. It's what makes you who you are. I just can't handle the waiting. Makes me so anxious. I'm sick with it." She stopped speaking, but he saw the rest in her eyes.

"Then I came home without her. That didn't help." He stared into her green eyes and made an enormous mistake. He spoke without thinking about possible repercussions. "Then come with us."

Shock widened her eyes as her chin dropped. "What?"

"The next time we go out, come with us. As long as it's a safe location, you can come on the next mission. If you can't go in the field, then sit with Pete. It might actually help if she sees a familiar face among all the hulking men or can hear your voice over the coms."

Instantly her features brightened with a Christmas morning smile. "Truly? You promise?"

Even as a dark sense of *holy shit what have I done* leached into his bloodstream, he smiled. "I promise."

New tears filled her emerald eyes. Elated, she jumped up, wrapping her arms and legs around him.

He savored just one last moment of having her in his arms, breathed her scent into his lungs. Setting her down, he struggled to put some distance between them. Where was Pete and his damn mouth when he needed him?

An utter asshole, he patted her on the shoulder impersonally then turned his back on her and walked toward Trent's. He didn't know which memory of her would be harder to bear, the tears, the smiles or the look of shock when he'd dismissed her.

He knew he'd never shake the memory of having her in his arms. He'd bear that beautiful scar for the rest of his days.

Fucking. Hell. What have I done?

Chapter Nine

Hours later, after everyone had gone, Rick left the cool air of Trent's home and ventured into the humid evening. He'd made a point of walking down and around the Walker's pond at least once a day, sometimes twice—once in the morning and again in the evening if he needed extra time to think. Needless to say, he'd been working the ever-loving hell out of his leg.

The sun sank the final few inches below the horizon, painting the evening in shades of purple and gray. Neither the gorgeous scenery nor the pain in his leg could distract him from the memory of Leigh's wet eyes. Every time he relaxed his guard, visions of her haunted him. Even in the brightest hours of daylight, he hadn't been able to shake them. Each time he lifted his leg and every single time his foot touched the uneven ground, the roaring throb in his thigh reminded him of the countless acres of forest they'd traveled.

All for nothing.

For all their sakes, he needed to get this wrapped up.

Gray light reflected off the pond, transforming it into a giant's mirror as he reached the slope's bottom. He barely noticed the serene view or the sounds of crickets and frogs having a party. He carefully stepped over a fallen log on the pond's far side and cursed the corner they'd been forced into.

As the light faded, fireflies—or lightning bugs, as Kylie called them—made their appearance. Flitting here and there, like glowing fairies in the grass and trees, even a practical man like him had to admit they looked magical.

He shook his head, freeing it of worthless whimsy.

Movement at the edge of his vision caught his attention and he turned. His breath caught and the world around him ceased to exist. On the opposite side of the pond, at the top of the rise, a siren sat atop a beast of a horse, reins in one graceful hand. A heavy, humid breeze blew by, pulling a strand of long hair with it. Not much more than a silhouette, he knew that utterly feminine form as well as he knew his own.

He'd certainly spent enough time admiring the long, lean lines and sleek curves.

His toes caught on a vine, twisting his ankle and wrenching his fatigued leg. Pain exploded in his already throbbing thigh. Stumbling, he crashed to the ground.

"Rick? Are you okay?" Leigh called out, her warm voice traveling through the warm air and across the pond. The sound of rustling grass moved closer and he pushed himself up off the ground to untangle his legs. "Hey. Are you all right?"

Standing, he brushed his palms clean and inwardly cursed himself. Any other time or circumstance and he had the agility of a damn cat. If he hadn't been mooning over Leigh, he would have been just fine.

More proof that he needed to get as far away as possible from her.

Coming around the pond's end, she urged the horse closer, making him feel like a clumsy fool. "I'm fine. I wasn't watching where I was going."

"Are you sure?" She stopped the enormous animal a short distance away. It flicked an ear and stared down its nose at him. Fireflies twinkled in the air around the woman and beast. Tilting her head, Leigh seemed to hold something back as she assessed him. "Would you like a ride up?"

Good god, she's gorgeous.

"Ah. No. I'm good." Like an idiot, to prove his point he stepped forward and his aggrieved wound screamed at him. He couldn't quite control his wince as his leg wobbled and it took everything he had not to crumple to the ground.

She sighed heavily, as if he'd disappointed her somehow. "You know, I figured you for a better liar and a smarter man. Is it such a bad thing to accept a helping hand? I won't bite. Promise."

"No, but he might." He nodded toward the beast she sat comfortably on.

Leigh looked down on him perplexed. "Tallahassee? She, not he. And she's a great mount. Gentle and steady."

"She's huge."

~

"She's not really that big, but she's a strong, reliable girl." She'd been staying up at the Walker's big house but had wandered down to talk with Kate. She'd been restless all day and looking for a distraction. With nothing else to do, she went down for a few minutes of girl time. They'd been sitting on Trent's front porch when Trent had come out and suggested she take a ride.

He'd innocently remarked how pretty the pond was and how thick the lightning bugs were around it. Then he'd gone as far to suggest that she take Tallahassee, pointing out how even tempered and strong she was.

The sneaky man had known exactly what he was doing.

Tallahassee stood patiently beneath her and stared down at Rick as if she didn't know what to make of him. Leigh didn't know whether to strangle him for his stubbornness or admire him for his seemingly endless supply of willpower. "Would you like a ride up to Trent's?"

Rick asked, "A ride?" He couldn't have looked more shocked if she offered him a trip to the moon.

"Yes." Leigh tried to sound neutral and not at all as if she weren't talking down to a stubborn three-year-old, but she wasn't sure she pulled it off. "Tallahassee and I can give you a ride up the rise and drop you at Trent's. You really should give your leg a rest. You've done too much. After the hours you spent looking for Addie earlier? You should be horizontal." She forced herself to stop there. As badly as she felt the need to do it, he wouldn't appreciate her fussing over him.

He looked from her to the horse and back to her. "No. I'm fine."

She couldn't take it anymore. This polite, impersonal distance between them frustrated her to no end. Enough was enough. "Rick. Your leg is shaking so badly that it looks ready to collapse. Please let me help you. She's strong enough to carry both of us. Promise." She stared down and willed him to be reasonable.

He ran a hand through his dark hair and turn his head to look over the pond. Then he spoke to it, refusing to look at her. "I—"

"Don't give me that bullshit. Man up and accept a helping hand for once."

He turned his head from the pond and looked back to her, a crooked grin on his face. "Man up and accept help? How does that work?"

She dismounted from Tallahassee and, holding her reins in one hand, stepped closer to Rick. "It is possible to do such a thing. It takes a strong person to ask for help. No one in their right mind would look down on you for that."

He stared down at her as if she were from another planet. "I don't care what anyone thinks of me."

"Then why won't you accept help?" Unable to stop herself she cupped his jaw in her free hand.

He closed his eyes. "I just can't. It's not who I am."

She shook her head. "Well, I have news for you, Superman. You don't have a clue who you're up against. Get. On."

He smiled. "I don't know about Superman. I'm pretty sure he never rode a horse."

"Well, tonight, he's going to."

"You really expect me to ride that?" He looked at Tallahassee as if she might breathe fire at any moment.

"Her, not *that*. Tallahassee is her name and, yes, I expect you to ride her." She took a small amount of pity on him and released his jaw. Taking his hand in hers, she drew him to stand beside her mount. "Put your hand here." Not giving him a choice or chance to escape, she took his hand in hers and put it on the saddle. Damn, he smelled good. Even in the hot, humid evening, his scent made her hunger for far more than a few light touches.

Then it hit her. Whether this meeting had been pure chance or the product of Trent's meddling, it didn't mean she couldn't use it to her advantage. "Put your foot here." She patted his outer thigh and pointed to the stirrup. She let her hand linger on the hard muscle as she met his gaze.

In the dim evening light, a well of fathomless heat

stole her breath. Something low in her belly flickered to life, warm and sultry.

"Leigh, baby." Quiet and grim, he started and stopped as if he didn't know what to say.

She swallowed the lump in her throat. He was worth the fight.

She battled the need to throw herself at him, beg him to see to reason. She called on the last few brain cells she had. Trailing her hand up to his waist, she kept the contact light, easy, but let him see her desire in her gaze. She might not be able to see it herself, but as much of it simmered inside her, she didn't doubt that it was visible. She wanted to ask him why he thought her opinion didn't matter. She wanted to know why he thought he had to shoulder the weight of the world alone when he was surrounded by a team of capable, willing friends.

She wanted to know why he acted as if he needed atonement. Was she making assumptions? Maybe, but she didn't think so. She'd lost count of the times she'd seen the shadows of guilt flash through his handsome features.

"All right, Clark. Mount up. She won't move until we tell her to." She ached to brush the lock of dark hair away from the nearly healed scrape at his temple. He'd needed a haircut before he'd been shot and it had only grown more unruly since. She loved the rakish look on him. She kept her hand light at his belt, waiting.

He looked at her in confusion. "Clark?"

"Oh, I'm sorry, Superman. You must have forgotten your disguise. No glasses."

He grinned and shook his head. As he looked back at Tallahassee, his grin faded. She took a small measure of pity on him. "Is it horses that bother you or animals in general?"

"That obvious, huh?" He sighed as if he'd just confided his greatest weakness. "As silly as it sounds, I've just never spent much time around animals. We didn't have any when I was growing up. After my mother passed away, I was sent away to school." He shrugged. "I just don't get them."

She resisted the urge to tease him. "Well, you don't have to understand Tallahassee. You have to trust her. She's stronger than you and Noah combined. Or I'll get Trent and have him drive down here to pick you up?" She grinned innocently. "I'm sure he'd love to come with the 4-wheeler and rescue you."

"Witch." The single word rang with something that sounded like admiration. "Fine. You got me. What do I do?" He sounded anything but convinced and her heart ached for the young boy who'd lost his mother and been sent away from his home and his remaining family.

"Watch me? Then do the same and sit behind me." Releasing his waist, she stepped back.

"Sure thing." The utter lack of enthusiasm warred with the meaning of his words. She didn't know whether to be amused or feel sorry for him. She mounted the horse, wishing she could help make his climb easier. She settled for being satisfied that he'd agreed to the ride. Patting the horse's neck, she tried not to look as if she were watching over him.

As she'd known he would, he copied her moves. Despite the weakness in his healing leg, he still looked strong, capable. At least until he awkwardly settled behind her and she felt the tenseness of his body from shoulder to hips. "Relax. It'll be easier on all of us. Hold onto me, and I'll have you up to Trent's in no time."

"Wait. Don't you have to take care of her before you

put her to bed or whatever horses do in their spare time?" Rick asked as she urged Tallahassee into a walk.

"I do."

His hands gripped her hips. "Just take me with you. I'll walk from there. I don't want to make you go out of your way for me."

"It's not a big deal to drop you off first. You really do need to get off that leg. Trent won't give you too hard a time. He's worried about you, you know. You scared everyone. You're the glue that holds them all together."

"They'd do fine without me. Each member is smart and talented. They don't know the meaning of the word quit."

"But you were the one that brought them back together, and you did that for Kate. I can never repay you for that, by the way. You barely knew her."

"I liked her immediately. She's good for Trent. Anyone would have tried to help her."

"No, not everyone would have. Too many people have become complacent. Far too often, at work, I see people turn a blind eye toward elderly neighbors who can barely make it to the mailbox, or hungry children just a few doors down. You nearly died for doing the right thing. Thank you."

His tone seemed flat, impersonal when he deftly changed topics. "My wound isn't that bad. Even super nurse Cara admitted it's healing well. You're right, I did do too much today, but it's mostly muscle soreness. Tallahassee shouldn't have to pay for my idiocy. The walk from the barn to Trent's is a shorter distance over level ground. You can show me what is needed to care for her. I'll need to learn someday, anyway."

"Why is that?"

"Well...considering on a silly whim, I bought a horse

farm that nearly rivals the Walker's in size, I should probably learn what it's all about."

"I didn't think you would want horses of your own. Why did you go with a horse farm?"

"I don't want them for me, but they would make a great smokescreen for Dark Horse operations and…" He sounded sad as his words trailed off.

She used his words from earlier in the day against him. "And? Come on, no teasing. Everyone knows the rule. You drop hints, you have to spill." She felt the rise and fall of his chest against her back as he contemplated heavy thoughts.

"Addie. She's not mine. Never will be. But each time I see a horse, I think of her and all the things she should have. The night of the fire out at Kate's? She risked a hell of a lot to check on Bonnie. She called us horse thieves and was fighting mad over it. She loves that animal. Hell, it was probably the only thing she had to call her own." He paused for a moment as she led Tallahassee up the rise then continued. If possible, he sounded even more forlorn. "You're right. I don't need to know anything about horses. No need." She ached with the need to comfort him.

She tried to draw him back to his comfort zone—business. "The location of Underwood Farms is near ideal for Dark Horse operations. It's not far at all from the interstate, but you'll have privacy. What is it exactly that you'll do with the business?"

"I haven't decided. I really haven't had time to put a lot of thought into it. It must seem like I have all the time in the world to everyone, but I have trouble concentrating on anything other than finding Addie and Sutton."

They came to level ground, giving them a better view.

Trent's home lay to her left and the stables to the right. She made her choice, urging Tallahassee right. Rick had lost a little of his tenseness, but he remained still and awkward behind her.

"Don't beat yourself up over it. You spend too much time taking care of everyone else. We're all willing to help."

He was quiet for a long moment then, as if admitting defeat, he replied. "As trite as it sounds, I don't know how to let go. For as long as I can remember, I've been the one to take charge. I've always wanted to, never once considered it a chore."

"It's the nature of your beast. I understand." Tallahassee neared the stable where she was housed. "Early on, my family encouraged me to go into nursing or medical school. There's not a lot of money to be made in my field, especially in our county. They wanted more security for me. I refused. From day one, I knew I wanted, needed, to go into social work."

"It didn't take long for them to give up the fight did it, did it?" Humor laced his voice. There was no disbelief or doubt in his tone, just acceptance and understanding.

"No. It didn't. By the time I was finishing high school, my parents were experts in all the ways I could be bullheaded. They were probably relieved just to see me graduate."

Shifting, he relaxed a bit. When he spoke, his voice rumbled just above her ear. Shivers raced from her nape to the base of her spine. "I heard Kate call you troublemaker the other evening. What was that all about? How can a dedicated social worker be such a hellion?"

"It's an old family joke. I got into some trouble early in high school. The name and the reputation stuck."

She stopped the horse at open doors large enough to

drive a train through. "Can you get—" before she finished her question, he'd already begun to dismount. She watched as he stepped down then discretely tested his leg. The instant he appeared satisfied, he reached up to help her down. "No, it's okay." She'd barely lifted one leg over when he gripped her waist and the world spun as he lifted her. She just resisted wrapping her legs around his waist. Instead she settled for bracing her hands on his shoulders. A moment later she felt the earth beneath her feet.

It wasn't the first time she'd noticed that his upper body strength hadn't suffered the least bit. His broad shoulders and flat abdomen filled out his tees to perfection.

With Tallahassee at her back, he'd boxed her in close enough to feel his body heat. His breath brushed softly across her cheek. Air charged with heat and long denied desire whispered over her.

Sweat beaded at his temple. He licked his lips, and forget keeping track of their conversation. She couldn't remember her own name.

He spoke in the quiet rumbling way she loved. "What did you do?"

She blinked. "Do what? When?" *Where? How? Who?* Thankfully, breathing was an automated function, otherwise she'd be blue in the face. She shifted her focus from the temptation of his mouth, meeting his gaze with hers only to sink into the depths of his dark as night eyes.

Liquid need pulsed through her.

"In school. What could you have done that branded you a troublemaker for years?" One hand squeezed her hip and the other tucked a stray lock of hair behind her ear. A cool breeze whispered through the barn. Horses shifted in the background, content in their stalls.

She blinked and took a breath. Then another. A single finger flirted with the skin just about her jeans. Her breath hitched somewhere between her sternum and her heart.

She swallowed. "Which time?"

He quirked a half-smile and shook his head once. "Why am I not surprised? Pick the one you got into the most trouble for." He reached out as if to teasingly tug her hair. His features softened and desire glittered in his eyes. His hand slowed and caressed down the length of her hair, all traces of play gone.

She matched his grin with one of her own. "I got suspended for pranking the high school's basketball star. I went to the thrift store and bought an enormous pair of granny-panties. Later, I attached them to his car antenna with superglue, like a flag."

"Why in the world would you do that?" His head shot back a few inches and his eyes widened.

"He was picking on one of the girls from the trailer park, saying really nasty things to her."

"And you stood up for her when no one else would." His face softened as he looked down on her."

"He was quiet, so none of the teachers heard the nasty things he said to her. Melissa, the girl I stood up for, was so embarrassed, she wouldn't say anything at all."

"It's no wonder you became a social worker. It's in your blood."

"It is. It's hard, sometimes heart wrenching, but I miss it even now. There's not any way I can get back to work until after he's caught, is there?"

"No. I'm sorry, there's not. I won't allow it." Regret

softened his voice.

"I'm trying to behave, really, but I don't know how much longer I can bear it."

He tilted his head in confusion. "Behave? How are you supposed to behave while you're here?"

"I'm trying to give you space, letting you do what you do best without interference. Part of me wants to be underfoot, asking a million questions about what you've found and what your plans are. I would only be a hindrance. If I could go to work, even for just a few hours a week, I think it was ease my restlessness. I don't do well with boredom."

"Give me a little more time and we'll get him. Hang in there, okay?" He kissed her briefly, sweetly then pulled back.

"Okay." She dropped her forehead to his chest and sighed. What else could she do? She looked up and met his dark gaze. "I trust you."

A flash of something dark and potent flickered in his eyes. He seemed hurt, torn.

Pulled closer as if by some invisible force, her body brushed his. The heat of his palm pressed flat against the bare skin of her lower back holding her in place. The other returned to her waist.

Blissfully helpless, she waited, star struck as his mouth descended. Firm, full, silken lips brushed hers. She parted, thirsting for his taste, so hungry for any morsel he'd give.

Tangling her fingers in the material of his shirt, she held on and succumbed. He groaned, the sound a delicious rumble. Thinking she'd won, that he'd finally surrendered to the unbreakable pull that bound them, she smiled beneath his mouth.

His kiss was everything she'd dreamed of and more.

Desire, fiery and fierce burned through her, all-consuming. His tongue met hers, seducing and claiming. He pulled away, only to return for more. They crashed together in a passion fueled maelstrom.

His hand swept up under her shirt, across the bare expanse of desire sensitized flesh, then pressed her front flat against his, crushing her against him in the most delicious way. Dizzy with need, her every cell seemed to reach for his with a desperate ache.

Tallahassee shifted behind her and brushed against her back. Rick pulled out of the kiss, rested his forehead against hers. He closed his eyes. Starved for air, their chests rose and fell in a matched rhythm.

Then without a word, he walked away.

In a not-so-subtle hint for attention, Tallahassee nudged her shoulder. She turned and reached for the reins. She run a hand along the horse's neck. Pressing her cheek to Tallahassee's side she closed her eyes to shut out the heartbreaking view. She might be a strong, independent woman, but that didn't make it hurt any less when she watched the man she loved walk away.

Chapter Ten

Instantly alert, Rick checked the caller ID and answered his cell. "It's nearly one a.m., Pete. What's going on?" With the youngest member of Dark Horse, it could be anything from the most random and trivial nonsense to Armageddon.

Pete's words came out quiet and rushed, tumbling one after another. "Sorry, but I might have found something and knew you would want to hear the news right away."

Rick sat up on the edge of the bed and closed his eyes, afraid to hope. He braced his elbows on his knees and swallowed before replying. "Yeah. I was awake. If it's anything remotely important, call at any hour. What did you find?" He hadn't slept well since the shooting, and each time Addie had slipped through his fingers, his insomnia had only gotten worse.

"Well, I've been digging through Tom Caudill's family tree, property history, and really anything connected to the asshole. I've covered the same ground over and over. Haven't found shit. I got tired of chasing my tail." Rick waited, hoping Pete got to the point sooner rather than later. "Everything's led me to a dead end. I've run numerous searches on Addie's mother too with the same result. Nothing."

Rick head spun with the speed of Pete's words. "Whoa, lay off the caffeine. You're going to give yourself a heart attack, and Crystal will have my hide."

His friend's speech slowed a fraction in an all too

serious and unPete-like way. "Not until we get her home, boss. I got my girls, and I may not have a lot of money, but I'll work three jobs and give them every fuckin' penny I have before I let them go without a single cookie. That girl needs a home and good people to care for her, too. If you and Leigh can't take her in, then Crystal said she'd sign us up for foster parent classes. We'll make room for her. The girls might like having a big sister."

Rick closed his eyes and hoped to hell they found Addie soon. Her loss had taken its toll on every member of his team. They all suffered for his failure. He chose not to reply to Pete's words, hoping he got to something important sometime before sunrise. His thoughts had pulled him out of the conversation but his head snapped up when Pete's information registered. "We know that Amanda Caudill was born Amanda Potter. Tom's property came to him through her. Amanda's father, John Potter, had two sisters, Bethany and Pauline. Pauline married Chuck Wilson at the age of seventeen. I ran a search on the properties on either side of Caudill's and came up with squat. The property directly beside the Caudill's belonged to Bethany Franklin. Just beyond the Franklin property is another large parcel that was deeded to Pauline Wilson until about three years ago. She passed away and the property went to the county for unpaid taxes. It was sold at auction and a new family built a new home there about eighteen months ago." Pete paused to take a breath, unintentionally giving Rick a chance to speak.

"Pete? Please tell me this is going somewhere. I'm getting dizzy." Maybe it took a brain that operated as fast as Pete's to process this amount of info. "If someone not related to the Caudills, Potters or even the Wilsons owns the property now, what's so special about it?"

"Caves."

Caves. That one words stopped Rick's heart. "Where on the property are the caves? Is it likely that she would know of them?"

"John Potter's parents purchased about two hundred acres in 1947. When they passed away, the land was divided into three pie-shaped wedges. John, Pauline, and Bethany each got an equal share. From the road, it's quite a distance, even to drive, but the caves are closer the center of the pie. There, at the narrow end of the wedge, the distance to the caves from Tom's place would be a fair hike, but not impossible, even for a half-grown child."

"A child who grew up in those woods."

"Exactly. Especially one who may have spent a great deal of time there with her grandfather, the Army vet."

"Fuckin A, Pete." The knot in his gut loosened. It was almost too perfect, made too much sense.

Could it really be that simple?

Eager and, if possible, even more wound up than usual, Pete spoke. "Boss, I only have one question."

Lost in his thought and hopes, Rick asked distractedly. "What's that?"

"When are we going? If I head out now, I can meet you in Potter county in about thirty-five minutes, maybe sooner since the roads will be empty at this hour."

Every cell in his body screamed at him to go now. Break protocol, skip calling in his team, grab his keys, and haul ass through the dead of night. He closed his eyes and clenched his fists. He couldn't ever do that to his team again. They'd all worried, sweated and even shed a tear or two over this girl.

They'd never forgive him if he did something so unsafe and unfair. They deserved so much better from him.

And Leigh. Dear god, Leigh. She'd been so patient, placing all her trust in him to do the right thing and to bring their girl home safely.

Their girl.

Shit. No.

"Try to get some rest if you can and be here at dawn. I'll wait until 0400 to call in the rest of the team to meet us here. Be here at 0500."

"Yeah!" Pete yelled into the phone.

When Rick heard Crystal shush her excited husband, he smiled, his heart a hundred times lighter.

~

Wanting his team to meet at five am, he'd waited until four to notify everyone except Trent and Pete. Pete had already been notified, and Trent had only to travel from one end of his house to the other in a fifteen second commute.

Rick was sitting at the dining room table, looking at satellite images of the area Pete had pinpointed, when Trent walked in. His friend ran a hand through his shower-damp hair and glared at him. "What's got you so fired up? We need to get you settled with your own woman. Maybe then you'll think twice about leaving her side before sunrise."

"Bullshit." Rick looked at his friend and frowned. "You would have been up within the half hour anyway. You have horses to pamper and who knows what else needs doing around here. You're the crazy one."

"So, what gives?" Trent took a seat at the table and leaned back, stretching.

"Got a call from Pete a couple of hours ago. He found a promising lead, possibly the most promising thing we've had so far."

He snapped to attention, all traces of snark gone. "Your girl?"

Your girl. There it is again.

Rick chose to ignore his friend's words and the tug in his chest when he answered. "There's another property that used to belong to the Potters not too far away from the Caudill land."

"And?"

"Caves."

Rick looked up at the sound of soft footfalls entering the room. Kate tied the belt of her robe and shuffled to the coffee maker.

"Kate, sweetheart. I told you to stay in bed. I'll make the coffee." Trent frowned in her direction.

"No, I got it. Are you headed out? I can help Harlan and the hands with a few things down at the stables."

"I don't want you wor—"

Kate cut off his sentence with one hard look then turned her back as she left the room.

Trent watched her walk away and spoke with nothing but affection and exasperation after their bedroom door closed. "Damn stubborn MacDonald woman."

"That little bit of woman has you so whipped."

"Absolutely." Trent sounded utterly pleased with the notion. "Who's coming in and when are we headed out?"

"Pete, Noah, Holloway, and Mayhem. They should be

here in about ten minutes or so. This is it. I feel it." Rick gave Trent a brief rundown of what he'd planned in the long hours since Pete's call.

Kate came back into the room, dressed in jeans and a faded tee. "Have you called Leigh? Do you want me to call her?" She opened a cabinet and pulled out three mugs, lining them up on the counter. She picked up the pot of coffee and began to pour as usual, caring for them all. He'd give her ten minutes, max, before she started fixing breakfast. It wouldn't do them any good to object.

A heavy rock settled in the pit of his stomach. He'd spent almost as much time battling his decision as he had planning the op. She would be supremely pissed and as badly as he hated to disappoint her, he had to. "No. I'm not calling her. You're not calling her. When we have Addie safely in hand, I'll call Leigh so she can be ready to meet us here."

Kate set the coffeepot on the warmer and came to stand in front of him. "I really think you should call her, or at least let me do it for you. She's been a part of this from day one. You know that as well as anyone. You were there that night."

"I was." It was also the first time he'd met Leigh. He'd never met a more beautiful woman. And her inner strength and beauty eclipsed the outer shell.

"Rick, this will shatter her." His own heart sputtered in response. Drawing on years of military experience and a childhood devoid of warmth, he hardened his resolve.

"I can't worry about that now. The only thing that matters is keeping everyone safe. Speaking of which, you are not to step one foot off this farm today. I mean it. I need everyone focused, including Trent." Steeling his heart and masking his face, he stared into her sad eyes. "Promise, sweetheart."

"You're making a mistake." The disappointment in her eyes nearly undid him.

"Then it's mine to make. You won't budge me on this." He couldn't let those big, sad doe eyes weaken him. "Safety first. As badly as I want to find her, I won't put anyone else in danger."

When loud footsteps sounded on the porch, a rush of relief swept through him. The front door burst open. "So what's the plan, boss man?" He'd never thought he'd appreciate Pete's presence as much as he did in that moment. He turned to his friend, dismissing the woman he'd come to love like he imagined he might a sister.

"Everyone should be here in a few minutes. I'll go over it then." He turned to his computer under the guise of looking over the topographical maps, all the while feeling like he'd kicked a puppy.

~

"Cookie! Wait for me!" Leigh heard Kylie's shout and stepped out of the way, placing her back against the wall leading to the foyer. About three seconds later, a tri-colored puppy ran clumsily for the Walker's front door. A pajama-clad Kylie chased after the little dog and, a moment later, Joe followed the pair out at a much slower pace, scrubbing a hand through sleep-mussed hair.

Helpless to resist, she followed them through the airy entryway and outside. The morning fog lay thick over the lush green landscape. A golden sliver of sun began its ascent over the horizon. She could just make out the seemingly endless sea of bluegrass, clusters of trees, and fence rails.

"Yes! We did it! See, Daddy, I told you we could do it!" A triumphant Kylie pointed to the puppy who'd just done her business on the front lawn. "No accidents!"

"Good job, pickle. You need to keep up the good work. Cookie's smart, but she still needs your help. I know Sandy are Harlan are really nice, but I want you to keep doing your best to not make a mess in their house. Cara won't be here this morning to help chase Cookie and pick up after you." Joe stepped down off the porch and leaned down to ruffle the pup's ears.

"I know. I'll be good. Pwomise."

"Don't forget your *r*. It's promise," Joe replied, almost absentmindedly. He turned and looked down as two vehicles pulled out of Trent's shorter driveway and onto the longer one that bisected the property.

Her stomach dropped to her knees. "Joe, where are they going?" It was just a few minutes before six. Yes, used to farm and or military life, most of them were early risers, but she was no dummy. Something was up, something big. Pete's old jeep still sat parked next to Holloway's SUV.

Joe said that Cara would be gone most of the day.

Her brother bent down to pick up a small red ball. He rolled it a short distance for Cookie to chase. When the little beagle mix pounced on it and growled, Kylie clapped. Leigh stared holes into the back of Joe's head and waited for a reply. "Joe?"

He would know. He and Cara were inseparable. He'd just told her two nights ago that beyond family, he'd never expected to love someone as much as he loved his daughter.

Then he fell for Cara. Leigh had seen firsthand how much Cara loved both him and Kylie. She'd faced her biggest demon for them and won. Cara would have told him where she was going and why. He placed his hands on his hips, and his head dropped as he looked down at his feet. Teasing Kylie, the puppy ran a circle around his legs.

He didn't have to tell her; she knew. Joe wouldn't be so reluctant to tell her if they had gone out on any other mission.

If they'd found a lead on Marcus Sutton, he wouldn't have hesitated to tell her. She'd be disappointed if they didn't get him, but not devastated. If they had an emergency of some sort, he would have told her. No reason not to.

Rick had a lead on Addie.

Her brother finally turned to face her. "Pete may have had a breakthrough last night. There's a property not too far from Tom Caudill's. Pete's research and topographical maps show that there are caves on a property that used to belong in the Potter family. They're headed there now."

A knife twisted in her belly. "He thinks this is it, doesn't he?"

"Yes, Cara said Rick's certain. He reviewed Pete's intel and went over everything with a fine-toothed comb. He told Cara that he hopes to have Addie here by lunchtime."

Hope and joy warred with anger. She didn't know whether to cry or kick something. Her brother certainly didn't deserve her anger, but she couldn't stand to witness the misery in his eyes any longer. He'd gone out with her to deliver supplies a few times when Rick hadn't been available. On the day they took Tom Caudill into custody, he'd been there *and* he'd called her when sheriff's department suspected a child lived alone at the residence. He knew better than anyone what finding Addie would mean to her.

She turned her suddenly blurry focus on her niece. "What time do you need to leave for work today?" She couldn't meet his gaze.

"I have to be in court at nine. I've got a while yet."

"Okay. Give me a little bit to shower, and I'll help Sandy keep an eye on Kylie today." Maybe her niece could distract her from the emotions rioting in her belly.

Did she dare hope that they'd found her? It seemed too good to be true. She needed to keep her hope that they would first and foremost. Addie was the only thing that mattered.

Not her feelings about broken promises. Not the reasons why Rick broke his word.

Addie. That's all that mattered.

Yet, no matter how many times she told herself that, it didn't prevent the pain's assault.

On her way to the shower, she grabbed her robe then paused. Bracing herself, she picked her phone up off the nightstand. No missed calls. No unread texts.

Rick hadn't called.

Chapter Eleven

Rick pushed yet another branch out of his way as they climbed up the shaded hillside. Tall grasses, weeds, and all manner of waist-high plants battled with trees in some of the densest forest they'd been in yet. With what felt like the millionth tree behind him and a short reprieve before the next, he wiped the sweat from his brow with his forearm. Even at this early hour, the humidity soared at ninety-two percent. He never could figure out how the air could be filled with so much moisture and not be pure water.

But then, the weather portion of science hadn't been his best subject. He'd been more concerned with figuring out what he'd done to make his father hate him.

Making sure his path was clear for the moment, he glanced to his left. About fifty yards over, James didn't look any less miserable than Rick felt. The pretty boy's face was already grimy, his olive-green tee soaked with sweat. Dark glasses shaded his eyes, adding to his grim appearance.

Rick had made the right decision in asking James to stay outside the cave and wait. He'd planned on going in to greet Addie alone, but they all unanimously nixed that idea. Under the force of all their glares, he'd agreed that Cara could go in with him. She'd briefly met Addie previously, and the girl had seemed comfortable in her presence.

He swatted a fly away and bit back a curse.

He just hoped like hell that they'd have one extra seat filled on the way back to Walker Farms. There, the girl would be safe and have plenty of loving with just downright good, women to care for her. He couldn't ask for a better family to care for her.

If they could only find and catch the wily thing.

Yeah, no question, she'll fit right in with the MacDonald women.

Once he managed that, he would be able to devote his attention to finding Marcus Sutton.

A glance to his right showed Cara easily keeping pace with him and James. Fifty yards over, he could just barely make out her small form moving through the brush and trees.

Pete waited back at the rendezvous point manning a computer that tracked them. He also watched the entrance to the overgrown gravel road where they'd entered the property and parked.

They'd given Noah and Trent a few minute's head start. They'd gone farther out in order to find a good vantage point. He wanted alert eyes up high, aware at all times of what was going on around them.

Noah had taken up a position on a rocky outcropping, lying low, overlooking the hillside. Trent had climbed a sturdy old oak halfway up the rise, where he also maintained lookout.

Rick couldn't afford any surprises this time.

If the girl was there, he wasn't going home until he had her. He didn't care how long it took. He'd stay out in the heat and misery a week, if that's what it took.

He stepped over a nasty tangle of vines, careful not to trip as he had by the pond. Could he have made a bigger ass of himself? Tripping, drawing attention to himself? Showing his weakness?

Of course, Leigh only cared about whether or not he'd hurt himself. Everything else had been his own critical perception. He held himself to a higher standard because of his belief in his capabilities, always pushing his own boundaries.

But memories of her sweet taste, the silken feel of Leigh's skin against the palm of his hand? The soft whimper of pleasure she'd made against him?

He'd never experienced finer and suspected he never would again.

Above all else, the memory that haunted him most was her utterly gorgeous, tear-filled eyes. The hope and happiness that filled them when he'd promised her that she could come with them.

He didn't doubt that she could keep up. If fact, she could probably kick his ass with those long, lean legs of hers.

He just couldn't bring himself to put her into any situation that might be remotely dangerous. Her safety had to come before all else. Although he hadn't done it on purpose, if she hated him afterward, well, that would be one less thing he'd have to worry about.

She wouldn't look at him like he was the strongest man in the world any longer. One half of their attraction would die.

"Boss." James spoke quietly across their connection through the headsets. "I see a rough trail, just a little to the east. Appears to head up the rise. It's small, but looks recently traveled. It's not much more than a small game trail, but it goes in the right direction."

He fought the relief swelling, threatening to break loose and overcome him. Though the signs pointed in the right direction, they were far from home free. He replied softly. "Stay on course, but keep an eye on it."

"Copy."

Well aware of the time, he checked his watch as a

matter of principal. 0900. "Team one, report." Considering he could see everyone on team one, the rollcall might seem unnecessary, but they never strayed from protocol.

Cara responded immediately. "Here. I'm good, boss."

James chimed in next. "I'm here. Sweaty and sticky, but I'm here. I don't remember volunteering for a job in the bayou, boss."

The mouth of the cave came into view between a cluster of scraggly trees. He beat his hope mercilessly into submission. There was no room for anything other than precision and stealth. He slowed his steps and doubled his caution. Another few steps and he wouldn't risk speaking. He couldn't give her any warning. This was it. He couldn't afford to breathe wrong. "Team two."

Trent answered. "I'm here. Despite the canopy, I have clear visual."

Noah's response came next. "It's all good, boss. I have you all in view."

"Team three?" Rick closed his eyes and waited a single beat for his last check in.

"Team three? Really? I want to be command center next time. I can't be a team all by myself, but I can be in command."

Rick reined in his exasperation. "Pete."

"Everything is good. Go get her, boss."

"Holloway, guard the entrance. Mayhem, you're with me." He didn't wait for their replies as he walked to the opening. The poor excuse for a cave wasn't much more than a tumble of enormous boulders, the largest of which had an overhang serving as a ceiling. It might be enough to keep the rain at bay.

Keeping silent when all he wanted to do was rage at glaring injustice that filled this girl's life, he dared spare a glance in Cara's direction. She was right beside him, rock steady, despite the suspicious moisture in her eyes. She nodded once in his direction, confirming her readiness.

Ducking beneath the shelf-like overhang, he peered inside the shadowed alcove. An old, battered backpack, a neat pile of trash, and a bundle of rags greeted him. He blinked damp eyes, and bit back another curse. He felt a light touch on his wrist and looked down to find Cara's hand, staying him.

He looked up at her in confusion as she spoke to the cave. "Addie? Sweetheart, don't be scared. It's me, Cara. Rick's here, too. You're safe." Movement in the dim hollow snagged his attention.

Up under the narrowest section, where the stone met the earth, the pile of rags moved. "It's about time you guys found me. My phone died days ago, and I'm running out of supplies. The family down the hill started locking their doors three nights ago."

Every molecule of air rushed out of him in one enormous gust. He braced a hand on the rock beside him and sucked in air, trying to fill the vacuum in his chest.

Cara turned to him with a bright smile, relief shining in her expression. She paused for a moment staring at him before she wiped dampness he hadn't been aware of from beneath his eyes.

Fucking tears. No wonder I couldn't tell it was her.

Cara took charge. "Come on, kiddo. Let's get out of here." She held out a hand to Addie and helped the girl up. "No games today, okay? We just want to get you out of here and to a safe place." Cara tilted her head toward the cave's opening, indicating that he needed to move.

He snapped from his stupor and nodded once.

Cara continued to speak, as if they were just ambling about on a Sunday afternoon stroll through the park. "Listen up, one of my Army friends is just outside the cave. Tall, dark glasses. He's with us. He's just extra protection. A little farther out, when we get to our trucks, you'll meet a couple more guys. They're on our team, and we couldn't ask for better. Okay?"

The dirty faced girl appeared to consider Cara's words for a moment before nodding her acceptance. But Cara had been burned once before. "I promise you, they're on our side. One more thing, sweetheart. They can run fast, too. The only reason you got away from me last time was a banged up knee. This time? It won't happen again. No tricks. The path out of here should be safe, but no matter what happens, you stay beside me, Rick, or James. You got me?"

"You said he's Army?" Addie fiddled with the long messy braid that hung over her shoulder.

"Yes, former Army. We all are. We've moved on now, but we served together a few years ago."

"So you trust him? Them?" Addie looked up at Cara and then to him, as looking if for his reassurance.

He spoke up. "Absolutely. That's why they're here. There's no one on the planet I trust more than my team. Mayhem, or Cara is right. It should be safe, but no matter what, you stay with one of us. We'll get you out of here."

Addie looked up to Cara with a frown of confusion. "Mayhem?"

"Yup. That's what they call me. If you want, when we're in the truck, I'll tell you the story."

"Cool." She nodded as if they'd all agreed upon a

restaurant for lunch, not heading out into a crazy, messed up situation.

Rick led the way until they were out and there was enough room to walk mostly side by side. James swept the wooded area around them with an intense gaze before he greeted her with a smile. "Hey there, sweetheart. Welcome to the party. Let's go get some grub, huh?" His words were friendly, but his posture stayed alert, tense.

"Yeah. I could eat."

James led the way, and Cara gestured to the girl that they should follow. Cara stayed, tight to her side, but she wore a friendly smile. Rick followed, bringing up the rear. They made their way down the wooded slope in silence.

Near the bottom, when the greenery thinned a bit, James looked back over his shoulder, companionably. "We'll call ahead to Walker Farms. I know a couple of women there who will be more than happy to put together lunch. Hell, maybe we can throw together a cookout this evening. I'll spring for the—"

Addie stopped dead in her tracks and interrupted, "Where?"

James kept his voice quiet, friendly. "Walker Farms, Trent and his families' horse farm. Big place, more than enough room for an army."

"No." Addie shook her head. "I'm not going there. No way." She turned to Rick.

A rock in his belly plummeted to the ground when he saw the fear in her pale eyes. "Addie, honey. It's the safest place. There are plenty of people to keep watch for strangers, and it's gated with top of the line security. It's the best place to stay until we're certain Marcus is behind bars."

She crossed her arms over her chest. "I'm not going. And if you think I won't fight you or find a way to sneak out, you're crazy. I don't want to be around a bunch of strangers."

Rick softened his tone. "It's only temporary. They have more than enough room for us there. You'll have your own room next to Leigh."

Her little chin jutted out, one hundred percent stubborn teenager. "No. I said I don't want to be around a bunch of strangers. Take me to your place, or I'll find a way out. I swear it." Rick knew that look of determination. He saw it in his own eyes every damn morning. He didn't know the first thing about teenage girls, but something told him he'd lose this battle.

Fuck. Me.

He bit back his urge to refuse. The last thing he wanted was to be cooped up with Leigh who would be anything but happy with him after he'd left her out of this. "Fine," he sighed. We'll go to my place. Cara will stay with us until someone can go and get Leigh." Damn, but she would be pissed at him. It couldn't be helped.

He'd kept one of his promises. He'd found Addie.

~

Leigh set a plate with a sandwich and fruit in front of her niece, then sat at the bar beside her. Little legs swung back and forth beneath the stool. "Awn't you eating?" Kylie poked an orange slice as if she expected it to crawl off the plate.

In a rare example of poor table manners, Leigh propped her elbow on the counter and put her chin in her hand. "Don't knock your feet against the cabinet." The little legs slowed as her niece picked up the sandwich and peeked between the slices of bread.

"If I have to eat wunch, why don't you have to?" Finally satisfied that her food was edible, Kylie took a bite.

"I'm an adult, and I'm finished growing." *Not to mention I'd likely vomit if I tried to eat.*

Kylie swallowed her bite then washed it down with a drink. "That's not fair."

"Nope, but that's just the way it is." She'd tried so hard to be her usual upbeat self with Kylie, but her insides tangled in mess of worry, heartbreak, and anger. It took everything she had just to engage her niece.

"Can I have a cookie? Me and Sandy made some wast night." Big, puppy dog eyes stared up, pleading.

Leigh ran a hand down one of the girl's chocolate brown pigtails and lightly tugged. "Say Sandy and I. And it's last, with an *l. Last* night."

Kylie scrunched her nose. "That's what I said."

Leigh sighed. "We'll see, if you eat your lunch."

Kylie took another bite of her sandwich and poked another orange slice while she chewed.

Heavy footfalls entered the kitchen. Leigh assumed it was Harlan coming in to have lunch with Sandy. She absentmindedly watched her niece until Kylie beamed a smile in the door's direction. "Daddy!" She threw her arms up in the air.

Joe walked straight to his daughter and picked her up. "Hey, pickle. How's my girl?" He never shied away from showing her affection, but there was something a little more poignant in the way he held her close this time.

He'd come home early.

Unease boiled until Leigh had to choke back her panic. She waited, knowing Joe would tell her as soon as he was able. In less than thirty seconds that felt more like thirty minutes, he looked her directly in the eyes. "Go pack, get everything. You're moving in with Rick. They found her."

A bubble exploded deep inside, freeing all the emotions she'd kept in a stranglehold. If she'd been standing, she likely would have collapsed from the overwhelming release.

Yet, she couldn't let them go just yet. She had too much pride to expose herself, even to two of the most important people in her life. She attempted to draw in a breath, made herself blink, and said the only word she could force out. "What?"

"Sis, they have Addie. Rick and Cara are taking her to his place. She's fine and so is everyone else."

"Aunt Wee? Awe you okay? You wook funny."

Leigh swallowed and forced out some words, hoping they satisfied her niece. "Yeah, baby. I'm okay. Uh. I'm going to get my things." She chanced a glance to her brother. The frown lines on his handsome features told her all she needed to know. She hadn't hidden anything from them.

With each step she took, she came alive. Her brain fired to life with questions and plans. Only one thing mattered. They had Addie, and she was safe.

Chapter Twelve

When she and Joe arrived at the door, Rick answered through an intercom with a terse, "It's open. We're in the kitchen."

With no idea what to expect, and feeling more awkward than she had at her first school dance over twenty years ago, Leigh walked into Rick's monstrous home. Accustomed to disappointment and afraid of being crushed by some unforeseen catastrophe, she'd refused to hope.

They walked through the silent, imposing home until they stumbled onto a kitchen that would make any Southern hostess swoon with envy. A filthy Rick leaned against one counter, arms crossed over his broad, sweaty t-shirt. Addie sat on the opposite counter, next to a couple of crumpled fast food bags. If possible, she was even more grimy than Rick. She picked at a spot on her jeans, appearing to shut out the world.

Cara leaned one hip against Addie's counter, just a few feet away from the girl, smiling. She greeted them brightly, seemingly oblivious to any tension between the scowling man and pouting teen. "Hey, guys. Come on in." Leigh knew better. Cara was anything but oblivious.

Joe walked straight to the slightly less mission-worn Cara, wrapped an arm around her waist, and tucked her close. Addie continued to pick at the invisible spot on her jeans while Rick continued to glare.

Oh boy. They were clearly off to a rocky start. She couldn't say that surprised her. She remembered the battles she'd waged against her parents when she'd been around that age. She couldn't imagine what kind of conflict had taken place when teen drama pitted against the hardheaded Rick.

She stepped forward and adopted a friendliness that nearly matched Cara's. "You've eaten? Good. We'll have to get some groceries stocked."

Cara went right along with her, as if there wasn't anything remotely tense happening around them. "I'm going to run to the store and pick up a few things. Help me make a list?"

Rick broke his silence and moved, pulling out his wallet then a credit card. "Good idea. Here. Get enough food for two or three days. Anything beyond that, I'll have delivered."

Cara looked from Rick to Joe. "Drive me?"

"Sure. Sis, need to add anything?" He looked reluctant to leave her, but he didn't have much choice. She hadn't missed that he hadn't acknowledged Rick's presence. At all.

"I'll be fine. I have enough clothes for a few days. I'll let you know if I think of anything else." She walked over and kissed his cheek, then whispered into his ear. "Don't worry about me, big brother."

He looked down at her as if she'd asked him to fly to the moon. He shook his head and muttered a single word. "Never."

Cara took one of his hands in hers and tugged him toward the kitchen's exit. "Let's go, big brother." They left, leaving her with whatever drama Rick and Addie conjured in the short time they'd been together.

She'd briefly considered continuing the happy charade and forging onward as if everything was rainbows and sunshine. But that bandage approach would only get them so far. Ultimately, they would all be better off if they started honestly and built a solid foundation for whatever came their way.

"All right, you two. What's going on?" Rick glared silently at the girl. If possible, Addie only slumped farther into herself, shutting them out.

Rick, a virtual granite statue, replied without even blinking. "She needs to shower."

Surely there's more to it than that? "She does."

Addie finally spoke. "He called me filthy and said I stink."

Leigh gave Rick an annoyed look then turned her back on him before speaking to Addie. "Well, sweetheart, you do need a shower. But he's a man and has no tact whatsoever. They may be smart about a lot of things, but they can also be idiots. I've got my bathroom bag with me. You're welcome to use my shampoo and soap."

Addie looked up to Leigh, making her heart stutter. Pale blue-gray eyes filled with a wealth of shadows and pain met hers. It took everything in Leigh's power to keep the tears at bay.

I can do this. One thing at a time.

"Where do we go?" she asked Rick.

He rubbed his hands over his face. She'd been so focused on Addie that she hadn't given any thought to him. He had to have been awake all night, not to mention whatever they had to go through to find Addie.

"Take your pick. There are six bedrooms and each has its own bath. I had the housekeeper stock towels and linens, but she won't be back until things are safer. Don't leave the house. I wasn't expecting to be living here just yet and need to run a check on the security system and figure out a few things." He stood straighter. "You can have the run of the house. I know there's not much furniture yet, but I'll take care of that tomorrow. The TV and satellite dish work. Make yourselves at home." He paused before repeating his earlier command. "Just don't leave the house yet. Once I have everything in place, I'll show you around the property." He walked away without another word.

"All right, sweetheart. Let's go explore this monstrous castle." Addie kept her head down, but followed her through oak trimmed archways and wide hallways. With no idea where to go, Leigh chose a random hallway leading down one wing. The first two bedrooms they peeked into were enormous with high ceilings, gleaming dark hardwood floors and matching crown molding. They were gorgeous and utterly empty.

They continued down the hall. At the end, they came to an open door. There waited another large bedroom with attached sitting room. Complete with large windows and wallpaper that she suspected might be silk, it was picture perfect. It also sat waiting, barren and empty. Addie followed, barely sparing the opulence a glance. Their footsteps echoed as they returned the way they'd come.

"Does he really live here? It's like an old haunted museum or something." The girl continued to look at the floor, but Leigh took heart in her simple act of initiating conversation on her own.

"He does. But I don't think he's owned it very long. He was hurt almost a month ago, so he was in the hospital for a bit. Since then, we've been staying out at the Walkers' horse farm for safety reasons, so he really hasn't had time get furniture or anything like that." They made it back to where they'd started their exploration. "Okay, I chose last time without much luck. You pick our path this time."

Addie quirked her head then pointed to the hallway farthest from the one they'd just traveled. "How bad was he hurt?"

Leigh led the way. "Pretty badly."

The girl spoke tentatively, as if she wasn't sure if her next subject might be off limits. "Did he get shot? I heard a lot of gunfire the day the guy took you away."

Leigh forgot that Addie had hidden in the woods and watched that day. Who knew what might have happened to her, if not for Addie's bravery?

"He was. A bullet hit him in the upper leg. He's come a long way, but it still gives him a little trouble now and then. Not that he'd admit it." They stopped at the first door and she slowly opened it.

The room's grandeur matched or, if possible, exceeded that of the first three they'd discovered. A new king size mattress lay on the floor in one corner. An unopened set of sheets and a single pillow sit atop it. On the floor beside it, a cell phone lay plugged into an outlet. The near empty room struck her as hollow and lonely.

The sound of running water registered and she quickly shut the door. "Well, I think this one is taken. Let's check the last two." Welling sadness made her words sound thick as she forced herself to move to the hall's end. Something about the thought of Rick, when he did so much to take care of everyone else, living alone in such a beautiful, but empty home tugged at her emotions. He deserved so much more than a home filled with nothing but echoes.

Directly across from each other waited two more

doors. Leigh shrugged and opened the closest. She stopped, mouth agape. A tall, four-poster bed in a lovely honey oak set in the middle of the enormous room. Matching furniture filled out the room. A pretty pale blue quilt covered the bed.

The same shade as Addie's eyes. Dear god.

"Wow. This one's pretty. What do you think? Do you want to take this one?" She walked through the room, as if they hadn't just fallen down a rabbit hole. "I'll turn on the shower to warm up the water." The bathroom wasn't any less luxurious than the rest of the house, but she got the water running before returning to the bedroom. She half expected to find the room empty.

Instead, she found Addie standing in front of a wide desk that faced the window. Next to the work surface was a tall stack of new, still in the box, art supplies. A mix of awe and fear glittered in her beautiful eyes.

The feeling that Leigh was embarking on what might be the most important part of her life whispered through her.

Please, don't let me mess this up for her.

She stepped out of the path to the bathroom and closer to Addie. She wanted to crush the girl close and never let go. Every instinct she had screamed that was the wrong thing to do. "Go on in, and check the temperature. Look for washcloths and towels. I'll be right back. I'll go get you my shampoo and stuff." She closed the door behind her and took a deep breath.

She retrieved her bags then returned to Addie's room. Digging out what she thought the girl might like to use, she sat the items on the bathroom counter and smiled. "Here you go. Use as much as you need. I think I have some pajamas that you can wear until Cara gets back with a change of clothes."

"Okay." Leigh was relieved to see that while she still

looked like she was headed to the gallows, she was at least cooperating.

"Well, then. I'll leave you be while you shower. Take your time, okay? I showered this morning, so I'm good. I'm going to take the room directly across the hall. Don't hesitate to come and get me if you need anything. Even if you just want to talk or hang out." She waited just long enough to make sure her words registered in Addie's shocked fog then Leigh shut the bedroom door on her way out.

Not giving a single thought to the room across the way, beyond its proximity to Addie and the escape that it offered, she walked in.

One step into the room, she stopped. The room was furnished much like Addie's and utterly gorgeous. Open and airy, filled with light and warmth, it was beautiful, comfortable, and *her*. The main difference? Her bed was a king with a white and a muted spring green quilt.

The same shade as my eyes. She set her things on the floor by the door and made her way to the bed. There she crashed face first into the soft bedding and let the tears fall. Months of stress, worry and hurt poured out of her and onto the pillow.

~

After waving goodnight to Noah, Rick closed the door to his room. He collapsed on his mattress and fired off one last order via text message.

Tonight – get some rest and spend time with your girls. Tomorrow, we're shifting all focus to M.S.

He figured odds were fifty-fifty that Pete would listen. He'd probably help his wife put their girls to bed, spend a couple hours with her, and then get back to his computer. Rick couldn't fault his team for their workaholic tendencies when that was one of the traits that brought them together in the first place.

He'd been awake for nearly a day and a half, but hadn't been able to rest until he had all the security details ironed out. Noah had volunteered to take the first shift, and he'd arrived early. Rick had been grateful for the extra set of eyes, and they'd gone over the grounds and ensured the security system worked properly. Each night, one of his team would come and keep watch until Sutton was found. Even though he knew his system surpassed most banks, he wouldn't be able to rest at night unless he knew a set of human eyes kept watch as well.

He and Noah discussed the possibility that Marcus might cut his losses and leave the country. They agreed that while that might seem like the best option for someone whose empire had been crushed, despite being wanted by multiple government agencies, Marcus would stick around.

Marcus wasn't much more than a grown schoolyard bully, and Rick had just smashed his sandcastle. There was nothing Marcus hated more than losing, and Rick had destroyed his operation and fled with his new toy, Leigh—two punches in the gut that he wouldn't be able to tolerate.

It was only a matter of time until he pounced. Rick knew it as well as he knew his own face, maybe better. He'd come looking for revenge, and the best way to punish Rick would be to hurt those he cared about. Anyone with two brain cells could see that meant Leigh and Addie were the most likely targets.

Rick would be ready and waiting when the asshole showed.

Thoughts of Leigh and Addie came to mind as he stretched out, lying flat on his back. He closed his eyes and hoped they'd been able to get some rest. The heavy pressure, that he'd expected to lift when they'd found the girl, continued to squeeze his heart.

He'd vowed to give the girls everything they could ever want or need. They deserved it.

Apparently, Addie expected the one thing he couldn't give. Him.

Or more accurately him and Leigh together.

As they'd driven up the driveway, James had coughed quietly to get his attention. He gave a subtle, single nod to indicate Rick should look in the backseat. Curious, Rick glanced in his rearview mirror. They'd sandwiched her between Cara and Pete, who'd done their best to occupy her with friendly chatter. When they passed the gates to the property, she looked around wide-eyed, french fry paused a mere inch from her open mouth. She remained silent until they'd walked through the front doors.

Once they'd entered the kitchen, Addie said her first words since they'd gotten in the cars for the long ride home, her quiet voice filled with awe. "This is where you and Leigh live?"

Not giving much thought to it, he'd answered honestly. "We don't live together. We're not a couple or anything like that. I just purchased this farm recently, but you two can stay here until we can be certain that everyone is safe."

Confusion colored her equally beautiful and filthy face. "You mean we're not all going to live together?"

Shocked by her assumption, and hating to disappointed her, he gave her a single word reply. "No."

She shutdown, ignored him and barely acknowledged Cara's friendly chatter.

Leigh had to be upset, likely seriously pissed at him. He couldn't say he blamed her, but he didn't regret his broken promise. Even in the midst of anger, upset and upheaval, she focused on the most important thing. Really, the only thing that mattered. Addie.

He owed her an apology. But it might be better if he didn't give it.

~

A sliver of dim light raking across her face woke Leigh from a dead-to-the-world sleep. As she struggled to clear the fog from her mind, a small figure tentatively entered the room. Her surroundings registered about the same moment she identified her late night visitor.

"Addie? Honey, come on in." She sat up and the last of the fog cleared away. "What's up?"

Dressed in comfortable pajama bottoms and matching t-shirt, the girl stared at her feet.

"Are you hungry?" She'd figured the poor girl would be starving. She should have checked on her after her shower. Instead, she'd collapsed and fallen into the deepest sleep she'd had in months.

Addie stepped inside and closed the door behind her. She was just visible in the dim glow coming from the bathroom nightlight. "No. I'm okay. Cara brought the groceries. We made sandwiches and had cookies before she left."

"That's good." She paused, wondering what must be going through Addie's mind. "Sweetheart, what is it?"

Slim shoulders rose and fell in defeat. "I can't sleep. I mean. I'm really tired, but it's too quiet. Can I stay in here? I'd rather sleep outside, but I think he would get mad."

Of course. She felt like a total heel. Addie had been sleeping outdoors for close to a month, if not longer. "Absolutely. Come on in. Rick just wants us to be safe. Where do you—?" Before she finished her question, Addie crossed the room and climbed in the bed. Not in eagerness, but as if she was afraid she'd lose her courage.

Oh, poor girl. I'm such a selfish idiot.

"Sorry, sweetheart. I should have checked on you. I must have been more tired than I thought. This bed is huge, and there's plenty of room."

Addie tucked a pillow under her cheek, frowned and looked accusingly at Leigh. "This pillow is wet. Were you crying?"

Leigh tried for a lighthearted joke. "Would you believe me if I told you that I drool in my sleep? Here, let's toss that one, there are about five more to choose from." She carefully pulled the tear soaked pillow free and handed her a substitute from the large pile she'd knocked to the floor when she'd gotten comfortable.

Addie took the new pillow, curled on her side, and looked at Leigh oddly. "You're not a very good liar, are you?"

Leigh could only laugh. "No, I'm not. I rarely lie. There's no point in it. I guess I haven't had much practice."

Addie inched closer, reminding Leigh of a starving, but wary pup. "That's not a bad thing. My dad was an expert liar. Why were you crying?"

Leigh pretended not to notice the way Addie crept closer and tucked the small ray of hope it brought her close. She'd have something happy to savor later. But, the little stinker had boxed Leigh into a corner. She'd just told the girl that she didn't believe in lying. Now she had to answer her difficult question.

Damn and shit.

"It's been a stressful couple of months. I've had a lot of worries bottled up for a long time. I think it was past time to let all the worry and stress out."

"Did it work? Do you feel any better?"

She thought for a moment then realized she did. "Yeah. I do."

Addie stayed quiet, mulling things over. Maybe Leigh should ask a question or two of her own. "What really happened with you and Rick? I'm no dummy. You can't tell me all the tension was because you needed to shower. He might be a clueless man, but there has to be more to it. I told you my secret. It's your turn to tell me something."

Addie flopped onto her back and stared at the ceiling. She sighed heavily. "It's stupid."

Leigh reached out and tucked a lock of silver blond hair behind the girl's ear. "No, if it upset you, it's not."

"How can you say that? You don't even know what it is."

"If it involves your feelings, his feelings, or both combined, then it has the potential to be something serious. Your feelings are important."

"I had this stupid little girl dream. He shot it down. It's not a big deal"

"Addie. Dreams are not stupid."

Covering her face with one arm, Addie admitted, "I asked him if you guys lived here together. Like, I thought maybe we could be a family and live happily ever after and stuff. Like I said, it's stupid."

"No. It's absolutely not stupid. Dream are important. What you need to focus on are dreams and goals that you can work toward. Your dream job. Places you want to see when you're grown, stuff like that. Those dreams turn into goals you can accomplish. When you hang your dreams on other people, well, those are just wishes. There's a difference."

"Like, no matter how hard I wished my dad would stop doing bad things, he never did?" Her sullen words were an ugly smack of reality.

She owed this girl honesty. Addie spent her entire life in a nest of ugliness and lies. The least Leigh could do was vow to always tell her the truth, even when it stunk to high heaven. "Yes, like that. I wish with all my heart things had been different for you, but there's no power on this earth that can change that. All I can do is vow to do the very best I can to be there for you from this point forward."

Addie whispered her quiet acceptance. "Okay." She didn't sound convinced, but Leigh took heart when she pulled the sheet up over her shoulder to get comfortable. Addie closed her eyes and eventually fell asleep while Leigh lay awake and stared at the dark ceiling for hours.

Chapter Thirteen

Rick woke at dawn, ready to tackle the day's agenda. As he quickly showered, he decided not to wait on the coffee maker's timer. He'd double the amount he'd added last night in preparation for this morning and a full day of computer searches, phone calls and about forty other random items that came along with hosting two women in his virtually unfurnished home.

He left his room, but instead of heading right, toward the kitchen, his feet carried him the opposite direction. He stopped in front of Addie's room. He knew logically that she should be in her bed asleep. He'd brought her home himself the day before. He'd seen Cara make her an evening snack and coax a small smile from her.

But the fear that she wasn't real nagged him. *Just one quick peek. Just this one morning.* That's all he would allow himself. Not wanting to disturb her, he opened the door just a fraction. The moment he caught a glimpse of her sleeping, he'd close the door.

Through the minute gap, he saw rumpled bedding. He chanced opening the door another few inches. Nothing. Concern took hold, forcing him to open the door wide.

Her bed was empty and the room was silent. Alarm beat in his chest. He stepped inside and listened. No noise coming from the bathroom and the lights were all off.

Shit. I don't even know where to look. He'd have to check with Noah, then they'd go over the security footage of all the areas surrounding the house. He turned on his heel and when Leigh's door came into view, his pounding heart stopped. He wrenched her door open in one hard yank.

In the dim light of the room, her head popped up, looking to him in alarm. Nestled into her side was Addie.

He mouthed a silent, "I'm sorry," and raised his hand in a signal not to worry. Concern shadowed her features as she pulled a tangle of hair from her face. He whispered in the heavy silence, hoping to ease her fear. "I didn't know where she was. Sorry to wake you. Go back to sleep."

She lay back on the pillow, but didn't look convinced.

He closed the door and hoped she'd be able to get back to sleep.

He needed coffee and work.

He spent nearly two hours checking his email and organizing a list of the day's tasks. His caffeine buzz had faded and he needed something in his stomach to soak up the next round of coffee.

He knew his time was limited. He wouldn't be able to keep the girls locked up indefinitely. Leigh hovered on the edge of stir crazy, and he didn't give her much longer before their captivity pushed her over. He needed a sharp mind like he needed his next breath.

As he opened a cabinet, he heard bare feet padding across marble floors. He set a bag of bagels on the counter beside the newly unboxed toaster and then turned. Addie stood in the large arched entryway, mussed braid over her shoulder and big eyes sparking accusation.

Shit. I hoped we were past yesterday's drama.

He hated to disappoint her. Hell, he'd give her the very moon if he could, but she'd asked for the one thing he'd forbidden himself.

Not knowing what else to do, he acted as if it was a perfectly normal morning in the Brady Bunch household. "Hey, squirt. Come on in. I was getting ready to fix something to eat. What would you like?"

She shrugged. "Doesn't matter. Not hungry."

He split two bagels and put them in the toaster. "So, were you looking for company? Leigh will probably be up soon. She's an early riser, too."

There was a definite edge to her voice when she snapped at him. "Probably won't be today."

Alarmed, he turned to her. "Is something wrong?"

"I don't think she got much sleep last night." She crossed her thin arms over her chest and lifted her chin in the air.

Unease prickled at the base of his neck. "What makes you say that?"

"Oh, I don't know. Maybe because she cried herself to sleep yesterday."

A kick to the balls would have hurt less. "How do you know that?"

A battle waged in the lines of her face. Coming to a decision, her little chin lifted even higher in the air. Her shoulders squared and her spine stiffened. "I freaked last night. Okay? Your house is too quiet, like a museum. It's creepy. I went to her room. She let me stay in there. Her bed is big enough for ten people. Anyway, her eyes were all red and puffy and the pillow I grabbed was wet. Like, really wet. She joked about it, but…" She paused, taking a deep breath. Then she stabbed him in the heart with her final words. "I know a thing or two about wet pillows and crying myself to sleep."

He felt about six inches tall.

"Sweetheart." *Holy shit, how do I handle this one?* He looked to the ceiling for a moment then focused on the pale eyes shooting daggers at him.

Then he heard the voice that never failed to grab him by the balls with its silken grip. "Hey, guys. Good morning. What are we having for breakfast?" Leigh walked up behind Addie and placed a hand on her shoulder.

"Considering I don't have any pots or pans yet, our choices are limited. Cara had enough forethought to get us a toaster yesterday, so there's toast, bagels, cereal and milk. I think she also got yogurt and juice. She also brought us a supply of disposable dishes and silverware."

"A bagel and coffee sounds good. What about you, sweetheart?" Leigh asked Addie as she nudged her further into the kitchen.

Addie scrunched up her nose in disgust. "Never had a bagel. I can eat cereal though."

He removed a plastic cup from a cupboard and filled it with cereal. From the front of the blue box, the giant orange tiger's smile mocked him. He added milk and a plastic spoon. "Here you are, my dear. A meal fit for a queen, served in the Evans family's finest china." When the bagels popped in the toaster, he removed one and asked, "Cream cheese or butter?"

When Addie looked at him liked he'd grown a second head, Leigh chose for her. "Try cream cheese. That's how I like mine." She went to the coffeepot and poured a cup. "You really need to get some dishes. All this plastic and foam makes me cringe."

"That'll make a great project for you girls today. I'll give you my card and you two can pick out whatever you think the place needs. Start with the kitchen and any personal items either of you will need for the next week or so."

"I need to contact my office and talk to my supervisor. She'll want to speak with Addie, and there's a mountain of paperwork to fill out. I need to start on that as soon as possible."

He and Addie spoke at the same time.

"No."

"No." If possible, the girl's response had even more bite than his.

Unfazed, Leigh tried reason. "Guys, this is really important. Rules have to be followed. School will start soon and, sweetheart, you've missed out on so much. We can't waste—"

"I'm not going. I'll run so far and fast you'll never find me. Not ever." Putting on a brave front, Addie planted her fists on the bar, but he didn't miss the fear in her eyes or the tremble in her lower lip.

Shit.

"Leigh, give me some time. You can order some home study courses or whatever testing materials you think she'll need. Hold off on anything that will put her name in connection with either of ours. Give me a little time, and we'll find him."

"You don't think there's any chance that he's fled the country?"

"No, I don't. I know Marcus well. Above anything else, he'll want revenge against me. He'll target you."

"I'm not going to some stupid foster home." Addie appeared to be on the verge of panic.

Leigh's face softened in sympathy as she opened her mouth to speak.

He overrode her. "No, you're not. You are staying here

with Leigh until I know you'll both be safe. As soon as any and all threats are gone, I'll do whatever it takes to make sure that you can move in and stay with her permanently."

"Rick." Leigh's words ached with longing and fear. "You can't promise something like that."

"Is that what you want?"

Her answer came quick and easy. "Yes. It is." Or at least that was part of what she wanted. He witnessed the unspoken dreams die in her eyes. "But it's a long, complicated process. And with my job? I just don't know if I can make it happen."

"It'll happen. I'll see to it. I have more lawyers than you have family. We'll find a way. Give me what I want, time. In exchange, I'll get you what you want. I swear it."

She glanced down and took in the fear on Addie's face. The girl looked up to her as if her very life lay in Leigh's hands. "Okay. I can buy the books she'll need."

"Nope. I want you two to outfit this kitchen with whatever you think it needs, down to silverware and napkins. Throw in some cookbooks, spices, the works. Maybe you can show her how to cook or something. Make some fancy desserts. Add the school books and anything else. Have everything shipped overnight. I'll have Trent or Holloway go over the packages with me before you open them. No arguments." He focused on Addie. "Cream cheese or butter, sweetheart?"

A small ray of hope bloomed in her sweet face. It wasn't enough, but it was a start. "I'll try the cream cheese. Thank you."

He suspected her thanks had more to do with much more than the bagel, but he simply nodded and handed her the rest of her breakfast.

~

Leigh closed the refrigerator door and looked across the kitchen just in time to see Addie's hand tilt the measuring cup midair. "Wait, no. That's not the powdered sugar!" Then she cringed as the girl dumped a cup full of flour into their icing.

"I'm sorry." She couldn't bear the crestfallen look on Addie's face. Over the past two days Leigh had tried her best to occupy the girl. Often, she acted as though she'd be punished for the slightest thing.

"Sweetheart, it's not a big deal. I promise. We'll just make another batch."

"But it's the second time I've messed it up."

She fought to find a way to make light of the mistake. Then she heard Rick's voice in the next room over as he spoke with Holloway. Inspiration struck. She whispered her plan. "I know. We'll see if we can talk Rick into doing a taste test. We'll ask him which recipe he likes best."

Addie's face scrunched up with doubt. "You don't think he'll get mad? It's gonna taste horrible."

"No. I don't." She believed her words, even knew them as fact. He was absolutely one of the good guys. She knew he'd play along and bend over backward to make their girl happy.

Shit. Their girl.

She needed to quit thinking that way. Addie would be hers and hers alone. It might not be everything, but it was the next best thing. She couldn't take that gift for granted.

She waved her hand to Addie and the bowl, whispering, "Quick. Go ahead and mix it in. We'll set the bowls on the counter for a taste test. Ask him to pick the frosting we should use on the cake."

Addie carefully turned on the hand mixer and mixed the flour in, doubt written clearly in her features. "Is it ready yet?"

Leigh could tell by the smell of chocolate cake in the air that it was close, but she did her best to keep Addie involved every step of the way. "Check the timer on the oven, hon. What does it say?"

Addie groaned and then answered. "Five minutes. That's like forever!"

Leigh laughed. "No it's not. It's five minutes. You can make it that long."

Addie turned off the mixer and pouted. "Yeah, but then it has to cool."

"That's right. See? You know what you're doing."

"Well, waiting and licking the beaters are about the only parts I remember. It's been forever since I've had cake. Don't know if I've ever helped with a made-from-scratch cake. I thought they all came in a box." With a skeptical face, she set her bowl of vanilla flavored icing next to Leigh's chocolate. Addie hadn't been able to decide which she wanted, so they made both.

"Well, I promise you can have a big piece tonight." She laid two spoons out, one beside each bowl of icing just as Rick walked in.

"What are you two whispering and laughing about? You're not causing trouble are you?"

"Of course not. We're baking, that's all. Go ahead, Addie. Ask him." Leigh's heart wept when the girl's eyes went wide with apprehension. Leigh looked to Rick, imploring him to play along.

Meeting her head on, he paused for a moment before asking Addie, "What do you want to ask me?"

Addie took a deep breath. She released it right before blurting, "We need you to do a taste test. We don't know which one we should put on the cake."

He pretended to think. "A taste test, huh? I can do that. I mean, who doesn't like frosting?"

Leigh gestured to the bowls and spoons she'd set on the marble island.

Rick picked up the first spoon and looked to Addie. "Which one did you make?"

Oh hell. If I wasn't already ruined for other men by this stubborn male...

Addie swallowed then pointed to the first bowl. "I made the vanilla. She made the chocolate one."

"Lucky me. Vanilla is one of my favorites. I always liked chocolate cake iced with vanilla."

Addie beamed. "Me too. That's the way my grandma made it a long time ago."

Rick dipped his spoon into the bowl of white icing. Addie froze. Without missing a beat, he put the sample into his mouth and then licked the spoon clean. "That's damn good icing."

Then he picked up the bowl of chocolate and looked at it suspiciously. Then he sniffed it. He set it on the counter and used the second spoon to scoop up a minute sample. Acting as if he were being forced to take medicine he didn't like, he touched his tongue to the frosting. Looking at Leigh with near comical suspicion, he finally put the entire, tiny bit in his mouth and forced it down with an audible gulp. "The chocolate is pretty good, but the vanilla is clearly the winner."

Addie laughed. "You're not a very good liar. The vanilla is horrible. I'll be more careful next time."

"I like it just fine. I think there's something fishy in the chocolate."

"You're whacked. The chocolate is amazing." The timer went off, signaling that the cake was finished. Addie smiled and looked at Leigh. "I'm going to go take my shower while it cools. Don't frost it without me!" She bolted out of the room.

Rick opened a drawer and, not finding what he wanted, he looked to Leigh. "Where are the damn spoons?"

Leigh pulled the cake out of the oven and set it on the counter, shook her head and opened the correct drawer. He pulled out a clean spoon and then dipped it into the chocolate frosting for a huge scoop. He put the entire bite into his mouth, closed his eyes and groaned. "My god. Have you tried this?" He opened his eyes and focused on her.

"Not today. I use that recipe all the time. It goes well with almost any cake. Put a thick layer on and I don't have to worry about leftovers." The sight of him licking his lips held far more appeal. The faintest hint of his scent teased her. Fighting the urge to slide closer, she discreetly stepped a few inches away.

"You haven't tried it?" Looking at her as if she were from another planet, he set his spoon on the counter.

"I don't need to. I've probably made it fifty times since my grandmother taught me how back in high school. I know it's good."

He dipped his finger into the bowl. When he moved to stand in front of her, a mixture of dread and longing washed through her. "Here. I insist." He held his frosting coated finger up to her mouth.

With her backside against the counter, she had nowhere to go. How could he not know that he tempted her with the very things he'd denied her?

Hoping to satisfy him quickly, get him out of her space before she capitulated and begged him to give in, she took a small taste of the huge dollop. She couldn't help but savor it. She closed her eyes. The creamy chocolate was always divine. Rich and sinful without going too far. Usually, the taste reminded her of summers spent with her grandmother.

But Rick, damn the man, eclipsed those memories with his heat, his scent, and the low timbre of his voice that rippled through her, leaving a sensual devastation in its wake. She fought the need to lean into him.

The pad of a single finger brushed over her cheek. Her eyes popped open in shock even as her sharp tongue failed her. He put his icing dipped finger back into his mouth sucked the last of the icing away.

He pointed with the finger on the opposite hand, the one he'd caressed her with. "You have something on your cheek."

She blinked to break the spell of desire spinning in eyes darker than the chocolate they shared, so close and so very tempting.

She sputtered. "Powdered sugar or maybe flour. I'm working on teaching her how to be neat in the kitchen, but, ah…we still have a way to go."

He raised that finger to his mouth and tasted. Her knees wobbled making her brace her hands on the counter behind her. His voice rumbled low, barely audible. "Sweet. Definitely sugar."

"Yeah. There was a minor incident when she set the open bag on the counter."

Breathe girl, breathe.

God, I am such a dork!

She forced herself to draw in air.

He tossed his head back and laughed. "Incident or explosion?"

"Truly?" She bit her bottom lip.

He didn't answer. He simply waited, looking anything but worried about the messes they'd made in his formerly immaculate kitchen.

"Both. It was an incident that caused an explosion of powdered sugar. I've already cleaned most of it, but I'll go over everything again when we're finished. I know it's a mess, but I'll take care of it."

He swept the cluttered room with a passing onceover. "It's not all that bad." Then a darker, thoughtful expression took hold. "It looks lived in. It's not a ghost town anymore."

Knowing there was a far deeper meaning behind his words, but unsure of the significance, she chose to keep things light. She ignored the heat running through her veins and smiled. "With Addie? No, it's definitely not a ghost town. For someone who was so stealthy in the woods, she definitely makes plenty of noise now."

He smiled and she had to press harder with her palms for support. "Kids are supposed to be messy and noisy. Let her do both, and don't worry about the clutter so much." His voice lowered in both volume and timber as he swept the room with his gaze. "I really don't mind."

Something warm and bright unfolded in her chest. "Rick, you've given so much of yourself, the last thing you need is for us to fill your house with utter chaos. I'll make sure to keep her out of your way. Everything will be clean before I go to bed."

"It's fine." For a moment, he looked as if he struggled with a great decision. Then his shoulders rose and fell. "I like it. The place doesn't look so much like a museum. It looks like a family lives here." Already close, he somehow inched closer without touching her.

"Rick..." She needed to say something, but as always, this man stole her words.

She needn't have bothered with the mere thought of speaking, because he kissed her. His mouth descended on hers and laid claim. And it was sweet and soft. Inviting.

She'd never in a million years have pegged Rick as capable of sweet, tender kisses, but the man delivered in spades. His lips merged with hers and he murmured unintelligible words into her. She felt, rather than heard their meaning as tremors of need rushed through her.

A need she couldn't fill.

She drew on every ounce of willpower she had and pulled her mouth from his. Weakened, she couldn't hold onto her composure any longer and the words tumbled out. "Please don't tease me with what I can't have. You have to know what I want. I... I heard you talking to Trent. I know what you said. I just can't."

He looked deep into her, but didn't appear to process her words. He stared and her mouth and dipped his head to hers. And damn it all to hell, she couldn't tell him no.

She let him and this time he was anything but soft. He crushed his mouth to hers in a fiery storm, claiming her with a ruthlessness that would shame a Viking conqueror. Clutching his shoulders, she gave up the fight, letting him in.

~

Leigh's graceful fingers curled into his shirt and, despite her words, giving him an unconscious greenlight. She opened, letting him in and he couldn't resist the temptation of her sweet surrender. She whimpered, a soft, muted sound that went straight to his groin.

Desire flared and whipped through him, awakening his desire.

He cupped her jaw in his palms and swept his thumbs over the curve of her cheeks. The silken heat of her lips beneath his, the hint of frosting on her tongue, and the warmth of her skin under his palms ignited needs he'd given his all to put to bed. Never in his life had he experienced anything more divine.

Fuck, I'm an idiot and an asshole.

How could he live the rest of his life without accepting a gift so precious?

One of the hands gripping his shirt flattened, putting pressure above his heart. He didn't care. He slid one hand along the angle of her jaw and cupped her nape. Tilting her head, he adjusted his mouth, seeking even more.

She gave as good as she got.

So lost in the moment and the sweetness of her gift, he failed to notice the light pressure of a second palm flattening next to the first, against his chest.

Leigh pulled back, breaking free of their kiss. Her lips were swollen and sexy, her breathing heavy, but it was the devastation in her eyes that broke him. Eyes damp like dew kissed grass in the springtime hit him like a freight train.

Her words gutted him.

"No. I'm sorry. I can't do this. It's all or nothing, Rick. I don't have it in me to play around. I wish I could, but I won't survive a fling."

"Leigh, baby. I—"

"No. I need to keep what pride I have left. If anything, you of all people should be able to understand that much. Just leave me be. I'll do my best to keep Addie quiet and out of your way so you can work. Just do what you do best and keep us safe. Find Marcus, so we can get back to our lives. Addie deserves a good one. I'll do my absolute best to give that to her. Just leave me be." Each word slashed at something deep inside him.

It was the same something that held his emotions and needs in check. She'd just wrecked the barrier he'd erected to keep everything inside.

She turned her head to the side, breaking their eye contact and loosening his hold on her nape. "Let me go, please. I'm going to check on Addie before cleaning up our mess."

He stepped back, giving her some space, but wasn't ready to give in and simply walk away. He couldn't. Something important just happened and he needed a moment to process the enormity of her words and their impact.

"Leigh—"

Bare feet smacked across the kitchen floor in a rapid-fire dance. "Hey, guys. Is the cake cool?" Addie bounded up to them, smiling brightly, seemingly oblivious to the tension. There was something in her eyes that made him think otherwise.

Having lost the moment, and still unsure of how to remedy the colossal mess he'd made, he stepped back.

Leigh immediately sidled away and walked across the kitchen to check the cake's temperature. The moment her back turned to him, Addie glared as if he was the biggest jerk in the world.

Maybe he had been.

Leigh faced Addie. "It needs just a little longer. I don't want your icing to melt."

Addie shook her head. "No way. We're not putting my icing on there. I want the chocolate frosting."

Leigh looked as if she'd like nothing more than to escape. "Well, I'll just go get ready for bed myself. I'll frost it after."

Addie practically jumped in front of her, blocking her escape route. "I know! Can we watch a movie? Please? Noah hooked up the new TV last night and showed me how to work everything. You don't have to do anything but sit and rest. I'll take care of it all." Then the devious little mastermind pulled out the big guns, her stunning, pale blue eyes. She used them mercilessly as she stood before Leigh and craned her neck, like a baby bird. "Please? There are so many movies I missed out on." Rick nearly laughed at her performance. It was just a millimeter shy of being comically over the top.

But it worked. Leigh was sunk.

She put her hands on her hips and pretended to think hard. "Okay. I guess one won't hurt. What do you want to watch?"

"Everything!"

Leigh smiled and shook her head. "There's no way we can watch them all. Rick might choke when he sees how many you ordered."

At the mention of his name, Addie turned her back to Leigh and focused on him. "You too? You work all the time and never hang out. You should watch with us." Only, instead of pleading innocence, he received a glare that defied him to go against her wishes, contrasting with the cheer in her voice.

She knew. The little stinker must have been eavesdropping. Hell, as focused on each other as he and Leigh had been, an elephant could have run through the room and neither one of them would have noticed.

Only Leigh had ever done that do him. And he knew, in his deepest core, only she had the power to hold him in a thrall so powerful an earthquake wouldn't register.

An idea formed.

"Sure, I'll watch a movie. What's your choice?"

She paused in thought for a moment then jumped as if an idea occurred. "I'll go pick one and start it. Don't be late!" Her bare feet smacked over the floor as she ran out as fast as she'd come.

Leigh turned on the faucet to start cleaning. She stared after Addie, dread written all over her pretty face. "Why do I have a bad feeling about this?"

"What did you two order? It can't be that bad. It's only eight. It's not too late to start a movie."

"I wasn't kidding when I said we got a little carried away. She was so excited to see all the options, I couldn't help but let her have a little fun." Leigh looked to the door and the hall leading to the family room. The dread on her face made him think she faced the gallows. "In addition to a bunch of random comedies, she ordered multiple fantasy saga boxed sets, with bonus scenes. How much do you want to bet, she's going to have me up all night?"

He smiled and followed after their girl.

Their girl.

Chapter Fourteen

Rick caught a glimpse of movement in the doorway and looked up from the monitors on his desk to see Addie standing there, her hair still messy from sleep. She covered her yawn and then waved a greeting. "Hey."

"Hey there. Good morning."

She stepped a couple of feet into his office. "Leigh's still sleeping. Did you carry her to bed, too?"

"I did. She was really tired, so I didn't want to wake her. How did you sleep?" He'd put her to bed in her own room. She'd been sleeping there and, as far as he knew, hadn't had any more trouble after the first two nights she'd spent with Leigh. The third night, they'd both slept with their doors open which gave them a view straight into the others' room.

"Okay. Don't really remember anything. Can I have cake for breakfast?"

"Why don't we have something a little bit healthier? I need a coffee refill, anyway."

"Would one of those bagels be healthy?" She asked this as if she already knew, or at least suspected the answer, but thought any play that might gain her a piece of Leigh's chocolate cake for breakfast was worth a try.

"Well, it's definitely healthier than cake, but I'm not sure it's truly good for you. Let's go see what we can come up with." He pushed his chair back from his desk.

"No. You keep working. I can refill your coffee and toast the bagels. You gotta catch the bad guy." Before he could stand, she vanished.

What is she up to?

Hell, he probably owed the kid a huge slice of cake for the magic she'd worked the night before. Not all of his furniture had been delivered yet, so a single couch was the only piece of furniture practical for them to watch movies on. Somehow, the child, who was no bigger than a minute, managed to take up half of the couch. She'd left him and Leigh with far less than their fair share.

He couldn't complain. Leigh had taken the middle, leaving him the outer portion. He had to hand it to Leigh, she'd done well. Stiff as board, she stayed awake for the entirety of the first movie, but shortly after the second one began, she'd started drifting off and her posture relaxed. Addie had fallen asleep with her head on Leigh's shoulder, so she'd been trapped. By the movie's middle, Leigh was out cold and with nowhere to go, she'd ended up leaning against his chest. He'd shifted, taking the weight of them both.

He'd liked it. A lot.

He couldn't remember the first damn thing about either movie, but he remembered Addie and Leigh's laughter and teasing. He remembered when Addie smiled at him, and how, when Leigh had shaken her head, the silk of her hair had brushed over his arm.

The light weight and soft warmth and contentment of having them with him was burned into his memory. He'd never had that, at least not that he could remember.

In truth, he could have woken Leigh at any point. She wouldn't have minded. Hell, she probably would have preferred it. He'd told himself that he didn't want to wake Addie. When she was fully asleep, he'd get her to bed.

He knew it for the lie that it was.

He hadn't wanted the moment to end.

"Okay. Coffee, bagels aaaannd cake." Addie appeared and drew out the *and* as if she were onstage, making a great presentation.

He took a tray that he didn't even know he owned and set it on his desk. "Cake, huh?" Sure enough, in addition to two bagels, smeared liberally with cream cheese, two thick slices of cake waited on dessert plates, that again, he hadn't even known he had. His mug of refilled coffee sat beside a glass of milk.

His house became more a home every second that these two females lived in it.

"So, what's the special occasion? Or, more accurately, what do you want?" He was having bagels, cake, and coffee for breakfast with a tween girl in his office.

Just be happy that she's here, she's safe, and seemingly no worse for the wear after spending the majority of her summer alone.

The two of them had been put through the wringer. Hell, after all they'd survived, they deserved cake for breakfast for the rest of their lives.

"What makes you think I want something?" She licked cream cheese off the side of her bagel.

He didn't bother replying. He sipped his coffee and looked at her.

Addie huffed then waved her food in the air, exasperated. "Do you like Leigh or not? I mean I *know* you *like* her, but what's your deal? You've been acting funny around her. Sometimes, when she's not looking you make googly-puppy eyes at her then sometimes you're all hard-faced, like a statue. How the hell am I supposed to know what to do?" Full of drama, she threw her hands up in the air again. Realizing she held food in one hand, she shrugged and took a large bite.

Rick set down his cup. "Googly-puppy eyes? I don't even know what that means."

She answered him with her mouth full, her words garbled. "Like this." She made an over the top, sappy, in love face that would shame any cartoon character. With her arms and bagel clasped over her chest, the only thing she missed was the beating hearts in her eyes.

Am I that ridiculous, or is she really that observant?

He guessed it was a little of both. In the world she'd lived in, keen observation had to have been necessary for survival.

It was also highly likely that he made a fool of himself around Leigh. This had to stop. He was only making them both miserable. What was the point of saving Leigh from a life of worry and danger, as he'd thought he'd been doing, when in the process he was breaking her heart?

"I look like that, huh? All googly-eyed?"

She nodded and added, "Googly-puppy-eyed. But sometimes you look like this." She made her face go stone hard and lifeless.

He laughed.

It hit him that he had laughed more in the past few days than he had in the last year, possibly even longer. And he was stealing that from Leigh. He'd been a dick.

"Well?" Addie looked at him like he was not only an ass, but an idiot as well.

"Well, what?" She'd lost him. This young girl, who had every right in the world to be an angry, bitter child, but had more wisdom than half the adults he'd ever met.

"What are you going to do about it? Like, I think you two should be a couple and all, but I don't like it when she cries. You shouldn't do that to her." There was something else beneath her words, more than what she was telling him.

"Go ahead. Tell me the rest." He gave her his undivided attention.

Every trace of comedy left her voice. "Well, I thought, and I know it's silly, but I thought we'd all be a family. Stupid, little girl dreams, I know. But if we can't all be together, then I don't want you to hurt her. Really. She's the nicest person I've ever known. She likes to do things with me. I can tell she's not pretending or just doing a job. She *really* likes me. I don't want her hurt."

"I won't hurt her again." The words left his mouth before his brain processed their meaning, but all the same, he meant them.

"You promise?" Doubt warred with hope and fierce protectiveness in her eyes.

How can anyone not love and cherish this child? Tom Caudill is an idiot.

"I promise that I will do my absolute best not to hurt her or you. I can't swear that we won't disagree over things or argue, but I'll be careful of her feelings."

"Do you love her?"

The answer was right there, instantly on his tongue. "I do." *Fuck me, I do.*

So, why was he pushing that away? His business was protection. If he couldn't protect those he loved, his word didn't mean shit.

"Then quit being such a bonehead!" She shook her

head at him and took a drink of milk.

He could only laugh. Despite her childish words, she was right.

To his left, on his desk, both his phone and his computer chirped. Instantly alert, he checked the feed from the security camera on one monitor. The screen was sectioned into several squares, each displaying a different location the property. He touched the square showing the gate at the main driveway. A dark sedan waited.

Addie caught his shift in mood. "What's wrong?"

"We have company." He frowned. He'd enjoyed his morning with Addie and wasn't the least bit excited to have a visitor darken their doorway, especially this one.

She frowned, mimicking his expression almost identically. "Who is it?"

"My father is here."

Addie appeared stunned. "You have a dad?"

"Yes. Why is that such a shock? I didn't hatch from an egg." He rose from his seat.

She thought for a moment then answered. "Well, you're..." She waved her hand up and down, indicating she was indeed talking about him "You're like Batman."

"Batman?" She could have knocked him over with a feather. He was flattered.

Until she spoke again. "Yeah. You know, rich and with all the high tech stuff but only grumpier."

Utterly baffled, he felt his eyebrows reach for the ceiling. "I'm a grumpy Batman?"

She grinned and followed him out of the room.

"When was the last time you saw Batman?" He stopped at the front door and looked to her.

"My grandpa had an old VCR and videotapes. He had a movie with the Penguin in it. He was creepy! Is your dad a nice guy like you?"

How he'd gone from being grumpy to nice, he'd never know. With no idea how to answer her question, he opened the door to his father.

A father that, other than his visit in the hospital, he hadn't seen in over almost two decades, despite the fact that, during most of that time, they'd lived within thirty minutes of each other.

Frederick Evans stood there, a near mirror image of Rick. The only differences were their age and their eyes. His stony father appeared to stifle a wince when he met his son's gaze. Not having a clue what to say, Rick waited silently.

His father stared back, equally speechless.

Addie broke the silence. "Hi, Mr.—" She turned to Rick and asked "What is your last name, anyway?"

He tipped his head down to answer. "Evans."

Addie turned back to his father. "Hi, Mr. Evans. Would you like to come in? We're having coffee and cake for breakfast." Then she looked to Rick. "That's okay, right? Leigh's trying to teach me manners and stuff." Her little nose scrunched on the offending word, *manners*.

"Hey, there you guys are. I wondered where you two had gone." Leigh walked in smiling, freshly showered and utterly beautiful.

Addie made the introductions while he and his father stood there, two gloomy statues. "This is Mr. Evans. I mean, the other Mr. Evans. I guess there are two of them now? Is that right?"

Leigh smiled at his father in welcome then answered

the question. "Yes, that's right. You don't have to call Rick that. He's…well, he's Rick. But, yes, you should give his father respect and call him Mr. Evans."

"Cool. We invited him in for coffee and cake." In her hurry to get back to her untouched cake, Addie grabbed his father by the hand and literally pulled him inside.

With nothing else to do, Rick closed the door and followed.

Speechless and likely shocked to find not only a woman, but a child in Rick's home, his father let himself be drawn to the kitchen.

"Here. Have a seat. I'll get you a cup of coffee. Leigh is a better cake cutter than I am. I can do it, but I'm messy. We have to eat here at the bar. They haven't delivered the dining room table yet. Leigh and I picked one out a couple of days ago. It's huge, like big enough for fifty people. We didn't get a super fancy one though. Leigh says the house already looks like a stuffy church and needs some personality, so we got one that looks like it was beat up. It's a rustic thing." Addie assigned his father a seat at the bar and went to get him coffee. When she opened the cabinet and touched the handle of a mug she paused and looked back to his father. "Do you drink coffee? Most adults do, but my dad didn't like it." Wariness on her sweet face, she waited for an answer.

"Coffee is fine, dear. Thank you." Then his father did something Rick hadn't seen since he was a child. Frederick Evans smiled a genuine smile that reached his eyes.

"Great." Addie beamed, pulled the mug down and poured him a cup. She delivered it and then looked around the room. "What? What did I do wrong?"

Leigh stepped forward and put a hand on her shoulder.

"Nothing, sweetheart. They're just stubborn, is all. You did good."

"Another hard-headed man thing?" Addie looked from his father to him and then to Leigh, who laughed.

"Yep. You could say that."

Addie looked up to Leigh, all innocence. "I told him he could have cake."

Leigh gave Addie's hair a playful tug. "I bet you did. I'll cut it. I assume, just to be polite, you'd like a piece also?"

"I already cut pieces for me and Rick. I'll go get them!" A purple and silver blur, she sped out of the room.

Awkward silence filled the room until Leigh spoke as she walked to the fridge. "Would you like milk or sugar with your coffee?"

"No, thank you. Black is fine." He smiled politely as she served him a piece of cake.

Addie reappeared with her tray. A moment later, she sat at the bar beside his father with her cake and milk. Leigh occupied his father with small talk while Addie ate. Only a few minutes later, Frederick was completely under their spell. And Rick hadn't said a single word to his father.

~

"Okay, kiddo. You are a mess. You need to put on real clothes, brush your hair, and clean the chocolate from your face." Addie hopped up from her stool and Leigh moved in, washcloth at the ready. Thanks to her niece Kylie, Leigh was no stranger to messes, but this girl kept her on her toes.

Leigh wouldn't have it any other way. She was a

miracle and Leigh knew that as Addie ran out the door, the young girl likely had no idea what kind of magic she'd worked. She diffused tension between Rick and his father—so thick, Leigh had felt smothered by it.

But it was time for the men to hash things out. She suspected this meeting was far past due.

"If you gentlemen will give me just a moment, I'll be out of your way. She's learning, but we still have a way to go in the cleanliness department."

Rick's father tilted his head and looked to her. "You talk about her as if she's new to the world or…I'm not quite sure, but something's different about her situation, isn't it?"

She wiped up the last of the crumbs and hedged. She had no idea what Rick would want her to say or not say. She assumed his father was a decent guy, but really, she had no idea. "Ah, yeah. Her past is a long and complicated story. I'm sure you and Rick have business to attend to. I'll leave you to it."

Rick spoke, his words harsh at first, but then softening and returning to normal. "No. Stay. He won't be here long. I'll have no secrets from you." Something powerful simmered deep in his eyes and words.

What is he doing?

She knew the two men had a rocky past, but she had a feeling that Rick's meaning went beyond his and his father's troubles.

It had something to do with them, as in him and her. And she wasn't sure she had it in her to stick around and find out what he was plotting.

He softly repeated his request, though it sounded more like a politely voiced order. "Stay."

What could she do? So she poured herself a cup of coffee and sat on a barstool at the counter's end.

Rick turned to his father. "What do you want?"

Leigh barely contained her wince at his abruptness.

"I wanted to make sure that you were all right after your injuries and had hoped to invite you over for dinner. I have some things I'd like to discuss with you."

"I'm not interested in taking over the company. I never have been and never will be. I'm doing what I want, and I have people that need me." Rick turned to her, looked into her, but continued speaking to his father. "They will always come first." His dark gaze trapped hers.

Frederick stood and faced Rick with a hopeful, weak smile. She didn't know what he'd done, or exactly what caused their rift, but she couldn't help but feel a little sympathy for the man. He genuinely appeared to care about his son. "Of course. I did not realize that you had anyone special in your life. That's wonderful news. They would be more than welcome to come. I would love to learn more about them. But what I wanted to discuss has very little to do with the business."

Rick returned his focus to his father. "I'm not interested and, as you can see, I've healed up just fine. There's no need for you to get sentimental. I'm good." A layer of finality laced Rick's harsh tone. His words might be simple, but his meaning was anything but.

"Well, son, I hope you'll reconsider, but if not, I understand. I'm pleased that you're doing well and have…people that are important to you. Truly, I can't tell you how happy that makes me. If you need anything or change your mind, please let me know. I'll show myself out."

Her heart ached for both men. Mirror images in both

their looks and iron wills, it was no wonder they'd clashed. She imagined that it hadn't been pretty when it had occurred.

Rick placed both palms on the counter and looked down as his father silently left the room. Wanting desperately to offer him some sort of comfort, she stood and moved to stand beside him. She placed a hand on his shoulder.

But what could she say to a man who had made it plain that he had no room for her in his life?

She had no choice but to remind herself of the pain that awaited her if she opened her heart even a fraction to offer him comfort.

Did that make her selfish? Probably. But there came a time in a woman's life that she had to put herself first. Turning away to leave, her hand trailed over his back as she walked away without saying a word.

Chapter Fifteen

"Whatcha doing?" Rick looked up from his monitor and the file he'd received via email from Pete to see Addie standing in the doorway with her tray. It looked like she had sandwiches for their lunch. It was the fourth time she'd brought him food at his desk. He appreciated it, even as it freaked him out a bit.

Glancing at the screen, he vowed to sort the new intel he'd received after a short break. It might prevent his brain from leaking out his ears. He'd almost made it past the Pete-ramble to the actual information he needed. He also had a surveillance report from Noah and James to review. They were on to something. Most of the pieces were there, but he was missing one, the most important.

"I'm sorting through my email."

"That sounds boring." She sat the tray in its now routine spot on the corner of his desk. She never offered him the extra meal she carried in, but her eyes always flicked from it to him until he took it.

"It is, but there's important stuff in there. It's just going to take some time to go over and figure out what it means." Off shore bank accounts. Intercepted emails. Shell companies and fraudulent charities. They had a virtual library of dirty information. The only thing they lacked?

Marcus Sutton's hiding place.

They were running out of time. Everyone on the team agreed. The more time Sutton had, the more opportunity he had to plan an offense. Not to mention that he and Trent had two

MacDonald women cooped up. It was only a matter of time before they had a rebellion on their hands.

Rick knew it cost Leigh a great deal to put her job—hell, her entire life—on hold. And she hadn't complained once. In the hospital, she'd stayed by his side every moment. He'd be stupid if he thought that safety and practicality were the only reasons why.

Practicality didn't have a single thing to do with the long hours she'd held his hand while he slept and healed. Her talking soft and low to him for hours on end in the ICU had absolutely nothing to do with safety.

He owed her so much and didn't begin to know how to set things right.

Addie turned her nose up at him and his "boring emails" but stayed silent, picking at the crust of her sandwich.

"What are you girls doing today?" He focused on her and picked up his sandwich, resisting the urge to peek beneath the bread. Hopefully Leigh had supervised its construction.

"Nothing much. We're supposed to make pizza for dinner. Maybe cookies, too."

He felt bad—cooking lessons and homeschooling would only hold her interest so long. They were all headed fast to stir crazy.

"I need to check on some things outside. Do you want to go with?"

Her head popped up. "Really?"

"Sure. No reason we can't take our lunch with us. Sandwiches are portable, right?" He held his sandwich in the air.

"Right!"

"Go put on your shoes and meet me at the front door

in two minutes, okay?"

"Okay!" She grabbed her sandwich and napkin then bolted out the door. He hoped they didn't find a trail of lunchmeat down the hall later.

He sent Leigh a quick text to let her know where he and Addie were going. After he opened the hidden safe in the wall behind his desk, he armed himself with a loaded 9mm. He secured it in a shoulder holster and pulled on a long-sleeve button-up to conceal it from Addie. He knew she wasn't immune to the danger they were in, but there was no need to put it right in her face. He and his team had secured his home and all the surrounding property, but he couldn't take any chances.

When he arrived at the front door, Addie waited, nearly vibrating with excitement. How had he forgotten that she was accustomed to spending so much time outdoors? "Ready?"

She smiled.

He opened the door and cautioned, "No running off. Stay nearby at all times."

She bounded out after him and stepped into the sun. Turning her face up to the sky, she sighed then she looked to him. "Where are we going?"

"Let's walk down around the stables."

She surveyed the sweeping, storybook view. "Jeez, it's like you have your own state or something. This place goes on forever."

"Not quite forever." He was thankful for that. The logistics of keeping the entire farm secured and under surveillance had been a huge undertaking. But, they'd done it.

"How many acres is it?" Wide-eyed she looked

around.

He tried to see it from her perspective. Seemingly endless acres of gently sloping and rolling meadows. A random assortment of graceful gray stone and cream painted, timber barns dotted the landscape. Each was topped with a pair whimsical cupolas. The farm, in its prime, had been featured in more than one magazine.

As picture perfect as it was, it possessed and air of loneliness. Due to their need to admit as few unknown people to the property as possible, the grass had grown a little too tall. He laughed at Trent's reaction the other day when he'd come by. His friend had been downright twitchy over the state of Rick's fields. Knowing the situation, Trent hadn't complained, but after he'd stared long moments at the ankle high grass, he said he'd send a trusted crew of his own to take care of it.

He hadn't given Rick any say in the matter.

But those overgrown fields were also barren, empty of life.

"The portion of the farm I purchased is just under three hundred acres. It was originally a larger property but the owner retired. He kept a smaller portion for a hobby farm, but had no need for the rest."

"It's really pretty, but it seems kinda lonely."

He couldn't deny the truth of her words. "It does. Maybe eventually it'll look a little more..."

"Alive? Less like a ghost town?" She answered for him disdainfully.

"Yeah, less like a ghost town."

She tilted her head to look up at him, worried. "It's okay. Really. I loved my little barn even though it didn't look very nice. I wanted a nicer place for my horses, but my dad didn't care. He spent all his money on drugs. Is your dad a bad guy, too?" Her quiet question caught him off guard. "It's okay. It's not your fault if he is. I know sometimes people who seem nice really aren't."

Hell, she's worried about me.

He couldn't fathom it. They paused and he leaned against a fence rail. "He's not a bad guy, really...He's not a criminal."

"Then what did he do to you?" She tilted her head and looked at him in question.

Well, hell. How do I answer that one? "He never did anything bad to me. He was just never there when I needed him. My mom died when I was young and things were...difficult. He made some pretty big mistakes." That might be the understatement of the year. He wasn't sure that he should tell a thirteen-year-old that his father had an extra-marital relationship while his wife battled cancer. "We never saw eye to eye on things that were important to both of us."

"I get that. Mine always ignored me. Like, totally forgot I existed. I stopped asking him for dinner and everything. I could feed myself, 'cause he never did anything to help me. But the one thing I really, really wanted, when I went and asked him to get feed for my horses, well, he kinda went crazy. He screamed and yelled and screamed and yelled some more. I thought he might never stop. Even when I started crying, like I tried not to, but when I couldn't stop it, I had to leave the house and go to my hideout. He's horrible. I...I wish I wasn't a part of him. Like I wish he wasn't my dad."

He'd never felt lower than at that moment when her words and their meaning registered. Yes, his father virtually disappeared off the face of the planet, abandoning him at the worst moment of his life. He hadn't been a good husband to his ill wife. Later after college when his father had tried to mend fences and draw him into the family business, they fought. And they had some brutal, nasty arguments.

But at that point he'd been a grown man and able to hold his own. He'd been able to stand up for his mother, even though she no longer needed it. She'd been gone for a decade.

He had never been a young girl, a child, forced to fend for herself. She had such an incredibly soft heart, much like Leigh's. For her to sit and watch her horses, the very best thing in her life wither away, unable to get them what they needed, well, he couldn't imagine the pain she'd shouldered alone. He imagined she spent more than just that one occasion in tears.

He'd always had a pantry full of food and, sometimes, even a cook or kind housekeeper. He wasn't sure he wanted to know the age she'd been forced to start fending for herself.

Yet, she remained a sweet and kind miracle.

He struggled to find some small way to shine a positive light on her past. "Sweetheart, I know science makes a big deal about it, but your DNA is only a small component of what makes you who you are. Your father only contributed to fifty percent of that. Your mother gave you the other half of your genes." He straightened and led them up the path to the side of the house.

Sourly, she groused. "At least I don't have his name."

Rick agreed, but wasn't sure he was supposed to admit that aloud. He himself had even been angry the Tom hadn't given Addie his name when she'd been born. Now, he wondered if that had been a blessing in disguise. It'd be one less stain on her life.

Instead of agreeing, he volunteered what little he knew

of her mother's history. "The Potters were pretty important people."

She scrunched her nose and looked down at her feet. "Yeah, right."

"No, really. I have the info in the files we created when we were searching for you. Did you ever think about the fact that your name is Potter? You lived in Potter County."

Addie scuffed the tow of her shoe in the grass. "A lot of people are named Potter. It's not special."

"Not true. It is special. The county was named after your great aunt, several times removed. Her name was Marjorie Jean Potter." He tried to put things in a light she might appreciate. "The area was extremely poor, but the kids needed a school. Most of them didn't attend because the nearest one was thirty miles away. She went to the mayor of Riley Creek, which was a teeny, tiny town then. He told her no, they couldn't afford to build a school. She didn't like that."

Taken aback, Addie squinted her eyes, straightening her neck in outrage. "But kids need school. Some teachers are even nice. The year before my mom died and things got bad, I went to school. I had a teacher who liked my drawings. She showed me a few tricks to make them better." She hopped over a knee-high boulder at the old garden's edge.

"Your great aunt agreed. Kids need school. She went toe to toe with the mayor. He kept telling her there was no money."

"She didn't like that, did she?" She smiled with the knowledge that his story would bring something better.

"Nope. I don't think she did."

"How did she get the money?"

"Marjorie was one of the few women landowners in

this part of the state. She offered a couple of acres of her own property to the town if they would build a school on it."

"Wow. She was really nice. Did he give her the money for the school?"

He gave his head a single negative shake. "Nope."

"That was a good deal. He should have taken it." She turned her head and looked at his beautiful, but lonely barn in the distance. The longing on her face tore at his heart until it bled. She needed a family, a life filled with love and light. Anything less was a crime.

He'd see that she got it, if it was the last thing he did. An idea sprung to life, spawning a new list of things to do, lessons to learn.

He smiled a wicked grin, playing the story up and letting her know that the best part was to come. "He definitely should have taken it."

She brightened, waiting for the good part. "What did she do?"

"She staged a protest. One morning when he got ready to leave for work, he opened his front door to find five women, all fired up and chanting. They blocked his door, refusing to let him past. He shut the door on them and snuck out his bedroom window. Do you want to guess what he found waiting for him when he got to work?"

Her eyes brightened. "More protestors?"

They walked along a curving path paved with smooth stones that led them into the old flower garden. "Yup. Six more mothers and three fathers waited. This continued for two weeks."

Addie stepped up onto a low rock wall that bordered a neglected flower bed. "He finally gave up?" She put her arms out to the side as if walking a tightrope up the inclined wall.

"Well, he got a whole lot more serious about finding the funds to build the school. When they opened it, your great aunt volunteered and helped teach." Without thought he held his hand out when she came to the high end of the wall.

"So...She was a badass?" She grabbed his hand and held on as she jumped down.

"Yeah, she was a badass. Just don't let Leigh hear you use that word, though in this case, I'd think she'd agree." He let her hand go. When the warmth of her little hand in his left, he realized what he'd done.

Her eyes shining with pride, she straightened her thin shoulders. "My grandpa was a badass too. He fought in a war. Had medals and everything."

"A veteran. Then he was definitely a badass. So you come from a long line of strong people who did good things. But I think the most important part of what makes a person who they are is the way the behave. Their actions and the things they say. The way they treat people."

"Yeah. I guess so." Her acceptance sounded half-hearted as she stared out across the empty fields. Knowing it wouldn't help, he just barely resisted the urge to reinforce his point. And he realized he wanted to be there to help her truly understand that lesson and others.

"Come on, kid. Let's go see what Leigh's up to. I have a phone call to make."

Trent Dawson just might laugh his ass off. So be it.

Leigh's bedroom door opened and Addie rushed in. She stopped dead in her tracks, looking at Leigh where she sat at her desk. "What are you wearing?" Disgust written all over her face, the girl stomped over, hands on hips. One would have thought Leigh had gone out, rolled in the mud, then dressed in a potato sack.

Without any idea as to where Addie's attitude came from, Leigh stood. "I don't have a lot of choices. Most of my clothes are at my house. Jeans can be dressy."

"Why didn't you pack nicer things?" She threw her hands up in the air. When she mumbled like an aggravated mother, Leigh had to bite her lip to keep from laughing. "I swear. How am I supposed to do anything with this?" She put one hand on her forehead then waved the other up and down gesturing to Leigh's clothing.

Leigh gave up the fight and laughed. When the joy bubbled to the surface, it erupted into full blown belly laughs. The hysteria felt wonderful.

Not the least bit impressed, Addie glared. "What happened to that dress you had on a few days ago? The yellow thing?"

"My sundress? It's not dressy, honey."

"Well, it's better than that." Adding pointed accusingly the jeans and top Leigh wore. Apparently, it wasn't what Addie had in mind when she'd insisted that she take a bath, relax and get pretty. She and Rick were to take over dinner preparations for the evening, giving Leigh a break.

She didn't mind cooking, or helping Addie with meals. Who knew what kind of kitchen disaster she'd find in the morning? The girl was so determined and excited about her secret menu, that Leigh hadn't been able to deny her.

She just hoped she didn't regret giving in.

"You really want me to wear a dress?"

Addie's pale blue eyes nearly bugged out of her head. "Yes!"

"Can I wear a skirt?" She walked to her closet and opened the door. "It's really all I have with me."

Addie huffed. "I guess it'll have to do."

Leigh smiled and bit back another round of laughter. "Give me just a couple of minutes. It won't take me long."

Addie's hands returned to her hips. "Fine. Five minutes and not a second longer. I'm going to check on Rick." She stomped out of Leigh's bedroom and closed the door.

Leigh had just pulled the skirt from the closet when her bedroom door opened and Addie's head and one shoulder appeared. "Your hair and makeup look really pretty. Can you teach me how to do the curls one day? And maybe the makeup?"

While she'd waited, she just taken a few minutes to add a few lazy curls to the ends of her hair and a little color to her face. "Sure. Anytime."

Addie nodded then disappeared.

Leigh heard her shout from the far end of the hall. "She needs five minutes, then I am done! Jeez, you grownups are a lot of work."

She exchanged the pale green and black skirt for her jeans. She slipped on a pair of strappy sandals. Making a stop by her mirror, she added lip gloss for some shine.

Hoping she passed Addie's muster, she sat down at her desk to wait. She'd been banned from the rest of the house while Addie and Rick had prepared dinner. She wasn't sure she wanted to know why they felt the need to hide their activities, but she told herself not to worry, at least for tonight.

Someone knocked on the door, breaking into her thoughts. Addie always announced her presence, often as she let herself in.

Rick.

She opened her door to find him dressed in a black tailored button-up and slacks. Men in business or dress attire had never appealed much to Leigh. A country girl at heart, she'd didn't have anything against them, really, but she'd always been drawn to men who appeared a little more rugged.

Until Rick Evans crossed her path. Polished, but not quite civilized enough to completely mask the dark undercurrent of lethal grace, he caused something in her chest to hitch each and every time she saw him.

Now? Forget the hitch. The sight of him, standing there, holding a bouquet of scraggly wildflowers, stopped her heart in its tracks. She'd seen plenty of handsome men in her life, but had never dreamed that a specimen as downright decadent existed beyond fiction. *Joke's on you, sister.*

His hair, still slightly shower damp, curled a bit at his collar and over one brow.

Words failed her, and she was forced her to settle on a one word greeting. "Hey."

He handed her the half-wilted bouquet. It was simultaneously the most pitiful and beautiful bunch she'd ever seen. "Addie insisted I bring you flowers. She picked them, but I'm not supposed to tell you that. She wanted me to take all the credit."

"I don't doubt that one bit. Your secret's safe. She demanded I wear a dress. Although I think anything less than a ball gown would have been a disappointment. My wardrobe is limited, so this is what you get." She gestured down at her skirt.

"Leigh, there is nothing disappointing about what you're wearing. You wouldn't be any less beautiful in jeans and an old t-shirt."

She shook her head. "Oh no, that wouldn't do for the organizer of this event. Any idea why this dinner is such a big deal to her?"

"No idea at all." His shit-eating grin said otherwise. Full of gentlemanly charm, he held his elbow out for her. "Shall we?"

Footsteps thundered through the house, sounding much like a herd of elephants. Addie appeared at the opposite end of the hall. Already dressed in pale blue pajamas, she tilted her as she looked them both over. "Just checking. I've eaten and I have snacks. Cara just got here. We're going to have a movie night. Just pretend I'm not even here."

She vanished as quickly as she'd appeared. Leigh laughed, surprised at how much noise a child who probably didn't weigh a hundred pounds could make.

"Another movie marathon? Poor Cara. You're going to owe her. Hopefully Addie won't be too hard on her."

"We have a deal. I suspect she'll keep her end of the bargain." A lazy, knowing grin spread over his face. Her toes curled. With nothing left to do, she took the flowers and his elbow.

A hundred butterflies taking flight low in her belly, she tried for lighthearted. "I'm still trying to figure out whether this is just teenager drama or something more."

He stopped at the patio door. His hands on her shoulders turned her to face him. The heat of his palms spread through her, bringing thoughts she'd tried so hard to ignore to the surface. There was nothing lighthearted in the deep undercurrents swirling beneath his simple words. "Definitely something more, for both her and I."

Making her best effort at a cheeky grin, she asked, "You wouldn't have anything to do with that, would you? Say like plotting my demise?"

The sly, sexy smile that took over his mouth just might be the death of her. "Never."

She gulped and pretended to be unaffected when she was anything but. Desire bloomed deep, its intensity shaking her.

His palms slid down the flesh of her arms in a sultry caress. He took her by the hand and led her to the kitchen where a picnic basket waited on the counter. Leaning close, he whispered, "Now, I want you to think about only one thing. What does Leigh Ann MacDonald want?" He took her hands, weaving their fingers together at her sides.

"Honestly, I don't even know anymore. I did. Then the world tilted, mixing everything up. Some things just don't seem as important as they used to." She didn't know what to make of their dinner. Rick and Addie told her they wanted to give her a break for the evening. Picnics and a sunset dinner? The setup felt more and more like a date.

They totally suckered me.

She should have known better. The two of them had so much in common that it was mind boggling. Why would they setup a date for her?

Rick had made it plain that he had no interest in anything beyond making sure Addie was in good hands. *Then again, the kiss we shared over icing a few nights ago took friendly to an entirely new level.*

Hungry. Sinful. Delicious. So far from platonic they might as well have been from opposite planets. Dinner for two didn't say, "Put your feet up and rest."

~

Addie walked down the hallway and almost bumped into Cara coming out of the kitchen. She carried a drink in one hand and a bowl of popcorn in the other. When Cara looked up she smiled. "Hey, kiddo. How's it going?" Addie considered that smile. It was real. She'd always had a knack for knowing if people were telling the truth or not. Faces and expressions weren't much different.

Cara was good people.

Good people. That's what her grandpa always said when he liked someone. *Mark's good people. The Parkers are good people. Beth, down at the store, is good people.* Maybe it made her sound like a country girl. She didn't care. She still considered it the highest compliment someone could give a person.

"I'm okay." She bit back the urge to babble on, revealing how she felt. As much as she liked Cara, she still felt awkward in the pretty soldier's presence. Addie enjoyed her company, but worried she might say or do the wrong thing. And she didn't want anything bad to get back to Leigh or Rick. She might be tired of staring at the same walls every day, but at least they were clean and safe. She had more food than she could eat in a month and both Leigh and Rick were so good to her.

Like real parents.

Almost too good, except they easily passed the smile test. She still couldn't believe this new world she lived in could be real.

"Come on in here, chickie." Cara tilted her head in the direction of the TV room. "Are we watching comedies or superhero movies?"

"You can pick. There are too many to choose from." She followed Cara into the family room and sat on the couch.

"Okay. Now, before we start the movies, tell me what's really going on. You're good with the poker face, but you can't fool me. What's up?"

Oh, shit. Addie looked down at her feet on the shiny wood floor. Cara had the smile radar, too. She knew better than to think she could outsmart it, but she couldn't do anything to screw up things here with Rick and Leigh.

"Come on, spit it out before you worry a hole in your bottom lip."

Her head snapped up to find Cara looking at her with concern. A long forgotten memory came to life, bringing a rush of happiness. "My grandpa used to tell me that."

Cara sat on the couch then sat her phone beside her. Just like Rick's, it had an app and access to security stuff on it. They never made a big deal about it, but they always had one close. "I think I'd like your grandpa. He sounds like a good guy."

"He was...I miss him a lot." She sat at the other end of the couch and crossed her legs.

"So, what's with the gloomy face?"

Maybe it would be better to tell Cara her worries? "It's not a big deal. I'm just getting bored. I don't want Rick to think

I don't like what he'd doing for me. I don't want to bug them."

"I think that's normal. Rick's working hard. The whole team is. It won't be long."

"I know." She wasn't sure she'd ever seen anyone work so hard in her life.

Cara turned on the TV with the remote. "You said your grandfather was in the Army?"

Full of emotion, worries and turmoil Addie nodded.

Cara got up and walked across the room to the loveseat. She picked up a large white plastic bag. She brought the bag over, then held it out for her to take. "For you."

Shock stole her words. What should she say? Do? What if Cara thought she didn't like it? She reached her hand out then before she came in contact with the bag, she withdrew it. "A present for me? I never get presents. We never had the money or dad was always busy with his...drugs." What did it matter anymore? Everyone knew what he did.

"This one didn't cost me anything, but I thought you might like to have it back. It's not a gift that most thirteen-year-old girls would like, but I figure you're special enough to appreciate it."

Curiosity stuck its claws in her. Addie took the bag. A little heavy and bulky, its weight shifted awkwardly in the bag. Half eager, half afraid, she opened it and looked inside.

"What?" She blinked. And blinked again. It was still there, the familiar dark greens and browns, a balm to her aching soul.

Pulling it out, she looked to the front. "It is. It really is." The name Potter was embroidered on the front. She rubbed a fingertip over the letters. Her breath left her on a shaky exhale.

"It's been laundered, so it's clean. I thought you'd like to have it back."

She dropped the bag to the floor and clutched it to her chest. She thought her grandfather's old coat was lost to her forever after she'd dropped it in the woods all those weeks ago.

"I don't know what to say or do." Tears welled in her eyes. Closing them, she bent her head and pressed the coat to her face.

"Just say thank you."

"Thank you so much. This is the best present ever." Addie thought she might have seen a hint of moisture in Cara's eyes too.

Then she threw a piece of popcorn at Addie. "Come on, sis. We have a pile of movies to watch. Did you save any cupcakes for us?"

Sis. She'd heard lots of people say it the same way they said sweetheart or honey to someone they liked. No one had ever called her that.

Does this mean I have a friend?

Chapter Sixteen

"Rick, what's going on here?" Leigh struggled to hold onto her focus. Trapped by the intensity of his dark eyes, she half-feared she might get pulled into their depths and never return. She took a deep, stuttering breath.

He released one of her hands to cup her nape. His words were quiet, but if anything, they were all the more powerful for their lack of volume. "Addie and I are waging war. We've decided what we want, and we're not stopping until we get it. We want you."

A stiff breeze could have knocked her over. A part of her had wondered, maybe even suspected, that the two of them might be working toward that end, but she hadn't expected Rick to be so direct. So very blunt.

But then again, the one thing he wasn't? A game player.

Releasing her, he drew her to the patio door and opened it. Torn, needing space, she walked out and away from him.

We want you. And there was no mistaking his meaning. He said *we* not *I* or even *she*, indicating Addie. Warring emotions burst to life inside her. Yearning. Curiosity. Fear. She didn't know what to feel, what to focus on.

She stopped at the edge of the cobblestone patio. She leaned against a stone pillar and crossed her arms over her chest. Resting her head against the column, she stared at the perfectly manicured lawn. The view spread out before her, storybook beautiful even in its loneliness. Day darkened, working its way toward night in a dazzling display of color.

He whispered close. "Be right back."

Nodding absently, she focused on an enormous, solitary tree in the center of a fenced pasture. Ancient and timeless, it would have withstood countless seasons and landscape changes as the farm evolved over the decades. It seemed lonely and somehow that only made her feel smaller, sadder.

Why had Rick changed his mind? What did it mean? After his denial, she'd convinced herself that they, or the relationship that had never been given an honest chance, couldn't be. The loss had hurt a great deal, so much so that the dull ache beneath her breastbone hadn't faded.

Now he'd changed his mind? Just like that?

She couldn't deny the prospect held enough temptation to lure a nun to sin, but what if he changed his mind again? The first loss had hurt enough to last a lifetime. She wasn't ready to sign on for another round of heartache.

Is Rick really offering what I think he is? The door behind her opened and closed, but lost in the tempest of her thoughts, she focused on the sunset. She couldn't afford to forget that it wasn't only her heart on the line. She might not know how they would get there, but she knew she wasn't giving up until Addie was permanently hers. That meant that any major decisions she made would also impact the girl who she hoped would become her foster daughter. She refused to screw that up.

He'd talked as if he and Addie had planned this…whatever it was, together.

Spinning, she found Rick behind her, basket in hand.

"You can't get her hopes up." Determined that he would see reason and put a stop to this game, she continued. She pointed her finger at him. "She's been through so much already. It's not right to draw her into some silly plan that doesn't have a chance of coming together. I won't have her hurt." Guilt stabbed her. She knew the last sentence was harsh, but she had to be strong for Addie.

Yet she knew that Rick would never in a million years intentionally hurt the girl he'd done so much for. He'd been the one beside her every step of the way when they'd searched for their girl. They'd worried and feared and hoped together.

They'd shared a lifetime of ups and downs in one season. "I'm sorry. I know you wouldn't hurt her. I have to keep her in mind for every decision I make. I don't want her to think she can have something that's impossible."

"Why is it impossible?"

"You and I? Together?"

He didn't respond, just waited.

Throwing her hands up, she released all her pent-up frustration. "Do I have to remind you that you shut me down? I heard you tell Trent that you thought I was the most beautiful woman you'd ever seen. You said I reminded you of an angel. Don't deny it. Those words burned themselves into my memory. I decided right then and there that I was declaring war on you." Poking his chest, she continued. "I would keep at you, battering at your hardhead until it broke."

He placed a single finger over her lips, cutting off her tirade. "You did break me." The solemn sincerity in his words maddened her.

She said his name against his finger. "Rick. You broke your promise."

Again, he took her hand in his and led her toward the nearest barn. "You're right. I did. Let's take this somewhere private. Addie means well tonight, but I don't want her eavesdropping and getting her hopes dashed before I've even begun."

Begun? He hasn't even started? Oh hell. She didn't have the kind of fortitude needed to withstand a Rick Evans assault. She wasn't sure Fort Knox did. *This isn't the way this is supposed to go!*

They walked hand in hand through the silent dusk. Reeling, she let him lead as she hoped with everything she had that she could survive the evening. Half of her wanted to run as fast and as far as she could go.

Her other half was desperate to explore the dangerous territory of their prior conversation.

I can't run away. I promised to be there for Addie.

Either one of them was a force to be reckoned with, but when they teamed up? She was well and truly screwed. Why hadn't she left him alone, letting him rot in his sulky funk? Shouldn't she have?

Possibly, but she never would have been able to live with herself.

Somehow, despite her inner riot of emotions, the walk over a corner of his property to one of the barns settled her nerves. The storybook scenery made her feel for a few moments that dreams could come true.

He stopped just outside the barn and facing her, took her free hand in his. He wove their fingers together. "I owe you an enormous apology. I was a complete bastard when I left you behind that morning. I knew it would hurt you."

"It did, very much so."

"I told myself that it was for your protection, but that was a lie. I used it to drive an even bigger wedge between us. It was a chicken shit thing to do. I'm sorry."

"Rick, I—"

"I don't expect you to accept my apology that quickly, if at all. It's not something a few nice words can easily mend. I just wanted you to know that I regret hurting you. Come on. Let's eat."

They walked inside and she stopped. Beneath the lofty ceiling sat the smaller farm table she'd ordered for his breakfast nook. In its center sat five mismatched candles.

Without a word, he seated her in one of the two empty chairs. He opened the basket and pulled out an assortment of random food. Grapes, berries, cheese, crackers, wrapped sandwiches, fruit snacks and beef jerky.

She burst into laughter. "I'm guessing Addie helped pack dinner."

Trying unsuccessfully to hide a grin, he pretended to be offended at her assumption. "What makes you say that? Maybe I planned this entire menu myself?"

"So fruit snacks and dehydrated meat with enough salt to kill an elephant are a part of your grand plan? Your seduction skills know no bounds." Damn, the laughter felt wonderful. She let herself fall into the happiness for a moment. Joy had been too far scarce over the past few months. From Kate's drama, to her brother's and hers. They'd all been put through the wringer.

He handed her a linen napkin and filled her wine glass. "She said you loved them. I believed her…a little bit."

"Well, that's not exactly what I said, but we'll go with it. I'm honored she shared some of her precious snacks with me."

"You should be. She also packed dessert." He removed a storage container. Pulling off the lid, he revealed four sloppily decorated cupcakes. Two of them had been under filled with batter and were too short. Another had cake bulging out and down over the sides of the wrapper. One was just right. Chocolate icing was smeared everywhere.

She blinked. "Did she make the frosting herself?"

He set two cupcakes on a paper napkin beside her plate. Then he lit the candles and sat down. "She said she used your recipe."

She blinked again, feeling silly that something as simple as homemade cupcakes and the knowledge that Addie had tried to use the things she'd taught her threatened to make her weepy.

A little lost and off-balance, she took a piece of fruit and savored the sweetness. When Rick burst into choked laughter, she paused. *Damn, he's got a great laugh. Is there anything he can't do?* "What's so funny?"

He set a stack of napkins on the table between them. Then he pulled one off the top and handed it to her. On it someone had drawn a man with enormous, adorable, cartoon, puppy dog eyes. The man in the drawing held a scraggly bouquet of flowers, offering them to a princess sitting on a toadstool. The princess had long flowing hair, wore jeans and tall pointed cap with a long ribbon waving in the invisible breeze.

Unable to help herself, she joined him in his laughter. "Oh, boy. Where did she get this idea?"

When Rick appeared uncertain, she paused. She'd never seen him so...speechless. "What is it?"

He appeared to give up some sort of internal battle before replying. "She told me that's the face I make when you're not looking. She told me I get googly-puppy-eyed when you're near."

"Oh. Rick…" What could she say to that?

He nodded to their meal. "Eat. Enjoy our gourmet feast."

Then she enjoyed their dinner. Rick gave her a break from heavy conversation, treating her to an odd, but somehow comforting meal. She hadn't realized what a toll the tediousness of past few weeks had taken.

By the time full darkness arrived outside and the candles shrunk to half their former size, they'd finished eating and discussing their hopes for Addie. There were so many issues to tackle. Legal issues. School. Socialization with kids her own age. Art lessons.

Whether it was the wine, the setting, or the company, her desire to run away faded. But no matter how relaxed she'd become or how hard she tried, the questions refused to hide. They demanded attention and answers.

It wasn't like her to avoid challenges simply because they might be difficult. Or at least, it didn't used to be like her. She'd learned the hard way that it was better to tackle any obstacle head-on and knock it out of her path—that way, she could move onto the next. Then she wouldn't have to waste time or headspace worrying about whatever current dilemma plagued her.

This? Rick's about face? Either way, it came with an equal chance that it might devastate her. Without him, she knew that she might never be whole. She could be a good mother to Addie, no matter what. But she might never be truly happy. She didn't want to spend the rest of her life a hollow shell.

What if she accepted Rick's change of heart and gave in? It could very well shatter her if things didn't work out. Which would be worse? Living her life in a drab, cold world devoid of love or experiencing it briefly and losing it? Which would be the better example to set for Addie? What did she want for Addie? Or her niece, Kylie? What would she tell Kate to do?

She'd want them to reach for the stars. Never rest until their hearts burst from happiness. Never ever settle for less than what they deserved. She knew what she had to do. The knowledge settled her jitters. By no means were they gone, but she was better for having made her choice.

Heaven help me.

Taking the bull by the horns, she stood and held out her hand. His dark eyes met hers full of barely banked curiosity. "Come on, rich boy. Show me around." Without hesitation, he stood and took her hand.

"Yes, ma'am." His grip sure and strong, he led her out of the barn.

"Tell me all about your grand plan."

"Which one? Work? Addie? Or..."

"All of them. Aren't they intertwined?"

He stopped and faced her. "Very much so."

Unable to resist, she poked him in the chest. "Then start there."

"Okay. If it's all so simple, then. Sure." Then he did. With the bright moon lighting their way, they strolled through the night. They held hands as they walked around three of the barns. Even as he downplayed the genius of it all, his vision stunned her.

Then she laughed. "You forgot one thing."

"I did?" Shocked, he turned to her.

"Yes. Sleep. You'll need to sleep, like maybe once a week. You might want to squeeze that in there somewhere." They'd made their way back to the patio, where their night began.

His wry grin made her heart flutter. "Maybe. I'll make a note of it."

"Be sure that you do." Unexpected, her next words slipped out, her tone lighthearted, but her words held deeper meaning. "You'll need a keeper." She hadn't intended to just throw her decision out there so blithely, but there it was. She leaned against her post, but this time she focused on him instead of the tree.

He was her tree, her future. When the truth of it settled inside her, it bloomed to life, vivid and real.

"Leigh. If I'm going to do this, if I have someone important in my life, she needs to be someone who understands why each part of my life is there and its importance. No single part is more vital than another." He cupped her jaw. "I can't think of any woman who fits that role better than you. I don't know that I can do it all alone."

"You could, I know it, but you shouldn't have to."

Palming her waist, he pulled her close. He touched his forehead to hers then, as if fighting some internal battle, he tilted his head and brushed his cheek against hers. She put her hands on his shoulders. Hands rubbed up her sides and down. His heavy sigh signaled he'd come to a decision.

She wished she knew what thoughts tormented him. His breath sighed over her mouth as he brushed his forehead over hers. Tightly sealing his lips, he closed his eyes. Coiled tension vibrated through the muscles of his chest.

Then the obvious conclusion finally hit her. He wanted her and fought against his desire. Part of him demanded he behave like a gentleman while the other half battled for what it wanted. Craved.

He needed her.

She was more than happy to help him with that problem.

Taking his face in her hands, she crushed her mouth to his. His hold on her waist tightened into a hard, desperate, branding grip. She loved it.

~

Fuck me, she's sweet.

The power of Leigh's honeyed mouth could bring him to his knees. The urge to lift her, wrap her legs around his waist and take her against the wall beat at him. The promise he'd made himself at the evening's start held him back, but when her slender fingers tangled in the material of his shirt, his will crumpled like a paper cup.

Tearing his mouth from hers, he drew on his last vapors of resolve. "Leigh, sweetheart. Stop."

She licked up the column of his throat. He felt her throaty, sexy reply deep in his balls. "Stop? Why?"

"I…I'm not sure I can control myself if you don't stop. I'm trying to be patient. Understanding." As he stared into her lovely eyes, something tugged his shirt free from his pants.

She's going to be the death of me.

Trapped by the beauty of her gaze, he couldn't move. A fingernail scraped over the skin of his lower abdomen. She leaned in closer and whispered into his ear, "You mean act like a responsible adult male?"

"Yeah. That." He swallowed and closed his eyes. The tugging at his shirt continued, gradually rising as she undid the buttons.

"Why would you want to do something like that?" She nipped his earlobe.

Why? Why what? He couldn't remember his own name, let alone follow a conversation with her devious fingers and mouth wreaking havoc with his senses. His libido fought to break free of the cage he'd forced it into.

Lust fueled the fire in his blood. "Leigh. You can't touch me. I want you too badly. I'm trying to not be an asshole." He prayed she saw reason and put an end to his torture.

Another nip at his ear. His shirt fell open. Two fingers walked down from one pectoral muscle.

"What if I want you just as badly?"

The air in his chest fled in one sudden rush. She wouldn't tease him. Even as he knew that as truth, as desperate as he was, he couldn't help but cringe at the thought. His one word response was more growling, hungry animal than human. "Leigh…"

She met his rabid beast with a sweet, sensual siren. "Rick."

He couldn't take it any longer. "Come on." He took her hand, intertwined their fingers and drew her around and back into the night.

She laughed even as her long legs struggled to keep

up.

"I don't see what's so funny." Impatient, he glared over his shoulder. He chanced another glance, half-afraid his surliness might turn her off or worse, scare her away.

Her smile, brighter than the moon, lit up the night. "You're about to seal the deal. What's made you so mean?"

"My house is too fucking big. Who the hell wants to walk a mile to get to the guest wing?" They came to the smaller patio that backed up to three of his guest bedrooms in the wing opposite the one where they had their rooms. The mood he was in, he couldn't trust himself to be quiet.

And if Leigh remained quiet, then he'd didn't know what the hell he was doing.

He pulled his phone from his pocket and accessed his security system. Praying he chose the room he'd had furnished in case a team member needed a place to rest, he used the custom-made app to unlock the closest door. He listened for the quiet whir signaling the lock disengaged. It was a wonder he didn't break the handle as he pushed it open.

Leigh, right on his heels, followed. He wrapped one arm around her waist, pulled her against him then slammed the door.

Her hands tangled in his hair. Their mouths met in a fiery kiss. Lips merged, tongues flirted, danced. When her fingernails scraped the flesh just below his navel, he groaned. Her tongue swirled with his and his already swollen cock hardened.

His hands slid from her hips, back to palm the curves of her ass. Pulling her softness flush against his body, he tore his mouth free and swore.

Angry at the delay, but needing more, he broke away.

"Too many layers. Clothes off." Desperate to feel the heat of her flesh against his, he yanked his shirt free. One loud thud sounded, echoing in the near empty room, as one shoe hit the ground. The second one followed as he pried it free with his other foot. Wanting to see everything, he impatiently flipped on a single light switch, filling the room with a soft glow. Far from fully furnished, the room held the one item he needed most. A mattress and box springs waited in the middle of the room. *Good enough.*

He fumbled with his belt, racing to get free. Eager, hungry, he pulled down his pants and underwear and sat on the mattress. He pulled everything free all in one go.

Looking up, he found Leigh, unbuttoning her blouse, a wicked smile lighting her face. Impatient, afraid to blink, he watched, torn.

Did he rip the clothes from her body, revealing the beauty hidden beneath, or wait and watch, rapt as she uncovered a little piece of heaven at a time? Either way, he'd die a happy man. Somehow, impossibly, his cock tightened further at thought of sinking into her delicious body, driving into her slick heat.

Oh shit, no. A sudden chilling thought threw cold water onto his lust driven dream.

"Damn it. Leigh, I don't have any protection with me. I didn't plan on things going this far. Never imagined that I'd be so fortunate. I'm sorry I'm not better prepared."

Her features softened. "I'm on the pill. Long story, but I'm protected." The siren appeared, all sex and sin. "As long as you're clean, you get a green light."

He nearly swallowed his tongue.

"Uh. Yeah. I'm good. I mean, I'm clean. Actually, it's

been a long time for me. Too damn busy."

"Then do your worst, big boy."

"Sweetheart, be careful what you ask for." His joy broke free and he grinned.

She finally, *finally*, dropped her blouse to the floor, revealing a lacy bra. He barely had time to appreciate it before the lace followed, landing on the blouse. Fire flashed in his blood.

Standing, unable to wait any longer, he hooked his hands in the waistband of her skirt. "Lose it or it won't survive another two seconds."

"It just slides down. Go ahead."

So, he did. Sliding his hands over her ass, he pushed the skirt over her slender curves until it met the tangle of clothes on the floor.

He stepped back to admire the view. She stood before him in nothing but a tiny scrap of lace, utterly gorgeous. His heart jumped and lodged in his throat.

She hooked her thumbs in the sides of her panties, shimmied, then removed them.

He drew in a single, slow, deep breath. "Come here." He crooked his finger. He'd never had such dominant, overbearing tendencies in the bedroom before, but with Leigh, he couldn't stop himself.

Something about her—her beauty, the sweetness coupled with sass—made him lose all sense of fairness. Forget chivalry, she turned him into a testosterone driven, starving caveman.

She answered his call and moved into his space. He might call the shots, but she had him eating out of the palm of her hand. Unable to wait a moment longer, he cupped her nape and crushed his mouth to hers. Eager, hungry, she matched his lust. Knowing that she craved him as much as he needed her only added fuel to the fire raging through his blood.

Hands caressed, mouths danced, breaths merged until every cell in his body came alive, yearning for Leigh. A contagious, ravenous desire consumed them.

Finally, able to do something he'd dreamt about for months, he lifted her by the hips and wrapped her legs around his waist. When the heat of her wet sex touched his abdomen, he swore. His cocked bucked. A precious burden he'd never grow tired of, he savored the weight of her in his arms.

He tumbled them to their sides on the mattress. In a mindless euphoric haze, they gave to and took from each other. Desperate, he moved down her body, reveling in the beauty of her honeyed flesh. He stopped at her breasts. He latched onto one beaded nipple and sucked the tight tip deeper into his mouth. Lavishing attention to the soft mounds, he wanted to gauge her every response but every sigh and moan fractured his focus. When he drew deeply on the hard, silken peak, she whimpered and bucked her hips.

With urgent, demanding, desire riding him, he cursed. There wasn't enough time in the world to explore and worship her the way she deserved.

He hooked one long leg over his arm and admired the sexy, hungry angel waiting beneath him. With his other hand, he found her wet, slick and ready. He notched the head of his cock into her heat. The last straw, her fingernails dug tightly into his shoulders urging him on. On a slow, sure plunge, he moved. Hot, slick, bliss gloved him.

A wicked grin spread across her face as she tangled the fingers of one hand in the hair at his nape. *Do your worst, big boy.* Fucking hell.

So be it.

Holding the smooth flesh of her ass in one palm, he slid out, the torture a delicious rasp over his hypersensitive cock. He returned her suggestive grin with his own. He readied to thrust again, but paused, caught by the beauty of her green eyes. "Leigh. I don't have the words." How did he define something so deep that it defied explanation?

She cupped his jaw. "We don't need words." Then she kissed him silly. They waged a mad, passionate battle, dueling until neither of them could breathe. He tore his mouth from hers, gulped for air, then slammed home.

Holding her in place, fucking into her, he drove them both to the edge of madness. Her short breaths came in faster pants. Her grin morphed into a mask of ecstasy as she arched, stretching her torso, unconsciously putting her gorgeous breasts on display. They bobbed with each hard slam. Fingers tightened on his shoulder and at the hair at his nape.

Rocking into her again and again, the rasping burn of pleasure maddened him, obliterating his composure. He pounded into her heat, watched the soft beauty of her eyes, and finally knew the meaning of home.

Her body tightened its hold on him. "Come on, baby. Give it to me," he whispered. "Let me have it."

She wrapped her other leg around his waist and held him closer. Breathing into each other, absorbing each other, they crested ever higher. Leigh's ragged breath hitched and her spine bowed as she cried out her release. Her body clenched his, squeezing, holding, giving him impossibly more pleasure than he'd given hers. Light exploded behind his eyes. Leigh's body milked him dry and filled with him ecstasy. Gasping, shuddering, they clutched each other and rode out the storm of passion.

Using the last of his strength, he rolled onto his back. She rested her head on his chest and heaved a content sigh. He smoothed a damp tendril of hair from her temple and kissed the smooth skin.

She returned his gesture by kissing his sternum, right above his thudding heart. Her quiet words stole his breath and sealed his fate. "I feel as though I've waited my entire life for this."

"Me too." He grasped her jaw and tilted her chin until she faced him. He stared into the spring green light of her eyes. "Me too, Leigh. All my life." Then he went about stealing the breath she'd barely begun to recover.

Chapter Seventeen

Leigh walked past Rick's dark office and paused midstride. A quick glance revealed that he sat at his desk.

Again.

She'd just seen the time on the microwave clock a few moments ago when she'd made herself a cup of tea. It was a few minutes after midnight.

With his brow furrowed, head resting in one hand, he stared at his computer monitor. His face was masked in pale blue light as he frowned at whatever the screen displayed.

Or maybe he scowled at what it didn't show him? The search for answers continued to eat at him. She couldn't imagine the pressure he'd put himself under as time dragged on. He continued to blame himself for their trouble. She hadn't been able to figure out if it was only his deep sense of responsibility and honor, or if there was far more than she was aware of.

Changing course, she entered the office. He didn't even notice as she walked up to the side of his desk. She picked up a cup of cold coffee then set it on an empty book shelf with her tea. His eyes flickered, following the movement of the mug, reminding her of a hungry animal watching food being removed from its cage. She sat in the cup's former spot on the desk. "Hey."

He blinked. Then he blinked a second time. Slowly,

life seemed to return to his body as he focused on her.

He scrubbed both hands through his thick, messy hair then finally responded. "Hey."

She poked him hard in the shoulder with a finger.

"Ow." He frowned and rubbed the spot. "What's that for? Sadist."

"Just checking. I wanted to make sure you were still alive. We didn't see much of you today, and it's getting late. Maybe you should take a break and look at things with a fresh eye in the morning." They'd seen so little of him that day, she'd briefly worried if he'd had second thoughts about the night before. Doubt had threatened to steal her happy glow, but she squashed it flat. She knew better. He wasn't intentionally putting space between them.

He was in work mode.

"I'm fine. I'll say goodnight to Addie in a few minutes then maybe spend a little longer going over everything. I just want to look over everything one more time."

"Rick, it's after midnight. Addie has been in bed for almost two hours. You told her goodnight when she brought you a bowl of ice cream." She pointed to a bowl half full of melted strawberries and cream on the opposite side of the desk. "You've gone over everything you have a hundred times. If you had what you needed, I have every confidence you would have seen it by now."

He leaned back in his chair and stretched his shoulders and back, reminding her of a great cat, waking early, flexing its muscles, and preparing for the day's hunt.

"Shit. Sorry. I'm missing something, I keep hoping that if I look at the pieces in a new light, I'll figure out what I'm missing. Getting frustrated that he's gotten one over on me doesn't help. I can't let our past cloud what's happening now."

There was that vague reference was again. Rick and Marcus had some sort of history. Could she get him to confide in her? It couldn't hurt to get him to talk about it, could it? She shook her head in frustration. "Driving yourself headfirst into a grave won't help anyone."

She went to the small fridge in the corner and got him a bottle of water. "Here. Drink. Flush some of that coffee out." She stood behind him and snuck her hands beneath the collar of his shirt. Tension knotted the already hard muscles in his neck and shoulders. She gently rubbed and massaged, hoping to ease at least a small portion of his stress. "How long have you and Marcus known each other?"

He dropped his head and groaned, the sound one of half pleasure, half misery. He'd probably been at his desk at least eighteen hours, if not longer. After a moment, he finally answered. "Since I was eleven years old. He'd just turned nine." There was something in his tone that warned her she wasn't going to like this story, but she knew that it was an important part of his life and their current conflict. She'd suspected that something significant lurked in their past, but would have never guessed that their history went back as far as childhood.

"You were only boys. What could have sparked so much hatred that it still burns more than twenty years later?"

"Jealousy. Heartache. Grief. Anger. It's all in there somewhere." He twisted the cap off the bottle and she stopped working the tenseness from his shoulders so he could take a long drink. He set it on the desk, but before she could resume the neck rub, he twisted and took her waist in his hands. Not meeting her eyes, he spoke soft, low and maybe a little desperate. "Come here." He pulled her around until she faced him.

"Hey. What's wrong?" Her heart bled for this man. He always put himself last and never asked for anything, even as he gave everything.

He pressed his forehead to her lower abdomen. "I'm failing you, both of you."

Indignation sparked. "Bullshit. You're doing no such thing."

"No, it's true. I can't do the one thing I'm supposed to be the best at. And while I'm wasting time, giving Marcus more and more opportunity to dig deeper into whatever hole he's crawled into, I'm also leaving Addie's care to you. I'd…" His words trailed off as he kissed her abdomen in apology.

"You'd what?" She ran her hands through his hair and tilted his head, forcing him to look up at her.

His words were so quiet she barely heard them in the still room. "I wanted to help." Then he straightened his spine and his voice grew to match hers in volume. "I wanted to help raise her. Be there for her. Just enjoy day to day life with her. With you."

Good god. If I wasn't already in love with this stubborn man…

She acted as if his words hadn't just tilted her world. "There'll be time for that when this is finished. I, *we*, have faith in you and your team."

"I wish it were that easy." He rested his chin on her belly and sighed.

"It's not an easy thing you guys are doing. We understand that it's going to take time. Now, are you going to tell me your story or am I going to have to pull it out of you?"

She caressed a thumb over the shell of his ear.

He closed his eyes for a long moment. "We met when his mother came to work as a housekeeper. Mom had just started feeling ill and had gotten her diagnosis. From day one, her prognosis was poor." He pulled her from the edge of the desk to sit on his lap. She wondered if the position change was so he could hold her close or so he didn't have to look her in the eye.

At that very moment, she would have given him the moon and the stars, so she let him have his emotional space, even as she lay against the solid warmth of his chest. She resisted the urge to strip his shirt away so she could get even closer. The fine cloth barred her from what she wanted.

"At first, they lived on the outskirts of town in a small trailer park. I rarely saw Marcus. I think once or twice she brought him with her when there was no school, but Anita did her job well and was rarely seen. Then mom started getting sicker and the harsh treatments only made her feel more so."

He stroked a hand tenderly up and down her back, as if she were the one who needed comfort.

"The sicker Mom became, the more we saw of Anita. I never gave it a second thought. A few weeks before Mom passed away, Anita and Marcus moved into the guesthouse. I didn't care, didn't even notice, until dad mentioned it. I saw Marcus in the kitchen a few times having lunch or dinner, but he never ate in the dining room where we had our family meals. I was worried about Mom, so I didn't speak to him much. I lived day by day in a fog of oblivion, utterly clueless about the world around me." He shook his head. "Never again."

His chest rose and fell beneath her as he took a deep breath. She looked up in time to see him press his thumb and forefinger into the inner corners of his eyes. She kissed the underside of his jaw and waited.

"I watched her get closer to death each day and there wasn't a damn thing I could do to stop it. One day, she told me to eat something. I was looking too thin. Eager to do anything she told me to, I went to the kitchen to get a sandwich. Marcus sat at the breakfast table eating his lunch. He was excited and chattier than usual. He sat there, legs swinging under his chair, babbling away. My head was in the fridge when his words registered. He said that it wouldn't be long until he and his mom moved into the big house. He already had toys packed."

Rick shook his head and resumed stroking her back. "In my, I'm-two-years-older-and-wiser brain, I brushed it off as silly little kid talk."

Oh, no. Oh, please, no. The heavy stone resting in her stomach only grew heavier as suspicion set in.

"Two weeks later, mom died at home. She refused to stay in the hospital during her final days. She wanted to be home in her bed, surrounded by the people and things she loved. It wasn't until years later, while I was in high school, that I remembered something. While she slept at home, in their bed, Dad was nowhere to be found. Most nights he slept elsewhere. He should have at least been in the same room in case she needed something."

"Oh no. Was she alone?" The words slipped out before she could call them back. No wonder there was so much animosity between Rick and his father.

His chest heaved beneath her. "No. She had around the clock care. A nurse waited nearby, always at the ready. They loved her, everyone did."

"Rick, honey, I'm so sorry. I can't imagine the pain

you shouldered alone." She tried to gently steer their conversation back on track. "Marcus and Anita didn't actually move in, did they?"

Gruff, angry and still grieving, he replied. "Nothing happened until two weeks after we buried my mother. Marcus had been present in the house more and more, but I hadn't cared, barely paid any attention to him. This time, when we came across each other in the TV room, he said 'Now that the sick lady is dead, we'll be moving in soon. Just a couple more days.' His words hit me like a blow. I snapped and yelled at him, screamed at him to take it back. He just stood there confused. He didn't understand why I was upset."

"Rick, you were both children."

"I know. He likely repeated what his mother had told him. My father heard me yelling and came to see what the fuss was about. He sent Marcus back to the guesthouse and tried to calm me down. Something in my sputtering rage got his attention. After I let it all out, he sent me to my room. I cried myself to sleep. The next thing I knew, Marcus and Anita were gone from the guest house."

"Oh, Rick." Her palm lay over his heart and she wished she had some way to heal the pain he continued to bear.

"I didn't see either of them again until about six or seven months later. Anita rang the bell and asked the new housekeeper to see my father. She stood there waiting, a suitcase in one hand and Marcus's hand in the other. He had a backpack over one shoulder and a suitcase of his own in his free hand."

"She didn't think she'd be able to move right on in did she?"

"Yeah, she did. Her belly was swollen and very round.

She was a strikingly beautiful woman. Waif-like, fragile appearing, and obviously pregnant. She carried my half-brother inside her. Maybe she genuinely thought Dad loved her. She might have figured pregnancy bought her a golden ticket. I don't know. I didn't even realize what her pregnancy or any of the drama meant until Dad came in and they started arguing. She started off sweet and teary eyed, and dad almost let her in. When a victorious light came over her face, he paused. The argument grew uglier. In her rage, she lost her temper and accidently revealed that she'd gotten pregnant on purpose. She'd seduced my grieving father from day one."

Words failed her, so she took his free hand, tangled her fingers with his and held tight.

"After they left, he and I fought. Less than two weeks later, he sent me away to my first boarding school."

"Did she…did he…? I don't know what to say. You have a half-brother?" As painful as his past was, she still wasn't quite sure how it amounted to so much utter hatred on Marcus's part. "Is that why he hates you? I mean, he's downright evil, Rick. It's all horrible, utterly terrible for you both but, even as my heart bleeds, I still don't get it. I'm sorry."

"I found out later, when I was old enough to search for my brother, that my father paid Anita a great deal of money to go away. She happily took it. She had a drug habit, and when she came into money, it only got worse. In just a few years, she went through all of the money and they ended up back where she started."

"But now she had two children to care for."

He tucked her head beneath his chin. "Yeah. I didn't know they needed anything. She should have gone into rehab. It guts me to think that they needed food or, who knows what.

I would have helped somehow if I had known. The house they'd lived in was foreclosed on and the three of them had moved back to the same trailer park. Anita overdosed not long after that. Marcus, who was a child himself, raised my brother, *our* brother alone. Looking back now, I don't think my father had any idea of what happened to them. I think he was overwhelmed by grief and guilt. It was just easier to forget they even existed." His hand tightened on hers.

"During spring break, my first year of college, I looked them up. Anita had already been gone a few years. Marcus told me in no uncertain terms that he didn't want me around Wendell. He stared at me with cold, dead eyes and vowed that he'd take away everything both my father and I held dear. He's shadowed me at every turn, never acting, but always making his presence known."

"He raised your brother alone while she wasted away. He thought he was going to get a better life, and then, in his childish viewpoint, you took it all away. Then he watched his mother slowly kill herself with drugs. Jeez. If he weren't so despicable, I could feel sorry for him."

"Yeah, but he's a grown man who's made all the wrong decisions for a long time. That's all on him."

"He didn't have any other family to turn to?"

"I had to do some digging to find Marcus and Wendell that first year and really had no idea what I was doing at the time. I did find Marcus's father, Darrell Sutton. He could have given Tom Caudill a run for his money in the shitty absentee father department. I drove out to his cabin in a little speck on the map called Barker Hollow. His home looked barely fit for animals to live in. He came to the door and sneered at me as if I'd crawled from the sewer." Rick's gaze lost focus as he got lost in the past.

"When I explained who I was looking for, it took a few minutes for any of my words to register. He finally remembered Anita when I showed him a yearbook picture I'd found. There was no denying her waif-like beauty. He denied having a son, but there was something odd about the way he spoke. He kept saying 'we' instead of 'I'. 'We don't want your kind around here.' That kind of thing.

"I left that hollow with the suspicion he knew more than he admitted. I also felt about ten times worse, knowing that Marcus's father made mine look like a saint. My family might have fallen apart after my mother's death, but its roots were sown in love."

"It's a shame when people have to go it alone. No one should have to live a life without family or friends. I'd survive without mine, but I'm not sure it would be a life worth living."

"No, Leigh, sweetheart, you'd be just fine. You'd build your own. You'd adopt people all along the way, bringing them into your light. Men like me are destined to walk alone in the dark. I don't deserve you."

Heart cracking into a thousand pieces, she stood, leaving the warmth of his hold. She turned her back on him, going to the open door. She closed and locked it, the quiet snick loud in the still, heavy air. Returning, she stopped before him. When he would have pulled her back into his arms, she shook her head and placed a staying hand on his shoulder. "Bullshit." She unbuttoned her short-sleeved blouse and let it fall from her shoulders as she spoke. "You are no less deserving of love than Addie is."

Without waiting for a reply, she yanked his shirt free from his waistband and stripped it from his body.

"Leigh, you don't have to do this." Despite his concession, she heard the desire in his husky voice. He wanted her every bit as much as he wanted to be the good guy.

"I know. This isn't pity sex. This is me, expressing my hunger for a man that is absolutely worthy of everything good the world has to offer. I found the man of my dreams, and I'm not letting him get away. Neither will I let him suffer alone. Is that okay with you?"

The light in his eyes flickered in the darkness, hunger coming to life. She sat on the desk's edge and took his face in her palms. Without waiting for a response, she set her mouth upon his, kissing away the sorrow. He tasted of pure sin. Sweet ice cream, a hint of coffee, and all man. Her man.

His hands found the clasps of her bra and sent it flying, freeing her aching breasts. Deliciously rough palms cupped their weight. His thumbs caressed over her nipples.

Desperate with need for this man, she pulled free and dropped to her knees. She unfastened his pants and freed his erection. Steel hard, eager, it waited for her. Her mouth watered at the sight. His body, just like his very character, defined raw, masculine, power.

She took him in her mouth and hands, working a labor of love to bring him pleasure.

Each of his groans rumbled through her, spreading tremors of dark joy through every fiber of her being. He cupped her jaw and swept his thumbs over her cheeks. She might be the one on her knees, but she felt utterly worshipped as he bathed her in praise. Love.

She flicked her tongue at the underside of his cock, making it buck. He groaned louder and longer. Lost in her own pleasure, she hummed.

Suddenly, strong hands gripped under her arms and lifted her from the floor. He set her on her feet and tore at the button of her jeans. It popped free, then he yanked the zipper down. "Rick, this was supposed to be my turn to give to you."

"I can't tell you how much I appreciate that thought. I also don't care. One thing I forgot to tell you about me? I'm as greedy and bossy in the bedroom as I am in life, maybe more so. You're going to have to learn how to deal with that." He pushed both hands into the back of her pants and beneath her panties, shoving them down as he went. His palms smoothed over the flesh of her bottom, down to the backs of her thighs. "Off." He punctuated his command with a light slap to one cheek. "All of it off. Now."

"Yes, sir." She answered him playfully, but she wasn't so sure that he didn't take her seriously.

She did as he'd instructed. Shedding the suddenly constricting denim, she bared herself to him.

"My turn to play. Sit. Open your legs." Her breath hitched at the image he created. Again, she complied, even as her heart stopped at his devilish grin. He took her place, kneeling on the floor, facing the desk.

"Here. Put your feet on the chair. He demonstrated by taking one trembling foot, kissing the top of it, then placing it at the chair's front edge, against the padded armrest. She placed the other foot on the chair's opposite side. He remained in between her legs, his rugged, virile presence saturating her with aching need.

She hadn't known it was possible to feel so vulnerable and overwhelmingly aroused at the same time.

Only Rick.

He swept his palms slowly up her knees to her inner

thighs. His dark eyes met hers. She felt pinned in place by the intense possessive heat simmering deep inside their depths. "Put your palms flat on the desktop. Don't move." She complied and felt the hard, cold wood beneath her hands.

"Sweetheart, you might want to breathe." His focus then left her face and moved lower. "You'll regret passing out and missing this." He blew a hot breath over the flesh between her legs.

Oh, my.

She grew dizzy as indescribable, decadent sensations rippled through her.

He braced his palms on the uppermost part of her inner thighs and opened her wide. Then he kissed her. His hot mouth closed over her pussy and hummed. He flattened his tongue, sweeping a long lick up the valley of her flesh.

Unbidden, a whimper of desperate need escaped her. She shifted her weight to one hand and grasped the top of his head with the other. Her fingers gripped his hair, holding on for dear life. Intense, bright joy whipped through her as he licked over her again, slowing his progress to a crawl as he came to her clit. When another jolt of electric bliss hit her, she didn't know whether to urge him on and beg him to never stop or beg him to quit before she fell so far deep into his spell, she'd never find her way back to sanity.

He flicked a light tap over her exposed flesh. "I don't think so. Palms flat on the desk or I'll stop."

"Damn you, stubborn man." She snapped her hand back to its former place on the cold wood.

"Relax." When he nudged lightly against her thighs she realized they ached from pushing against the hands holding her open. She took a deep breath and tried to do as he said.

Relax. She almost laughed at the absurdity of the idea. He was giving her what was possibly the most erotic experience of her life, and he wanted her to relax?

He returned his attention to his task, licking the dampness from her, loving her as every bit as thoroughly as she'd worshipped him. When she thought he couldn't push her any higher without tipping her over the edge, he inserted two fingers into her pussy. Another whimper escaped.

"So very sweet. I could play here all night. I'd happily keep you on edge until dawn." He worked her flesh until her arms became weak from the tension. All sense of time disappeared as he worked her with his hands and mouth, leaving no part of her untested, unloved.

When he'd teased her into a whimpering, half-sobbing mess, he stood. Grasping his cock in hand, he touched the head to her hypersensitive flesh. He circled her sex, gathering moisture and taunting her.

She bit her lip in a stubborn attempt to keep from begging him to take her. A knowing, cocky grin spread across that delicious mouth she loved so much.

She'd do anything for this man.

When he finally slid home in a slow, wicked glide, she broke. She clutched his shoulders with both hands. He whispered into her ear, a rough but tender, reassurance. "Hang on, love."

Then he pounded into her, a hard, wracking, desperate rhythm. Each blow, a delicious shock that filled her full of him and mind-blowing pleasure. Wave after wave of exquisite pressure crashed through her as flesh slammed against flesh. Bliss bloomed deep in her center, rolling out to fill every single pore. Her breaths hitched. Her pulse skyrocketed. Her pleasure soared.

Thrusting harder with each rapid blow, he pistoned into her. His chest heaved, his hands on her hips tightened. He completely owned her.

His movements shortened and quickened until he jackhammered into her. Her sex tightened on his, gripping, squeezing. Stars exploded behind her eyes, light shone through her, burning away everything except Rick and the ecstasy consuming her. His arm tightened around her waist and anchored her. His heavy pants brushed her ear. Taking his mouth in hers, she nipped his bottom lip and scraped her fingernails lightly over his nipples. He groaned into mouth as his back arched, pushing his hips tight against hers.

He laid her back against the cool wood of the desk and slammed his cock deeper. Another wave bliss ripped through her, sharper, brighter and she cried into him, a desperate keening sound of joy.

Gripping her hips, fingers biting into the flesh of her cheeks, he came, filling her. He groaned into their kiss, and she wrapped her arms around the wide breadth of his shoulders. Their breaths mingled as their gazes met, holding each other in the still of the night.

Chapter Eighteen

Something about Leigh's words the night before stayed with him. She went past accepting the darker parts of his soul and straight into loving them. He might not deserve it, but he'd be a fool to turn it away.

The nagging sensation wouldn't go away.

He reviewed their night. Not a hardship. Leigh was nearly as beautiful on the outside as she was the inside. The only thing that topped the physical pleasure they enjoyed was the strength of their emotional connection. Given his childhood and the rough relationship with his father, that was something he'd never expected or even hoped to have.

Family.

Sure, he had his father, but he was closer with the members of his team than he was his own flesh and blood.

"Hey, Rick. We're going to go swimming. You wanna go with us?" He looked up from the computer monitor to find Addie with hope shining in her smile. Her bright eyes never failed to lighten his dark moods. Each day they seemed to grow brighter.

"I wish I could, but I'm busy. Maybe tomorrow." Regret filled him, matching the disappointment that flashed in her eyes.

But instead of turning her back on him, she entered his office and sat in her seat in front of his desk. She looked down picking at an invisible speck of lint from her long t-shirt.

"You always say that." Something tugged at his heart,

freeing a memory from his childhood.

He'd been sitting on the edge of his mother's bed when she'd first fallen ill. "He always says 'maybe tomorrow, Richard.' Tomorrow never comes."

His mother had hugged him close, and tried her best to soothe the hurt away. He couldn't remember which promise his father had broken that day. There'd been so many. It wasn't hard imagining Leigh soothing away Addie's hurts.

Filled with guilt, he looked to Addie. His motto had always been that friends and family came first. He'd claimed Addie as his. Sure, they had legal stuff to settle. But one way or another, he'd make sure it happened.

She had to come first.

He had to start thinking like the father he wanted to be, not that father he'd had. Otherwise he was no better.

Something sparked, reminding him of his conversation with Leigh just the night before.

Father.

"You know what? You're right. Give me five minutes to pass this work on to someone else then I'll come out and join you two.

"Really?" Joy lit her expression.

"Yep. I promise. Five minutes. If I don't have trunks somewhere, I'll find scissors and make some."

She laughed. "Silly. You do. Leigh ordered you some when she ordered my swimsuit. She put them away in your closet."

"Of course she did. She thinks of everything."

It was her turn to say, "Yep. It was the same day you made sure the pool guy was safe to come and fix the pump. I can't believe you have an indoor pool! Leigh says that maybe when this is all over with, we can have a pool party and have everyone over. It won't even matter if it's at Christmas! I can swim and watch it snow!"

From day one, Leigh had turned this cold, lifeless house into a home. He didn't think she'd intentionally done it, but everything she touched spelled home and love.

Family.

Shit. That was it. How could I have been so fucking blind?

Fathers.

He'd been so focused on Marcus's business dealings, properties, contacts, and finances, he hadn't paid much attention to the bastard's family.

"Go on and don't tell Leigh. I want to surprise her."

"Okay!" She was out the door like a shot.

He picked up the phone and called Pete.

He quickly finished that call, then made another. He stood, then had another thought. He sent a couple more messages to Pete. The last one read, *Final order for the day. spend some time with your girls tonight, all of them. Give Crystal my thanks and love.*

Then he went and found his swim trunks.

~

Rick started his SUV and backed out of his garage. Watching his surroundings closely, he drove them down the winding driveway. Placing his hand on Leigh's knee, he reminded himself to be patient. He'd wanted nothing more than to run headlong into the search, guns blazing. It would have been a dumbass move.

This required patience. He'd always had a steady supply, but the past few days had worn his tissue paper thin. After his call to Pete, the kid had gotten busy, energized by a new lead. He'd dug fast and deep and, miracle of miracles, he'd managed to find pay dirt, even on a man who didn't know the first thing about the internet or technology. Their link to Marcus had been right in front of his face the entire time, he'd just had to open this eyes.

Then the hard part came. Surveillance. They'd spent four long days watching, waiting in the woods until finally, they found him. Marcus Sutton might think he was smart, but even his deviousness had its limits. Snakes always returned to their nests.

Rolling green pastures and neat fencing rolled by as he drove. Leigh rode beside him and a notably agitated Addie sat in the middle seat behind them.

She'd been so happy and seemingly carefree around them at his place that he hadn't once thought about what leaving their little private compound might do to her. Stupidly, he'd thought she'd be excited when he told her they had information and were going after Sutton to end this. He'd framed the plan in a way to make it sound like a vacation or escape from her prison, but when the color drained from her face, his stomach had fallen to his feet.

He hated upsetting her, but didn't have any choice.

Leigh had promised to stay by her side the entire time, but that had only marginally alleviated her tension. Even using the carrot of touring Trent's stables and checking in on Bonnie hadn't lessoned the anxiety in her sweet features.

His gut twisted with guilt as he wished that he could

do this another way, but even as Leigh had pointed out, Addie would have to leave the house eventually. School had already started in most districts. Even if they homeschooled her, she needed to get out and experience the world. Today was only the first step of many Addie would have to take.

Leigh turned to look at Addie, trying once again to soften the blow they'd dealt her.

"Sweetheart, I promise, you'll adore Harlan. He's an even bigger, gruffer teddy bear than Noah. He loves kids. You'll have him eating out of your hand in no time."

"I wish I could be there to see it. I've never seen a man melt so fast as when Kylie came running up to show him her new puppy. A snowman in the Arizona sun stood a better chance than Harlan."

Addie finally spoke, her voice not much more than a tremulous whisper. "Is the puppy still there?"

"She is. Cookie belongs to my niece, Kylie. She's an energetic little thing, but as sweet as they come." Leigh reached back to pat Addie on one knee.

Addie tilted her head in question. "Which one?"

Leigh pulled at the upper half of her seatbelt to get more slack as she focused on Addie and her question. "Which one what, sweetheart?"

Rick looked in the rearview mirror. Addie nibbled on her lower lip. She stopped to ask, "Which one is sweet?"

Leigh answered. "Ah. Well, both of them, I guess. I was talking about Kylie, but the description applies to both, really."

Addie turned her head to watch as he drove onto the main road. "My grandpa said sometimes animals resemble their owners."

Leigh straightened, sitting back in her seat. "In this case, I can safely say the Cookie and Kylie are two peas in a pod."

In the mirror, he watched Addie face forward. So serious, she spoke as if she were asking permission to perform brain surgery. "I'd like to play with the puppy, if Kylie won't mind."

Thinking of little Kylie, he replied, honestly. "Honey, she won't. She'll be thrilled to have someone new to talk to. She's the very definition of social butterfly."

"You said, what's his name? Harlan? Harlan and his wife are nice?"

He slowed the SUV as they came to the turn leading them to Walker property. "Ridiculously nice. I swear."

Her little shoulders rose and fell with a deep breath as she steeled herself. "Okay."

"O—" He barely got the single syllable out before she continued.

"You'll come back to get us, right?" Addie began with a plea, then ended on an order. "As soon as you're done." He looked in the rearview mirror to see her little fists clenched tight. Her shoulders were straight and her eyebrows tight.

Damn, but she kills me. Straight through the heart with an arrow.

"Absolutely. The moment this is finished, I'm coming straight to you two." He turned the car onto Walker property.

"Okay. Be careful." Another order.

He gave her the words she demanded. "I promise." The moment he closed his mouth, he realized they weren't empty words. He meant them. He wanted—no, needed—to come back and be a part of both their futures.

Leigh took over the conversation, giving him a break as he drove them through the enormous property. "What do you want to do first? Oh! A friendly warning, Kylie will likely pounce the moment she realizes she has company. Once she finds out you like animals, it's all over. I probably won't even have to give you a tour. She'll steal you from me."

They came to Trent's house and Rick parked. He got out and opened Addie's door only to find her still sitting in her seat. He held out his hand to her. "Come on, sweetheart. I promise these are the best people."

"They're good people?" Her pale eyes shone with wary hope. He didn't quite understand it, but there was something in the way she said the words "good people" that held weight.

"Yes, good people." He took her hand in his and helped her down. He gave her hand a little squeeze then let it go. They walked around to join Leigh, who'd pulled a large tote bag from the back seat and was throwing it over her shoulder. He'd encouraged her to pack a few overnight things for them both, but she hadn't wanted to make a deal out of packing, fearing it might add to Addie's anxiety.

The front door opened and Cara came out, shaking her head. She gave him a wry grin as she headed their way.

Leigh greeted her. "We don't have all that much. You didn't have to come out to help, but thank you."

Cara called down from the porch. "It's okay. James and Noah are at it again."

"Damn." He didn't need two of his team members at each other's throats right before they headed out. "How bad?"

"On a scale of one to ten, I'd give this one a three. They went back to the Thirsty Beaver last night."

Leigh's head went back in shock. "Why would they go to a dump like that?"

"James bet Noah that he couldn't win back the money he lost at the pool table the last time we were all there. He was a hundred dollars in the hole and ready to make his move when all hell broke loose. He walked away before recouping his money." She leaned against the rails, glowing with amusement, when she could have been traumatized by almost being assaulted by Boyd Campbell, a ghost from her past.

"He should have said something. I would have reimbursed him. It was a work-related expense. You guys are supposed to track all expenses." He didn't know why he bothered. He'd repeated that a hundred times over.

She shook her head, silently laughing at him, and pushed back from the rail. "Sure thing, boss."

He wasn't sure he wanted to know, but had to get to the bottom of their current drama before they could get on with more important matters, like work. "What happened last night to set them off?"

"A woman."

"Not this again?"

"Yep. Noah saw someone who caught his eye, but as usual he's slower than molasses."

"So, he's pouting because James made the first move, while he stood back and did nothing. Again."

"Pretty much. They'll be over it in five minutes, if they're not already."

Leigh spoke up, surprised. "They found someone worth asking out at the Thirsty Beaver? I mean, I don't mean to sound like a snob, but…"

Cara laughed. "I get you. They said there's a new

waitress, and she doesn't look like she's from around here. Who knows what her story is? Poor girl, caught in the middle of Ramsey and Holloway drama, and she doesn't even know it." She came down off the porch to greet them, and he couldn't have been more thankful when she met Addie with a bright smile. "Hey, kiddo. You ready for another adventure?"

Addie nodded.

"You'll love it here, so much so that you might not even want to go back to Rick's boring museum." Cara winked playfully, and he could have kissed her. "Come on. You want to see Trent's house first? Kate ordered pizza for everybody. She can't stand the thought of Trent or the crew going on a mission with empty stomachs. You've already met all the guys, so you'll fit right in."

Smart.

She pointed out that Addie was in the presence of people she already knew and who cared about her without saying it outright. She tucked Addie under her shoulder and escorted her inside for pizza, as if they'd been friends forever.

He turned to find Leigh shutting the car's backdoor. She looked down at her feet before finally meeting his gaze, her lovely eyes so solemn. "I'll give her a little bit to eat with the guys and then get her out of your hair so you can get to work. I know you'll need to plan. We won't stay long."

"It's okay. I planned for extra time." He took her hands in his.

She released a choked laugh that sounded suspiciously as if it hid a sob. "Of course you did." She turned her head to look over the horizon.

"Hey. What's this?" He took her chin in hand and turned her to look at him. She pulled a hand free and casually swept a tear away. She pressed her lips together and shook her head. He pulled her into his arms and held her tight. Tucking her head beneath his chin, he breathed in her sweet scent and closed his eyes. "We'll get him, and I'll do everything in my power to come back to you in one piece. You have my word."

She shook her head again and sniffled.

Guilt clogged his throat, reminding him that he'd broken his word to her before.

Chapter Nineteen

Marcus leaned back in his desk chair and steepled his fingers. He rested his chin on the tips as he ran through his plan again. It was foolproof. He knew it as well as he knew the sun would rise in the morning.

Too easy. It'll be too damn easy.

He smiled.

His office door opened and Wen walked in. Fresh from a shower and a few weeks free of drugs, he didn't look half-bad. *Shame it wouldn't last.* He'd give his brother a week, two tops, before he gave into the weakness that he'd never outgrow. Along with their mother's beauty, he'd also inherited her propensity for self-destruction.

That was something no amount of money or care could fix.

Wen flopped down in the chair across from his desk. He asked a question, but sounded as though he didn't expect anything new. "What's going on today?"

How typical. That was the root of Wen's problem. He lacked any sort of ambition. Content to amble through life, he never looked for more.

"Today, it ends. The bastard owes me. He ruined her from day one. This is my chance to get them all at once."

Wen sat up straight, his baggy sweatshirt hanging loosely, much like the hair always in his face. "What? With Rick? Really?"

He just resisted the urge to roll his eyes at his brother's

naiveté. "Yes, really. He's playing right into my hands. He'll watch his little world crumble and then he'll die. It'll all be accomplished by nightfall."

"Sweet! You're sure you've got everything lined up. No holes in your plan?" What looked like genuine interest filled his brother's face as he leaned forward. Marcus half expected him to pull his chair closer, ask for details, and demand the right to participate. He knew better. Wen had the initiative of a doorstop.

He didn't bother hiding his disdain for Wen's lack of confidence in his plan. "It's airtight. I assure you, I have everything in place."

Wen tilted his head and looked at him, considering.

Well, well, well. A couple of weeks clean and suddenly brother dearest think he's smart.

"You're sure? You look…wound tight. Like, more on edge than usual. It's not like you." Concern filled Wen's eyes.

He laughed it off. "I'm not the one with an addiction that makes me desperate enough to stick a dirty needle in my vein."

Wen winced. "Ouch. That's harsh, but I guess I deserve it. Still, I'm worried about you."

Indignation rose. "You're worried about me? Do tell."

When his brother tilted his head in that considering way again, his blood boiled.

Stupid brat. Doesn't he remember who raised him?

Wen paused before finally answering. "You haven't been eating. I had to bring food to you last night and remind you twice to eat the damn sub, even though it was right there at your elbow."

"I wasn't hungry."

"It's almost two in the afternoon. I bet you haven't eaten today."

Marcus didn't bother with a verbal reply. He just glared.

Wen kept at him, pointing his finger as he asked, "What about sleep?"

"Wen..."

"Yeah, yeah. I know." Wen through his hands up. "You have dark circles under your eyes and your hair is a little shaggy. You've let your fingernails go. When it comes to hygiene and appearances, you've always been a perfectionist. I'm supposed to be the slob. It's almost like we've swapped roles."

He glanced down at his hands. Then he told himself not to run them through his hair. "Bullshit. Just because you've been a good little boy for a very short time doesn't give you the right to criticize me."

"Bro, I'm not trying to insult you. Promise. I'm just trying to look out for you. When was the last time you had a shower?" His brother asked as if he'd proved some monumental point.

"When I bathe, clip my goddamn toenails, or take a fucking shit is none of your business. You can get off your throne now. In fact, I recommend it."

An odd look flickered through Wen's features before disappearing. "Sure. No sweat."

"Good."

Wen stayed silent for a moment then switched topics. "When are you leaving? Can I go?"

"Since when are you interested in anything beyond finding a piece of trash to screw or your next high?" He pretended not to notice the hurt that flashed across Wen's features.

His brother straightened his shoulders. "Since today. It's past time I grew up and started wat—helping around here. Maybe I'll learn something."

Marcus threw his head back and laughed. "You don't have the slightest idea how business or the real world works. You'll get yourself killed."

Another flash of pain slashed across his brother's face, then disappeared as he fought to hide it. "I don't like this. Rick's smart. You're smart, too, but it stinks, Marc. Let me go with you."

"No fucking way. You're clueless. You couldn't plan a trip to the park, let alone a complex operation."

"Look, I know the commando shit isn't my thing. It's always been yours. I'm clean. You know I haven't had a hit in weeks. Let me go with you. I want to watch you take them down. She was my mother, too."

"You want to see how a real man operates? Fine, let's go. If nothing else, you might actually learn something."

Wen pursed his lips before replying, "Cool. What's up first?"

"First? We make a phone call." Leigh MacDonald would be at his mercy in a very short time. He could almost hear her desperate cries now.

~

Addie remained close to Leigh's side as Kate showed them around. She couldn't say she blamed the poor girl. No matter how welcoming every single person they'd encountered was, the enormous horse farm remained a strange place. The sheer size of the Walker's operation continued to boggle Leigh's mind, and she'd spent a great deal of time there. She could only imagine what it must feel like to a child.

They entered the largest barn, and Kate led them to a stall. With her soft voice, Kate summoned the horse inside, a tall bay with a white patch on its muzzle. "This is Nash. He's a big guy, but as sweet as they come, at least to the ladies. He's new to the farm and still giving Trent and the boys the cold shoulder. He likes me, and I bet he'll adore you."

Addie stepped closer and followed Kate's instructions for petting the big horse. She beamed until Leigh thought that she could almost see real light shining from her. *Jeez, she's a pretty kid.* She'd always thought so, but true happiness only magnified the loveliness of her fine-boned, doll-like features.

"See, I knew he'd like you. You've got the touch too. Be careful or Trent might try to steal you away from Rick and Leigh. He'll put you to work." Kate continued to closely watch Nash and Addie.

"Hey. Speaking of work, I thought Trent wasn't too happy with the idea of you helping out here." Leigh felt like a heel. She'd been so focused on her own troubles that she hadn't given much thought to the major upheaval in Kate's world. Yes, her cousin was far safer now, but security didn't always equate happiness.

"He's still not thrilled with the idea, but he's decided anything that keeps me occupied on the farm is better than anything that takes me away from it. Even if we weren't restricted by our current trouble, he wouldn't want me to leave at all. Any time I mention my house or Riley Creek, he changes the subject. He's distracting me at every turn, but it's actually kind of cute."

"How are the repairs on your place coming? Any idea what you'll do when it's finished?"

"The fire damage to the outside has been repaired. Even Trent agreed those repairs had to be a priority. Of course, with everything that's been going on, getting him to take me out there to check on progress has been near impossible. As usual, Uncle Robert has been a godsend. He's helped check on things for me. Even if I can't see the repairs myself, knowing he's keeping watch is nearly as good."

"Yeah, Dad mentioned he'd been out there to check on things, but he didn't give me a lot of details. You know how he is." She shook her head in amusement. Her father was as good as they came. Worked hard every day of his life and always put his family and neighbors first.

"That, I do. All work and very few words. I think he saves them all for Kylie." Kate laughed and gestured to the next stall. "Addie, do you want to meet Barton?" She moved down and crooned directly to the big gray stallion. "He's been a little restless, but deep down he's a good boy."

Leigh smiled thinking of how tightly little Kylie had wrapped her grandfather around her jelly-coated finger. For Leigh's father, the sun and moon had less sway over his life than his only grandchild. "Hey, Kylie could coax a stone wall into conversation."

"Very true." Kate looked from Barton to Addie. "Hey, how about we go see Bonnie? I bet she'd be happy to see you."

Addie stopped. Her face paled.

Leigh's placed a hand on the girl's shoulder. "Addie? What's wrong? Don't you want to go to the other barn? Bonnie looks great. She's housed with several other foals and in good company."

Addie's bottom lip quivered and she shook her head. "That's okay. Maybe some other time. I...I'm tired. All this walking has made me tired. I'm not used to being outside so much anymore. Can I go take a nap?"

Her excitement at offering Addie a treat long gone, Kate ran a hand down Addie's braid. "Offer stands anytime, okay? If you change your mind or feel better, just say the word." Kate met Leigh's gaze briefly, concerned. "I'm going to stop by Trent's for a bit. "Holler if you girls want company later."

If Leigh wasn't mistaken, she'd seen a flash of moisture in her cousin's eyes before she'd turned away, jean clad legs carrying her into the bright sun.

Concerned, she moved in front of Addie and spoke softly. "Hey. What's wrong? Kate was only trying to be nice. She didn't mean to hurt your feelings or upset you."

Fear flashed across Addie's face. "Oh no. I didn't mean to make her mad at me. Promise."

What in the world? "Sweetheart, she's not mad at you."

"Are you sure? Then why did she go away? She's nice. I don't want her not to like me." She bit her bottom lip.

"I'm absolutely sure. I think she's probably worried that she hurt your feelings somehow. That's the last thing she wanted to do." She took Addie's hand in hers and gently tugged her toward the big open doors. "Are you going to tell me what's got you spooked?"

Addie trailed along, her clammy hand firmly in Leigh's. "You're sure Kate's not mad at me?"

"She's more like my sister than even the closest friend. I'm certain. Spill."

The humid air lay heavy and still around them as they walked along a fence line in the silence. It wasn't long before Sandy and Harlan's home came into view. Leigh bit her tongue, waiting and hoping Addie would confide in her.

Finally, she spoke, breaking Leigh's heart. "I miss Dream, I mean Bonnie. It was a silly name, I know, but all I could think of when she was born. I miss her a lot. I'm afraid to see her. I'd probably cry and look like a baby. I don't want Kate to think I don't appreciate her taking such good care of my, I mean, her horse. I'm happy Kate is taking care of her, and that she won't be lonely. I just miss her. If I see her, I'll probably start blubbering like a girl!" She threw her hands up in the air exasperated.

Even as Leigh felt for Addie's heartache, she laughed at her last few words. "Like a girl, huh? That's not a bad thing. You have a soft, kind heart. That's a rare and wonderful thing. Don't be ashamed of it."

"I guess." Addie groused.

"You know what the good part about gushy, girl feelings are?" She lightly punched Addie in the arm, punctuating the word 'girl.'

"What?" Addie looked at her with suspicion.

"We get to wash them down with dessert. Let's go see what Sandy has in the kitchen. She always has something sweet to snack on. Harlan has an enormous sweet tooth."

"Okay."

From her back pocket, her phone rang, startling them both. They looked at each other and laughed. She pulled it out looked at the display, which showed an unknown caller. Not wanting to leave anything to chance with Rick and his team out in the field, Leigh answered. "Hello."

"Hello, beautiful. How are you?" A voice summoned directly from her nightmares answered. She stopped, breath freezing in her lungs. The sun shone brightly in the mid-eighty degree weather, yet ice leeched into her bone marrow.

Marcus.

"What's the matter? Don't you have anything to say? I've missed you, terribly. You shouldn't have run away from me. I'll make sure you remember that next time."

"Leigh?" Something gentle tugged her hand. "Leigh, what's wrong? Should I run and get Kate?" Addie's voice finally broke through the fog of terror brought on by Marcus's call. Her hand shook, vibrating the cellphone against her ear.

Addie, pale and scared, stared intently at her. She shook Leigh's hand, attempting to get her attention. "Stay here. I'll go get help."

Leigh fought to find her words. Taking a deep breath, she reminded herself that she had to keep it together. The last thing she wanted to do was scare Addie further. Her words came out in a whisper, but at least they came as she looked to the girl. "No. Don't." She swallowed her terror. "No. I'm okay."

Addie looked anything but convinced as she scrutinized Leigh. "Are you sure?"

That average, everyday male voice couldn't disguise the pure evil in Marcus. He spoke at the same time as Addie. "Is that the little brat from out by the quarry? I remember her well. Tell her I said hello."

Just like that, somewhere deep inside, a switch flipped. Every minute molecule of fear flashed, morphing into white, hot, protective, anger.

Oh, no. He's not getting anywhere near my girl. Not. Happening. Her spine snapped straight. The rage burned so fiercely, she didn't know how she contained it. She half-expected fire to explode from her fingertips.

How did she handle this? Rick was gone, and since Marcus was on the phone, they hadn't taken him down yet. She could tell Joe. Hell, she probably *should* tell Joe. He was at work, but she could get a hold of him.

"What do you want?" She smoothed a hand down Addie's braid and smiled, but her girl wasn't fooled. Concern warred with curiosity in her sweet features.

"I thought I'd be a giver and let you in on a little secret. Your man is headed into a trap. He's followed my breadcrumbs, and he's getting ready to jump into the oven." His gloating hit her, a sucker punch to the gut.

"What have you done?"

"See, those breadcrumbs are leading Rick and his band of merry men out to my father's shack on a wasted trip. They'll get there and find nothing but a grouchy old bastard with a loaded shotgun."

Something insidious curled heavy and lazy in her belly. She'd heard Rick say something along the lines of "father" and "digging deep" when James had come out for night duty a couple of evenings ago, but she'd been so focused on Addie, that she hadn't paid attention to the details.

As she sifted through her memory Marcus continued to gloat. "At this very moment, I have Frederick Evans in my sights. He's sitting at his desk, looking over paperwork. I hope it's his will. Very soon, it's going to be a shame if his affairs aren't in order."

She struggled to control her breathing and looked out over the horizon. The beauty in the storybook scenery seemed wrong somehow as she listened to a madman talk about killing. No matter what happened in the past Frederick didn't deserve to die. It would devastate Rick. He might act cold toward his father, but ultimately their past wouldn't cause Rick pain if he didn't care about the man.

If anything happened to him, Rick would carry the weight of guilt for the rest of his days.

She looked down to Addie and turned the phone away from her mouth as she spoke quietly to her. "Everything's okay. Let's go." She indicated the direction of the house with a tilt of her head and put the phone back to her ear. Thankfully, Addie complied even as she didn't look remotely convinced by Leigh's words.

When Marcus spoke again, it took everything she had not to crush the phone then throw it against the closest barn wall. "Are you still listening, beautiful?"

At least that was one thing she could answer without giving anything away to Addie. "Yes."

"Good. Now, unless you want Rick's daddy to die, you need to do me a little favor…"

Chapter Twenty

Rick closed his eyes, picturing his team's whereabouts on the map in his memory. "Boss, it's hot as hell out here. This Indian summer shit is for the birds." Holloway's hushed curse came through Rick's earpiece. "I vote that next time we take down someone who lives in Hawaii. No, forget the heat altogether. How about Alaska? Surely there's an asshole who needs to be taught a lesson in Anchorage."

Rick sighed. He knew they'd secured the surrounding area and that was the only reason Holloway dared run his mouth, but it didn't stop him from wishing he could reach through his mic and slap the back of his friend's head.

"Shut it, asshole." Noah's deep, quiet voice filtered through next, a rarity and even more powerful for its scarcity.

James ignored it, but his new commentary held a note of seriousness. "Seriously, sweat stains aside, this reeks worse than last week's trash. I don't like it."

Before Rick could agree, Noah put in his two cents. "For once, I agree with his runaway mouth. I have a bad feeling about this."

"Guys, for what it's worth, I agree, but there's no going back. Cara just reported in. Target A is on the go. Be on your toes. We're finishing this today." Earlier that morning, he'd received word from Noah who'd been doing surveillance that he witnessed increased activity at one of their observation points.

"Hell, yeah. I'm not saying I think we should back out. It just feels off. Like we might have missed something. Pete? Did you dot your *i*'s and cross your *t*'s?"

Pete answered. "Only dick flappin' in the breeze is yours, playboy. I'm in position, hunkered down in the old treehouse. Feels like I'm at home."

Unsurprisingly, Holloway's mouth continued, but his uncharacteristic words made them all pause. "By the way, Ramsey, Sylvie, the little brunette at the Thirsty Beaver? She shot me down. She wouldn't tell me why, but she wouldn't meet my eye when I made my play. She kept looking over my shoulder at something behind me. Pretty sure she was watching you clean up at the pool table. You might want to revisit that Beaver soon. Shit, I mean revisit *the bar*, not that beaver. You know what I mean, damn it."

"She tied your tongue in knots, playboy? Hell. Maybe I do need to go back to the Beaver."

Remarkably, James did shut it, at least until he had something to report, updating Rick on his progress through the surrounding forest. "I'm at the creek's northernmost point. I'm ready to move on your word."

Rick replied with what he remembered of the area, one he'd easily committed to memory. "Good. If you look east, you should see two boulders. The largest is probably about waist high."

"I see it and the two lazy rats keeping watch."

"I doubt they have much training, but be on your toes."

"Copy. I'll wait there for your word."

"Remember, I've brought in two extra team members. Trent's in the field with you, so if my second takes over, you might want to stop the wisecracks. Big brother isn't as fun as I am." Rick's focus narrowed to a pinpoint. Nothing registered beyond the steady green pinpoints on the digital map displayed by his phone. Each dot, an important piece of his tactical plan, represented a member of his team. No single dot was more important than any other. Beyond their importance in his plan, each one was a member of his family and that role held far more weight.

Trent, right on time, reported in. "I'm in position, seventy-five yards out. You were right. I have a good view of the front entrance from the old shed. I have the third bogey in my sights. Over."

They'd been observing Marcus's lazy crew for two days. His inexperienced men didn't have the slightest idea they'd were being watched. They'd followed until one of them led them to the townhouse Marcus was staying in. Last night Trent and Noah had placed a tracking device on the bastard's car.

With a swipe of his finger, he brought another map onscreen. Cara was in route. With another swipe of his finger, he switched to another map and confirmed she was on the move in a rental car, following Marcus and Wendell. As he watched, Cara's car slowed and stopped in an unexpected location. She was just a few hundred yards short of a rest stop on the edge of the highway. The second blip on the map indicated that Marcus's car had pulled in and parked.

Shit.

The screen of his phone went black for a split second, then displayed an incoming call. Frustration and confusion battled for headspace as he looked at the odd number. When he'd first set up the *Do Not Disturb* function in his custom phone design, he'd blocked all incoming calls except for a very select few. He couldn't have phone calls breaking his concentration. On the way to dismiss the call, he paused.

Recognition slammed home. It was Addie's number for the cell he'd left her back at that shack she'd lived in. Damn, it seemed like ages ago, but hadn't been much more than what, a couple of months? He remembered making her number one of only three contacts able to reach him at all times. Trent, Pete, and Addie. He'd need to add Leigh's soon.

Impatient and a little worried, he answered. "Hey, Addie. What's going on?" She was a smart kid. He figured she would have understood his need for focus.

"I know you're busy, but I have a problem. A big problem."

"Sweetheart, can Leigh or Kate help you with it? I'm a little busy." Even now, he itched to flip back to the map displaying Cara's still car.

"Well, that's my problem. I'm okay, but Leigh's gone." Something in her voice got his attention, even when he knew she had to be mistaken. Leigh wouldn't have left Addie or the farm.

"Are you sure? Maybe she's in the shower or walked down to see Kate? Kylie could have dragged her away to look at something. Kylie is a pro at stealing people." Anxiety scratched at his nape, even as he tried to reassure her.

"I'm sure. Kate's in the kitchen with Kylie and Sandy. They're making a big dinner for everyone. Leigh told me she had a headache. She was going to take some medicine and needed to lay down for a nap. I tried to lay down and rest, too. I must have fallen asleep. When I woke up, she was gone. She's not in our room or bathroom. Her purse isn't where she left it, either."

His anxiety evolved into fear, but Leigh knew how important it was for him to have no distractions. His mind raced. "Have you asked Kate or Sandy if they've seen her?"

"Not yet. Rick, it was the phone call that came in that scares me most. She seemed real scared for a minute. She got mad, like *way* mad. And then she pretended everything was okay, but I knew she was lying. She never lies to me." Her quiet words hit him with the force of a ten-ton asteroid.

"Phone call? When did she get that? What did she say? Repeat everything you can remember."

As Addie relayed what she could of the call, his fear transformed into terror. "Sweetheart, you did the right thing by calling me, but I've got to get off here and see what I can find out."

His focus on the maps blown, he closed his eyes and concentrated on the small voice coming through the phone. This little girl and the woman who'd taken her in held his heart, his everything, in their intertwined hands. "Good. I know she's worried about me being scared and wouldn't leave me alone here, even with people she likes. I know her. She wouldn't do that to me." Her little words strengthened into ones of hard won confidence. "She...I think she loves me. I know she wouldn't leave me alone when I'm scared. What if he gets her? You have to find her."

Cara's voice sounded in his other ear, breaking into their conversation. "Shit, boss?"

"Hang on, Mayhem." He continued to focus on Addie. "I'll find her."

"Promise?"

"I promise. I won't come home until I get her back."

"He's in big trouble, isn't he?" Rick thought he might

have heard a hint of a smile in his girl's voice.

Even though she couldn't see it, he sent her one of his own, a lethal grin full of predatory anticipation. "I gotta go. I'll call and update you as soon as I have her."

Her small, unsure voice returned. "Okay. Rick?"

"Yeah?"

"Be careful. I love you." He had to strain to hear her soft words, ones that couldn't have been easy for her to say. She was every bit as strong as Leigh. No two females belonged together as much as those two did.

"I love you too, kiddo." When the words broke free, they opened something inside him, a warm, soul-freeing, release.

Damn. When was the last time I told anyone that? It had to have been before his mother died. He hadn't even given those words to Leigh. She deserved them. If anything happened to her before he had a chance to give them to her, he'd never forgive himself.

The phone disconnected and he tucked Addie's sweet gift deep inside for later. Keeping his shit together had never been more critical. He quickly checked his missed call log and found five missed calls from Leigh. No messages.

She'd needed him and hadn't been able to reach him.

Fuck.

Simply keeping her under lock and key wasn't good enough. She was a brave, fiercely independent woman, one totally capable of walking by his side. She'd been a saint through this entire ordeal, but he'd be a fool to think that she'd always be content to wait in the wings while he ran off into danger. She needed more than just a bodyguard, she needed a partner.

He still had things to set straight, but first he had to finish this once and for all.

"Mayhem? Go ahead." With a wretched feeling slithering in his belly, he pulled up the map. Her car still sat parked along the side of the highway. He closed his eyes, bracing for confirmation that his suspicion was truth.

She spoke, the stress in her voice transmitting clearly through his earpiece. "They've pulled into the rest stop. We've got a problem. A huge problem."

~

The steering wheel stuck to Leigh's damp palms as she turned off the highway and into the rest stop. She took a deep breath, shifted into park and looked for the car Marcus had described. A dark gray four-door with tinted windows waited at the end of the row. She could just make out two figures inside, one in front and one in back.

Echoes of Marcus's threats replayed in her head as she turned off the ignition and exited the car. *I get you. Rick gets his daddy. He can't have both and, let's face it. I'll have much more fun playing with you.* Bile rose in her throat. She dropped her keys and phone in the cupholder so Frederick would be able to take her car and call for help. She hoped he'd go straight to Rick. She'd called both Rick and Joe several times with no luck.

He'll come for me. I know he'll come for me.

She knew with every fiber of her being Rick wouldn't stop until he found her. Even now, he hunted. If Marcus had set a trap, Rick wouldn't be fooled for long. In no time, he'd regroup and he'd be hungrier, more determined than ever. She'd survived one round with Marcus. She'd survive another.

Feeling as though she walked down a plank over shark infested waters, she made her way down the sidewalk. Even as the late afternoon sun beat down, chills crept into her very bones. She followed the instructions and opened the back door. Instead of Frederick Evans waiting to trade places with her, she found Marcus. With one arm stretched casually along the seat he held a black handgun. The dark eye of its muzzle stared straight at her. He waved her in with the other arm. "Come on in, love. At this very moment, one of my men has a gun trained on ol' Fred. You wouldn't want me to get impatient. Let's go."

Marcus slipped his aviator style glasses down his nose. Arctic eyes glittered, daring her to disobey. When they made a slow sweeping survey of her, she shivered. He caught the subtle movement and grinned.

He wore a dark gray athletic shirt and black fatigues, but they appeared new and... maybe even expensive? His boots looked like they were fresh out of the box, nothing like the ones Rick or her brother routinely wore. Theirs were well used, practical. Everything Marcus wore seemed more about appearances.

When he slid mirrored glasses back into place, she almost sighed in relief, freed from his icy stare.

Getting inside, she hoped she hadn't made a terrible mistake. Chances were, she had, but she would not step back and allow Rick's father, an innocent man, to die. She'd never be able to live with herself if she hadn't acted, allowing the worst to come true.

The moment she closed the door, the locks quietly engaged. In the driver's seat, a thin man—younger and far less polished than Marcus—turned back to greet her. His blond, longish hair fell over one eye. "Hello." Something familiar in his features nagged her. "Nice to meet you. Sorry it's not under better circumstances." He seemed genuinely happy to meet her as he smiled.

Then it hit her. His mouth and eyes. Minus the warmth that entered Rick's eyes whenever he looked at her, they could have been mirror images. The bone structure of their faces were miles apart, Rick's full of masculine angles and planes, and the driver's fine, almost to the point of frailty. But these new eyes were identical to the warm, dark chocolate ones she loved so much.

How odd to find something so dear in someone so despicable.

She remained silent and focused on keeping her nausea under control.

A shark smiled with more warmth than Marcus, and he looked her up and down. "So pretty today. Wen, let's go. On to our next stop! Oh, and Leigh? I lied. I don't have ol' Fred yet, but I will. We're headed there now. What can I say? I'm a bastard. When I'm finished taking away everything Rick cares for, he'll wish he were dead." Her stomach lurched when the meaning of his words hit her.

God, I'm such a fool. She'd only made a bigger mess for Rick to clean up.

"What did I tell you, Wen? Everything planned out to the last detail and foolproof."

She smoothed her hands over her legs and prayed for time.

Marcus's hand drifted over her shoulder to her nape. He swept gentle caresses there, ignoring the gooseflesh he'd conjured as if it were the most natural thing in the world. She turned her head toward the window and her focus snagged on the rearview mirror. Wendell's gaze met hers. It had to have been her imagination, or maybe their resemblance to Rick's eyes, because for a moment she could have sworn they softened with sympathy.

Craziness.

It was likely her subconscious searching for a lifejacket in the storm.

The scenery passed them by, a growing palette of greens as they headed father away from civilization and deeper into a woodsy rural area.

Marcus spoke to Wen about the plans to rebuild his business from the ground up. She knew that she should probably commit as much of it to memory as possible, but couldn't bring herself to care. Instead, she called up the faces of everyone she loved and wished she could write them a goodbye letter to be delivered if she didn't make it out of this alive. As time wore on, and the highway whirred by, she worried that she might not get to see any of them again.

But no matter the pain blooming in her heart, she refused to shed one tear. She'd put herself in this position. She and Marcus held the entirety of the blame.

They exited the highway onto a long and winding stretch leading them into the heart of hill country. The narrow road led them to yet another lane, this one unlined and far narrower.

She almost felt at home.

"How's it looking?" Marcus's question broke into her thoughts. As Wen remained silent, she realized he must have been speaking to someone on the phone. "You're sure we're all clear? No sign of Evans?" He paused for a moment, then snapped. "Rick, the younger one, you idiot!" Unable to help herself, she listened intently, hoping for some sort of clue.

"Good. He's still chasing his own tail. No, don't go check. I want you boys nearby. Wait for my word."

What wisps of hope she had evaporated as she heard his confidence return.

They traveled the narrow lane until it brought them to an aging stone fence and iron gate, set with an enormous, ornate *E*. Wendell stopped the car, but before he could speak into the security box, the gate swung open.

He drove them down the driveway and halfway around the pavement circling a large fountain. He parked in front of beautiful but imposing double-doors. The lovely heavy dark wood appeared to have been there from the dawn of time.

"I've always admired this place. It stinks of old money and class. Silly me, at one time, I thought I belonged here." Marcus spoke fondly of the home that, long ago, he'd known for a very short time. Appearing to shake off the nostalgia, he toughened. "Let's go. We've got business to attend to. Wen, you go first. Gorgeous, don't try anything. I was trained by the best, and there's no outrunning a bullet."

She followed his lead. They strolled up to the front doors as casually as if they'd been invited to dinner. Then he jerked her to stand in front of his body, and he pressed the gun's muzzle to her temple. She closed her eyes, filled with more regret than fear.

When the door opened, followed by Frederick's sharp inhalation, they popped open. "What in the world? What's going on here? Marcus Lewis is that you?"

"It's Sutton, not Lewis, not Evans. I'm a bastard not

worth claiming, remember? Let us in or she gets to decorate your front-step in blood and brain matter."

Frederick's head snapped back in horror. He immediately opened the door wide and stepped to the side, giving them room.

"Hi, Mr. Evans." Wendell made his casual greeting as they walked in.

Marcus snapped, losing a fraction of his composure. "Idiot. You don't call him mister, he's your father."

Wendell paused in the dim entryway to look at his reflection in an ornate framed mirror. He raked a hand through the ever-wayward shock of pale hair. "I know that. It just seems weird to call him Dad when I've never seen him before today. I've never been like you. I don't do formalities. The uppercrust is such a stuffy place. I never really understood why people like it there." Wendell shrugged, comfortable with his brother's ire.

Ignoring his brother, Marcus gave her a hard shake, jolting the pistol against her temple. "Show us to your office, Fred. You're going to give me access to all your accounts. I need funds to restart what Rick destroyed. I'm collecting what the two of you owe me." He jarred her again, as if to make a point.

Shaken, Frederick led the way through a house that was as lovely as it was dark and impersonal. Dark paneled walls led them down wide hallways. Silence hung oppressive and heavy. An enormous grandfather clock sat like a sentry at the hallway's end. The tick-tick-tick counted down like a bomb.

So sad and lonely.

She ached for the little boy had who lost his mother so

young, then was dealt another vicious blow when he'd been sent away from the only home he'd known to live with strangers.

Frederick indicated the office door with a welcoming gesture. His eyes remained pensive and alert.

Like father, like son.

"Wen, lead the way." She felt Marcus jerk his head toward the door. "Fred, you follow. Times wasting. Pull up your account information. Start with your personal financials. We'll go from there."

Frederick crossed a large room, straight from a Sherlock Holmes novel. She half expected Dr. Watson with his pipe to emerge from a heavy door on the rooms north wall. Rick's father sat stiffly in his leather chair, framed in the big picture window displaying the manicured front lawn. "The process is quite complex and takes some time. I—"

Marcus shoved her into the middle of the room and barked close to her ear, "Quit stalling. Just get it done."

Barely controlling her wince, she closed her eyes and hoped.

"When you have the transfer ready, I'll give you the account number."

From a distant memory, her father's words came to her. A practical man without an ounce of fancy. *Leigh, hopes and dreams are fine things, but the real world is a hard, often cruel, place. To get anywhere, you have to be on your toes and work for what you want.* Her young heart had been stung by the thought that he didn't believe in something as lovely as hope, but at the core of it, he'd been right. A person had to work to obtain their dreams. She couldn't just sit under the clouds and wait for magic to bless her.

She had to watch and wait for the opportunity to make something happen. Waiting for Rick was fine, but she'd be an idiot if she didn't keep her eyes open just in case a chance for escape occurred.

"Wen, stop being a slug and keep watch."

"Sure." He walked to the corner and leaned his side against a shelf filled with leather bound books. "Pretty place you have here, Mr. Evans. Looks like a golf course."

His head snapped around when the door in the middle of the opposite wall opened wide. Marcus's body went tight as he turned them to face their meeting's surprise addition.

Her brother stepped out, handgun raised and pointed directly at Marcus. "Let her go." Relief washed through her at the sight of Joe in old jeans and boots, standing in the dark doorway. He'd come out of uniform. *Where is Rick?* Cold, barely controlled fury hardened the face she'd once thrown snowballs at.

"I don't think so. Fred? Get to work. Nothing's changed. I'm holding all the pretty cards right here in my hand." He gave her another shake to make his point.

Joe's gaze flicked to hers, commanding her with a single glare that said *behave and don't do anything stupid.* If she wasn't up shit creek, she might have laughed at the absurdity of Joe expecting her to follow his orders.

Currently? She absolutely would.

"Uh? Marc? Maybe you should listen." She chanced a glance at Wendell. White as freshly fallen snow, he stared at a point somewhere behind her and Marcus.

Marcus snapped at his brother. "This is why you'll always be a failure. You don't have the balls it takes to get anywhere. You're a fucking disgrace." She sensed that

Marcus's attention was fractured as his body subtly shifted from Wendell to Joe and back with each word.

"But, Marc, you don't know what's—"

Marcus's voice raised in volume. "You're the idiot. I know everything, you stupid pup!"

"Is that so?" *Rick.* At the sound of his quiet, steely voice behind them, her knees nearly gave way. Then she heard the distinct click of a safety being flicked off behind them. "I'm thinking there's one or two things you haven't figured out yet. Leigh? Baby, are you okay?"

She struggled to take in a deep breath then answered shakily, "Yeah. I'm good."

Wendell raised his arms in the air as another man she knew stepped into the room. Detective Jake Bowie. Talk about a triple threat. She couldn't think of anyone she'd rather have coming to the rescue than these men.

The hand holding her upper arm squeezed harder as Marcus trembled behind her. She couldn't tell if the increasing tension came from anger, fear, or frustration. But it didn't matter, did it? Any combination of the three spelled bad news. She still had a gun aimed at her head in the middle of a standoff with no easy way out.

Her heartbeat thundered in her ears as her gaze connected with Wendell's across the room.

He took a step toward them, pleading. "Marc, bro, listen. If we walk out of here, then we can make another plan. There will be plenty more babes later. She pretty and all, but I've seen and done hotter."

"Idiot. They're not going to let us walk out of here. It's not about her. What do I have to do to get that through your thick skull? This is about getting our due. They owe us! You never let an opponent get one over on you."

Frustration pinched Wendell's features. "But, Marc, they're also family. We've never had famil—"

"Shut. Up. You have no idea what you're talking about. Family? You want to know what family will get you?" The metal against her temple disappeared and Marcus jerked her aside as he aimed his gun at Wendell.

Something that looked like resignation crossed over Wendell's face. "Shit, Marc. Was it always going to come to this?"

Cold, detached and utterly heartless, Marcus replied, "Probably."

"If you despise family so badly, then why'd you get so obsessed with them?"

She looked to her family, Joe, and thanked the heavens for what she'd been given. He flicked his eyes to the floor and her heart stuttered.

"You mother fucker!" Marcus bellowed and fired.

She dove onto the floor and her cheek smacked the hardwood as a second shot thundered. A hard body landed on top of hers. She squirmed and struggled to draw in air. The heavy weight, shifted a minute fraction, letting her inhale. The small breath carried Rick's scent and she could have cried with relief.

Then she had a terrible thought. "Rick?"

"Shhh. I'm fine. Stop squirming. I'll let you up as soon as they're both unarmed." Heavy footsteps moved through the room.

She rested her head on the floor and waited. "Ease up a smidge, big boy. I can't breathe." The weight of his body lessened as she listened to Jake call for medical transport for two. He kissed the top of her head.

Rick's chest rumbled at her back with a terse question. "Dad? You okay?"

Frederick released a shaky breath. "I think so. Leigh, my dear?"

"I'm good." And she was.

At least until her brother responded. "Only until I we get this taken care of. When I finally get my hands on her, she might not be. Stubborn brat."

She could've quaked beneath the fury in his voice if she didn't know him as well as she did. As furious as he'd been, he'd also been terrified that he wouldn't be able to help get her out of the danger she'd put herself in. She responded to his name calling wryly, wishing she could stick her tongue out at him, only so she could watch him roll his eyes. "I love you too, Joe."

Rick's weight lifted and he helped her to her feet, but when he spoke, it wasn't to her or anyone in the room. "Copy. Bring them to the front lawn. I'll pass the info to Bowie. Jake? How is he?"

Jake looked up from where he was checking Wendell's pulse with one hand at his neck. The other hand pressed a growing red stain over a thin chest that rose and fell with rapid, shallow breaths. "I don't know. His pulse is still strong but he's losing blood fast. How many men are there?"

Rick answered. "They're marching three of Marcus's crew in now. They'll meet your officers on the front lawn. Keep me updated on Wen. I need just a second." He pulled her by the hand out into the hallway.

"Where are you going?"

"I have a phone call to make." He pulled his phone out

of a pocket in his dark fatigues.

What in the world could be so important? She waited, confused, as he put the phone to his ear. She faintly heard half a ring before someone on the other end picked up. A little voice spoke. "Rick?"

"I have her. We're both safe."

Oh dear. Poor Addie! The waiting and not knowing must have been torture.

She barely heard her response. "Really? Promise."

Rick smiled. "I promise. She's right here beside me. I'm holding her hand. We're going to stuff the bad guys into ambulances and then we'll be home as soon as we can. We're going to have to answer a lot of questions, so it may be a while. Stay with Kate or Sandy, okay?"

Rick tilted the phone so it was a little easier for her to hear. The little voice strengthened. "Okay. Don't let her go! I love you guys." The sweet words hit her like an anvil as Rick's dark eyes met hers.

"We love you, too." He answered for them both then disconnected. She burst into tears and smashed her face into the solid heat of his chest. "Hey. What's this for?" He pulled her back so he could look at her.

She wiped her tears away. "Sorry. I guess it finally caught up with me. I was fine until I heard her say those magic little words. I'll get it together in a minute."

"They are pretty damn powerful, aren't they?" He caught a tear she'd missed with a gentle sweep of his thumb. "Sometimes, especially when someone hasn't said them in a long time, they can be hard get out."

She could only nod.

He cupped her jaw and kissed her. His mouth met hers

full of sweet promise and delectable heat. Too soon he broke the contact and met her gaze. "I love you."

"Oh, Rick. I love you too. I love you so much."

Wrapping her arms around him in a tight hug, she thanked her lucky stars for everything she'd been blessed with and vowed to never, ever take it for granted.

Chapter Twenty-One

Four long hours. Rick sat on the couch and watched his father finally walk Detective Bowie to the hallway leading to the front door. He took Leigh's hand in his and raised it to his mouth. He kissed her knuckles, savoring his first quiet moment with her since he'd seen Marcus hold a gun to her head.

They'd received word a little while ago that the gunshot wound to Marcus's heart had proved fatal. Joe had taken no chances.

Rick had checked on Wendell, who was faring on slightly better. He'd made it out of surgery where the trauma surgeon had done her best to repair the damage done by Marcus's bullet. He was and would be listed in critical condition for some time. Marcus had a history of using hollow point ammunition and the damage from his bullet had been devastating.

He heard the front door shut. "I'll be right back." He kissed the top of her head and rose to meet his father.

Rick was smacked with the changes in his father brought on by time. He appeared tired, maybe even a little frail. He'd never been weak. To Rick, he'd always been tall and strong like an old oak tree.

But even the strongest trees weren't immune to the effects of time.

His father held his hands together over his abdomen as if not quite sure what to do with them. Still, he had manners fit for dinner at the White House. "I would offer you two dinner. I know you must be starving, but I don't have anything prepared. The moment you called to tell me Marcus was moving, I sent my staff home. We could have sandwiches and soup, if you'd like?"

"No, but thank you, Dad. Here in just a few minutes, we're going to get Addie. We've called her a couple of times, and she knows everything is okay, but she won't rest until she sees Leigh in person. I don't want her to worry any longer than necessary."

"Of course not. You should take care of your family first. Always. I…I didn't. I made too many mistakes and lost mine. I wouldn't want the same for you."

Rick reached a hand out behind him, knowing Leigh would come and take it. When she did, he pulled her into his side. Without hesitation, she wrapped her arm around his waist. "Dad." The word still felt awkward on his tongue, almost as if it were a foreign word he couldn't master. "This Saturday afternoon we're having a barbeque at my house. It'll be more of a burgers and beer crowd. You're more than welcome to join us. Bring swim trunks. Addie and Kylie can't get enough of the pool, so things might get a little wild. It should be entertaining if nothing else."

When his father appeared surprised by the invitation, he felt like an utter asshole. He had virtually no one left, other than his employees and household staff. The thought didn't set well.

"I…I'd like that. What time?"

"Four o'clock. There's no telling how long it will last."

"All right. Thank you."

Leigh softly squeezed his waist in approval.

"Mr. Evans." Leigh slipped out of his hold so she could give his father a kiss on the cheek. "Please come. We'd love to have you."

Not able to let her get more than an arm's length away, he drew her back to his side as they walked down the hallway. They stepped into the night air, and he released a heavy sigh. It was finally over.

He walked her to the passenger door of his truck which Noah and James had dropped off a little while ago. He opened the door but before he could help her in, she stopped him with a hand over his heart. "I'm proud of you. I didn't know we were having a cookout, but I'm so very glad you invited your father."

Not sure how to process her approval, he focused on the easy part. "The idea came to me a little while ago when I was talking to Joe. He wasn't too happy with me and the way I hurt you when we found Addie."

"Oh. I didn't even realize. I've been so caught up in everything. I'll talk to him and—"

He put his hands on her waist. "I, *we* know. It's okay now. We've worked it out. He's still not thrilled at the idea of me taking his little sister away, but he'll come to terms with it eventually. I can't fault him when it's because you two are so close. I'm happy you have that."

She played with the collar of his shirt. "You're stealing his little sister, huh? What exactly does that mean?"

Taking both of her hands in his, he held them over the center of his chest. "I know this is not the best time, but I want to make this permanent, you and me, forever."

The was an audible hitch in her chest. Her eyes widened as if she was afraid she'd misheard him. "Forever?"

"Forever. We don't have to put a ring on it tonight but, yeah. That's where I'm headed with this. What do you think? Not that Addie and I will give you much say in the matter."

"Yes. Forever sounds perfect."

Epilogue

"Addison Jolene!"

Holy crap. Addie dropped her pencil and looked up from her sketch of the flowers she picked earlier that day.

Rick never hollered. Even when she'd dropped cake on the rug in his office. She'd known the rug had to have been an expensive one. A lot of the things around his—no, *their*—house were, but he never yelled. Not even when she cursed or broke a plate in the kitchen. Glass shards had gone everywhere, but he'd only closed his eyes and taken a deep breath. Then he'd picked her straight up and carried her out of the room so she wouldn't get glass in her bare feet.

What had she done? She jumped from her desk chair and hurried. Leigh waited at the end of the hallway with him, but she was smiling. Then she winked. It was nice, but Leigh was always kind. Addie couldn't give it much thought, because Rick looked so serious.

Rick crossed his arms over his chest in what she'd come to call his "boss-man" pose. "I have a problem."

She looked to Leigh for a hint, but she wasn't budging. They were in on whatever this was together. *Damn it. I mean, darn it.* She was really trying not to curse, at least out loud, but still struggled sometimes. "What's wrong?"

Rick answered. "Follow me." He turned and led them through the maze of rooms until they went out through the big mudroom. He opened the door and held it open. When they were all outside, he took Leigh's hand in his and walked across the backyard. "Addie, I have a problem."

"What is it?" She couldn't figure out what was going on. She didn't think she was in trouble, but she just didn't know.

"See, I bought a horse farm, and I don't know the first thing about animals." He continued leading them across the property. They headed toward the closest barn, but a flash of something gray caught her eye in the opposite direction. She turned her head to see the front of Trent's truck coming onto the driveway. As it carefully turned off the main road and around the gate, a horse trailer came into view. "Seems like a pretty silly idea, to have a horse farm with no horses."

Her heart stopped. Torn between bright hope and fear that she wasn't wrong in her guess, she couldn't breathe.

"Come on. You're falling behind. We've got work to do."

She picked up the pace, practically running to keep up with his long strides. She looked up, hoping to find a hint, but he had his face locked up tight. *Damn—darn it. He's still in boss-man mode.* "What's going on?" She looked to Leigh for an answer, but she had some sort of weird face going on. Was she trying to hide a smile? Maybe she was just holding in a sneeze.

She tried to pay attention to Rick and keep up with his long legs, but got caught by the movement of Trent's truck. It was halfway up the drive. The trailer behind it was really big, but that didn't mean anything. He was a horse guy and always wore barn clothes and boots. He was probably just stopping by to talk to Rick.

"I think it's time we expanded your list of chores.

You're doing a good job so far, but it's not enough." He stopped at the corral and turned. He leaned back against the rail and crossed his arms over his chest.

She heard the rumble of the truck as it neared. It pulled to a stop behind them but she didn't dare look. Doors opened and when they closed, she felt the loud thump in her chest.

"What chores do you want me to do?" She didn't mind. When she'd lived by herself, she did pretty much everything. She and Leigh worked on a lot of things together and it was kind of nice. She could do outside stuff too.

She refused to turn and look when she heard more opening sounds behind her.

Trent's opening the trailer. I'm not looking. I'm not looking. Nothing but wonderful things had happened since she'd come to stay with Rick and Leigh. Life was almost too perfect. Sometimes, when she woke in the mornings, she didn't want to open her eyes, afraid that it still might be a dream.

Trent called to her. "Addie, can you open the gate? I seriously doubt Mr. Shiny Shoes knows how. You've got your work cut out for you, sweetheart. Definitely, braver than me." She held her breath and moved to do as Trent asked. Her hands shook, but she got the latch on the second try and swung the gate open.

Unable to bear the suspense any longer, she turned. Trent was leading a dark chocolate mare down the trailer's ramp. She tried but couldn't hardly draw air into her lungs.

Kate came to her rescue. Addie hadn't even realized she was there until Kate pulled her into a gentle side hug. Then she bent down and whispered into Addie's ear. "Breathe, sweetheart. Take a big breath and let it out. It's going to be okay. Trust me?" She squeezed her hand.

Addie couldn't find her words, but managed a small nod. Kate smiled. "I remember when my dad brought our first two horses home. Jack and Ms. Priss really weren't anything special, just a couple of old horses. When he led them out of that rickety old trailer it was love at first sight."

Trent murmured something to the horse before releasing it into the paddock. Then he returned to the back of the trailer.

Kate pointed to the horse. "That's Seraphina, or Sera. I helped Rick choose her. You'll love her; she's an absolute doll. I thought she'd be a good match for Leigh. Isn't she a pretty thing?"

It was all she could do to nod.

Trent led a second horse down the ramp. "That big guy is Apollo. I thought he'd make a good match for Rick."

Still at a loss for words, she nodded.

"I'll be right back, okay?" Kate patted her on the shoulder and took Apollo's lead from Trent. She walked him to the paddock. After running a hand down his neck, she removed his lead and returned to Addie's side.

Leigh came to stand with them. She took Addie's hand in hers and squeezed as Trent ambled over. "What Kate was too kind to say is that Apollo doesn't know the meaning of the word run. He's a big, steady slowpoke that even a chicken like Rick can't fall off."

She knew she should laugh at his joke or say something nice, but she still couldn't make her mouth work. He went back up into the dark trailer again.

A minute later he brought a third horse out. It was a pretty reddish brown color, much like Apollo, but smaller in size like Sera. Kate made another introduction. "That's one of

Apollo's girls, Gypsy. She's three years old. Trent says she's the only one good enough for you to ride. He's always picky, but when he's selecting a horse for family, he's even more so. She's steady, and listens well, but she's fun, too. I think you'll like riding her. I'll be right back, okay?"

She might have nodded again, but then again, maybe not. She watched Trent remove Gypsy's lead before coming to lean against the inside of the rail. Quietly he asked, "You doing okay, kid?" His pretty storm gray eyes were soft in concern.

Somehow she found a word, a single word. At least it was the right one. "Yeah."

"Good to hear it." He pointed behind her and nodded like he wanted her to look at something.

She turned and froze. Kate was walking down the ramp with Dream, or Bonnie. Kate led her straight to Addie and handed her the lead. "I'm returning her to you."

Lost, overwhelmed with emotion, she looked around floundering until she found Rick. He stood, arms crossed over his chest, watching her closely. "Pretty silly to have a horse farm without horses, huh? What do you think of your new chores?"

Her mouth opened and closed but nothing came out.

Kate patted Bonnie's neck. "I thought, if it's okay with you, that I could come by in the mornings and help. I can show you how we've been feeding them and help you get a routine started, if you want? Trent went through the barn with Rick and made sure everything was ready. Of course, Leigh has experience with horses, too, but if you need anything at all I can be here in less than fifteen minutes. Trent or I will be more than happy to take your phone calls or come out to help. Even if we aren't available and something comes up, Trent always has stable hands on standby. And there's Harlan, too. He taught Trent everything he knows. Is that okay?"

Finally, finally, her mouth worked. "Yes. Please. Oh. Please." It wasn't much more than a whisper, but she was happy to know that she hadn't lost the ability to speak. She turned to Rick. "You bought them? They're really yours? They're staying here?"

He genuinely looked perplexed. "What would I do with horses?"

Trent rolled his eyes and pointed to Rick. "See? He's clueless. What did I tell you? You've got your work cut out for you, honey. What kind of fool spends a fortune on a place like this when he doesn't know one end of a horse from the other?"

A sudden image of Rick staring at a horse's behind and scratching his head popped into her mind. Laughing, she looked back to Bonnie and Kate.

Oh, no. "I can't take your horse! You took care of her and love her and…she's yours."

Kate met her gaze dead on, and Addie thought there might have been a hint of dampness there. "Nope. I loved her, still love her, but she's always been your baby. I'm finding out the hard way that I can't keep all the rescues. I have to send them on to their forever homes. I'm just a pit-stop."

Trent came over to pull her into his side, where he spoke gruffly to the top of her head. "You're not a pit-stop."

"I don't know what to say." For a brief moment, she tried to stop the tears from falling. Then she gave up and let them fall.

Who the hell cares? These are my people, and they love me.

About the Author

As a teen, International Best Seller, Amy J. Hawthorn, fed her reading appetite with fantasy and horror stories. Then she stumbled upon a pretty book cover—complete with a bare-chested, sword-wielding, Highlander. That Highlander and his author showed her the magic of a Happily-Ever-After.

She has read her way through Kentucky, Arizona, Southern California, and then back home to Kentucky, where she's living out her own Happily-Ever-After. The only person surprised by her Best Seller title? Amy. Her friends and family are laughing and saying I told you so.

ALSO BY AMY J. HAWTHORN

Protecting Kate: Dark Horse Inc. Book 1

Catching Cara: Dark Horse Inc. Book 2

Azrael's Light: Demon Runners of Unearth 1

Sunlight's Kiss: Demon Runners of Unearth 2

Dillon's Gift

Lacey Temptations: Crave 1

A Craving For Two: Crave 2

Discover the latest updates at
amyjhawthorn.com

Made in the USA
Middletown, DE
08 September 2024